JUL 2021

Yesterday
or
Long Ago

Yesterday or Long Ago

An Evraft Novel

Jenni Sauer

YESTERDAY OR LONG AGO
Copyright © 2021 Jenni Sauer
ALL RIGHTS RESERVED.

All characters in this book are fictional. Any resemblance to persons living or dead, events, or locales is purely coincidental.

This book or any portion thereof may not be reproduced, redistributed, or used in any manner whatsoever without the express written permission of the publisher except for the use of brief quotations in a book review.

Paperback ISBN: 978-1-7345096-4-9
Ebook ISBN: 978-1-7345096-5-6

Cover Design by Megan McCullough
http://www.meganmccullough.com/

Published by Ivory Palace Press
https://ivorypalacepress.com/

To Yentl for being the Amya to my Rinity and to Selina for being the Gibbs to my Tov. I've been lost without you both.

And to everyone who didn't leave when it would have made sense or been easier to go. Thanks for being the ones who stayed.

Pronunciation Guide

Characters

Alana—ah-LAH-nah

Alaric—al-uh-RICK

Allomina—al-oh-MEE-nah

Amya—AH-my-ah

Bina—BEE-nah

Carrigan—CAIR-uh-gihn

Comina—Coh-MEE-nah

Cosima—Coh-SEE-mah

Dalen—DAHL-en

Elisandra—el-ih-SAHN-druh

Favager—FAH-vah-gehr

Isambard—is-AM-bahrd

Norah—NOHR-ah

Rinity—rih-NUH-tee

Siphone—sih-FAH-nee
Twila Setki—twihl-AH SEHT-kee
Zhadidock—ZAH-dih-dok

Planets and Places

Alisethian—al-ih-SETH-ee-uhn
Elassi—uh-LASS-ee
Englever—EN-gleh-ver
Liosa/Liosi—LEE-oh-sah/LEE-oh-see
Mahsirian—mah-SEER-ee-in
Philosanthron/Philosanthrian—phil-oh-SAN-thrun/ phil-oh-SAN-three-un
Taras—tair-IS

Chapter 1

You had to have money or military connections to be allowed in the Liosi Royal Library; Rinity Garrick didn't even know who her father was.

The Library had high, vaulted ceilings that went up three levels, so that you could see the floors above you from the long row down the middle that cut through them. There was a neat line of tables, at one of which Rinity sat. The levels were filled with shelves and shelves of books, stuffed with everything from ancient, dusty tomes to volumes that had released that same year.

It had somehow withstood the Philosanthrian invasion and rule. Had lived through the Revolution that had been fought just miles away. If Rinity closed her eyes, she could hear the history and stories the books told, their whispers a language all their own, though Rinity had come to understand it sometimes, when they let her.

"Membership card, please."

Rinity looked up from the book in front of her, over the stack of volumes she planned to read next—and maybe a few she planned to smuggle out—to see the Library Steward a few tables away. He checked the membership cards of those seated and then moved on to the next table to perform the same check.

They usually only checked at the door and left everyone inside free of such interruptions. Did they know she'd snuck in? But she'd done it for years and no one had ever been suspicious before.

She slipped from her seat and ducked down a row of bookshelves. Making a point to walk with purpose, she made her way down the rows, like she was going somewhere and not on the run from the Library Steward.

It shouldn't have made a difference, not really, whose blood poured through her veins. She had Will, after all, the man whose name she bore and who was more father to her than she deserved. But she was Liosi and there was nothing more important than money or military valor. And if you didn't have those things, you could only succeed by being connected to those who did.

Until she knew where she'd come from, she'd always be the civilian who didn't know if she could walk through the Library door with her head held high. She probably couldn't. But it'd be nice to know with certainty.

She turned a corner and nearly ran into a Librarian. The woman scowled at Rinity as she adjusted the stack of books in her arms. "Can I see your membership card, please?"

Rinity knew that in her ripped denim leggings and faded tee she didn't exactly blend in with the blazers and pressed trousers and long skirts. She rather thought it was a nice outfit, but she understood that it didn't exactly scream wealth and privilege. She should have asked to borrow something from Amya; but it'd be such a hassle to do that every time she wanted to read books.

So, she turned and started in the opposite direction. The Librarian yelled after her—were Librarians even allowed to yell?—but Rinity didn't stop.

She ran, weaving her way through the rows and rows of books. There was more shouting behind her as she reached the end of the row of shelves and she made a split-second decision. Using the shelves as a ladder, she scrambled up. She reached the top and found she could just barely reach the bottom rung of the railing that ran the length of the next level. She grabbed hold and hoisted herself up.

Her feet on solid ground once more, she rushed off before another Librarian caught sight of her.

She headed through the rows of books and came to the hall at the far end of the library. She hurried down it as voices sounded behind her. In a panic, she grabbed the first door handle she saw and slipped inside.

The room was an office and she cursed herself because even though it was empty, there was no second exit. Even if no one thought to look in there for her, at some point whoever the office belonged to was sure to return at some point.

The office was neatly kept and beautifully furnished with a thick carpet beneath her booted feet, a sturdy wooden desk with a chair behind it and two in front, several carts with books arranged neatly on them, and bookshelves that lined the walls. There was a sense of peace and order and Rinity wished for nothing more than to take up residence in that sanctuary.

But she had no business being there and she needed to find a way out if she didn't wish to go to prison—sneaking into the library would probably get her a fine. But if they found out she was borrowing books without permission...

She looked about to survey her options. The window seemed a viable option until she looked out and found it overlooked the river that ran through the heart of the Liosi capital. And she was three stories up.

Prison was better than breaking multiple bones or possibly drowning.

The only door was the one she'd come through, so that wasn't an option. She could open the door, but she'd have no way of knowing what was on the other side. It was a good way to walk right into the trouble she wished to avoid.

She looked up and saw that on the wall near the ceiling, above the bookshelves, there was a vent.

It would do.

She climbed up. Then she eased the cover off the vent and set it down in the top of the bookshelf so she could hoist herself into the opening. After she maneuvered herself so that she faced out, she settled inside and pulled the vent cover back into place behind her.

She realized her mistake as soon as she was closed in—the vent was too small for her to turn around in; she wasn't going anywhere.

But it was too late for her to do anything about it because the office door opened and a young man slipped inside.

He looked exactly like a hero in a story ought to. His blond hair was so bright Rinity wondered if it glowed when he was in the sun, as white as an Elassi's. It contrasted his dark skin, which was smooth and unmarred. He wore a shirt of deep yellow, tucked loosely into a pair of gray pants that looked brand new—unlike the ripped and faded ones Rinity wore. The pants were cuffed to show off a pair of polished boots.

It looked the perfect outfit to adventure in—perhaps to pour over an ancient prophecy or decipher a hidden message. Maybe even rescue someone in need, like the Lord Nash of legends.

He must be a Librarian, Rinity concluded, though he seemed a shade young for the position. She guessed he was around her own age at eighteen or nineteen.

He crossed to the desk and as he did Rinity felt a tickle in her nose. She couldn't sneeze. Oh, *victory*, she couldn't sneeze.

He sat down in the chair and immediately began spinning in it and Rinity had to look away. She was not going to think about how attractive the Librarian looked as an expression of joy spread across his face.

Her nose tickled again and she tried the trick Amya had taught her—mouthing a word that began with 'w' and putting extra emphasis on that letter.

It didn't help.

The tickle grew stronger until she couldn't hold it back anymore. She drew in a sharp breath and buried her head in her arms in hopes of muffling the sound.

Still, it was a sound, and it rang through the vent.

"Stars give you strength," the Librarian said, almost automatically. His words were the superstitious blessing one traditionally said when a person sneezed; it wasn't commonly used in passing anymore but a well-read Librarian could have adopted the habit.

He rose and shuffled to the vent. "Is someone hiding up there?"

Rinity wasn't stupid enough to answer that.

He sighed. "That was dumb. What I meant was, I know you're hiding up there, so you might as well come down."

"No, thank you," Rinity said, her voice coming out smaller than she intended.

He gave a little shrug as he turned and Rinity's heart pounded as she realized what he intended to do.

"Please don't go get a Guard!"

"Why would I do that?" he asked easily as he grabbed a chair—not the one behind the desk but one from the other side that didn't spin—and dragged it over to the bookshelf as if he were coming to rescue the heroine of a story.

Not that she was a heroine. She was villager #3 at best.

"I wasn't doing anything wrong," she told him because she wasn't.

It wasn't fair that she couldn't read at the Library simply because she didn't know who her father was—and he probably wasn't anyone important anyway. It was stupid to have rules about who was allowed to frequent it. They were just books. It wasn't like they were anything dangerous.

But, of course, they were dangerous. They were books.

And there was nothing more dangerous than a civilian with ideas.

The Librarian climbed up onto the chair, so that his feet were on the arms. He balanced himself on the top of the bookshelf with his arms crossed across it, his chin resting on his arms.

"So, what're you doing up here then?" he asked, like he was curious about the answer, as if they were having a friendly chat about hypotheticals and not about a girl hiding in a Library vent.

"I forgot my membership card," she lied. "And I—well, I didn't want to create a scene."

He snorted at that and Rinity loved the sound of it. She pushed back the thought because it didn't matter that he was attractive and heroic and had the cutest snort. Even if he didn't turn her over to the Guards, he'd want nothing to do with her once he learned the truth about who she was.

Or as much of the truth as she knew.

"I'm pretty sure you already made one," he said, the humor warm in his voice.

"I didn't want to get thrown out." It was easy for him to laugh because he'd never had to worry about getting thrown out of a place before. He'd never had his blood questioned and sneered at. "It's embarrassing."

And it wasn't fair.

"You're absolutely right, such a scene would have been unfortunate, Miss...?" He trailed off and there was silence between them until Rinity realized he was waiting for her to supply her name.

"Rinity."

What had she just done? When you were lying to someone, you didn't give them your real name.

"Rinity," he repeated and her regret faded instantly. She liked the way her name sounded when he said it.

"And you are?" Since they were handing out names...

"Tov," he said and ducked his head.

"Like...?"

"Prince Tov," he finished with a nervous little smile as he looked back up to meet her eyes. His were a soft brown, like the worn leather of her favorite book, and a little murky, like the waters of the Englever River. "Like every other kid is named Tov, after the Prince, it seems."

It was true. She'd talked to a Tov on her way there. It was strange though, because it was more common for civilians than the ranked and connected, and usually in boys a little younger than the Prince himself. But he worked at the Library, so surely he was connected. And he was already young for a Librarian. She doubted him younger than her earlier assessment.

"So, we've established why you're up there," he said finally. "But you can't just stay up there."

She shrugged, then realized he couldn't see it. "I could."

"Not forever," he argued and there was an earnestness to his voice, soft and sure.

"I mean, I could."

"All right, fine. I'd prefer if you'd come down. Is that better?" He looked at her with an adorable, pleading expression and she hated how it made her heart beat. Was that how Lady Cecily felt when Lord Nash rescued her from the Zhadidock?

"Why?" She was stalling. The longer she kept him talking, the longer she could stay up there.

He offered her a little smile that could power an entire city for a month with all its radiance. "Because I want to get a better look at you. Cute as you are through the vent."

He had no way of knowing that; he couldn't see her that well in the vent. Maybe she ought to stay up there, because he'd probably find her less cute if she came down.

She shook her head, only to move it a little too vigorously and hit it up against the side of the vent wall. She gave a small hiss.

"Are you okay?" His voice was laced with concern.

"I'm fine."

He frowned, peering at her through the cracks in the vent as if he could properly examine her that way. "You ought to come down so I can take a look."

"Very smooth," she said with a laugh. Only Will and Amya and her stories made her laugh like that; why was she laughing at the Librarian? "Someone might come in. And what would they say if they found you alone in your office with a girl?"

"My...alone with a girl?" he said. "Who cares what they say?"

She laughed, because he was an idiot with an adorably dorkish smile. "You should. It's your reputation that'll be on the line—Royal Librarian with a girl in his office? How the rumors will fly."

"They'll fly a lot faster over the girl in my vent," he pointed out.

"Not if they don't know I'm here."

He sighed in an exaggerated way. "But just think of all the work it will be for me—I'll have to smuggle you in food and you'll probably want books to read too, and well, I think taking care of the girl in my vent is above my paygrade."

She laughed again without thinking but stopped herself almost immediately as the sound rang in the vents; she'd never noticed how strange her laugh sounded before. Did he hate it?

He sighed again, less dramatic that time. "Okay, fine, what if I promise I can get you out of here without getting caught? Will you come down then?"

A thrill ran through her at the promise of a daring adventure with the man who was clearly born for such a thing.

"Why would you do that?" she asked. "What's in it for you?"

He shrugged. "For one thing, I'll save myself from all the rumors that are supposedly going to fly about us. And, like I said, I'll get a better look at you."

"I'm cuter up here," she assured him as a list of all her flaws flooded her mind. He wouldn't much like her when he saw her, she was sure of it. "But you're right, I can't stay up here forever. You promise I won't get caught?"

"*Rook di goo.*"

Well, if he was going to be that serious about it...

"Okay, you get down and I'll come down," she agreed.

He shifted to get down and grabbed onto the top of the shelf as he slipped and lost his balance.

"Are you okay?"

He offered her a shaky smile as he moved a little slower that time. He kept a firm hold on the bookshelves as he descended. "All clear."

She gently pushed on the vent cover and meant to grab it but it slipped from her fingers. It fell with a crash as Tov cried out.

Chapter 2

"Are you okay?" Rinity asked as she scrambled out of the vent.

If she killed a Librarian, she'd be in so much trouble. And even if she hadn't killed him, she'd probably scarred his perfect face for life. Though she was sure he'd wear the scar well and be as dashing as ever.

The vent lay on the floor next to Tov, who stood holding his head with a frown. She hurried to climb down the bookshelf to stand beside him.

Victory, what if it was bad?

She shook off her racing thoughts as she scrambled onto the chair he'd used to climb up and talk to her. They were about the same height so she needed the chair to gain a better vantage point.

Except his hand was in the way. She pulled it away to find he was bleeding. She let out a little shriek as she drew back, nearly losing her balance. She managed to catch herself just in time, and looked back to Tov to find him scowling at her.

"If you don't want to get caught, stop making so much noise."

"You're bleeding." The bright red seeped into his platinum curls.

He looked at his hand, covered in blood, and his frown deepened. "Is it bad?"

"I don't know!" Rinity exclaimed. She'd killed him. He was going to die a slow, painful death bleeding out and it would be all her fault.

"I should probably find a medic," he said thoughtfully, like he was open to discussing other ideas, as he pressed his hand back to the wound.

"'Probably'?"

"Okay, I should go find a medic," he amended. "Which is the perfect distraction. I'll just let everyone know I'm bleeding and..."

"I can slip out the back."

"Right," he said with a nod and then winced. How badly had she hurt him?

"I'm sorry," she said. She should have said that straight away.

He offered her a smile that lit up his whole face and warmed her far more than it should have. Rinity wanted to blame it on the heat, but the building was air conditioned. "I'd do it all over again, just for another five minutes with you."

Oh, *victory,* he was smooth. He shouldn't say things like that and she shouldn't feel the things she was feeling when he said them. He wasn't Lord Nash and she wasn't a prin-cess worthy of being saved. She started to shake her head in protest.

"Please?" he said. "Just say you'll come back?"

She sighed, her willpower weak at his pleading expression as blood trickled down his face. Or, perhaps, she just wanted to use those as excuses so that she felt justified in her response. "Okay."

"Promise?"

She drew in a breath. "I promise I'll come back."

"*Rook di goo?*" he pressed.

She sighed. "*Rook di goo.*"

He took her hand in his—the one not covered in blood—and pressed her fingers softly to his lips. She felt herself sway, unable to stand properly all of a sudden. "Until next time, Miss Rinity."

He slipped from the room, presumably to find a medic.

As Rinity walked back to her apartment building she felt heavy and not just from the heat. It was sweltering, the city begging for a release from the relenting humidity that came from existing on a rainforest planet. Even walking along the river offered little relief.

But Rinity's mind wasn't on the heat, it was on Tov, the Librarian.

She'd sworn on her life to go back and see him but that wasn't the real her. She'd lied to him, straight to his face, and whether she let it go any further or stopped it there, it was already too late.

It wasn't some fantastic adventure novel, where the hero saved the girl and they lived in merry bliss for eternity. Rinity wasn't even particularly in need of saving.

Her feet pounded on the pavement of the sidewalk, slower than the pounding of her beating heart. The tall buildings that stood high and proud around her, looked down on her small frame in disapproval. As if they could see into her thoughts and knew just how foolish she was to think about a Librarian—noble and goodhearted and kind—in that way.

She'd been so distracted she'd forgotten to take a book with her—it wasn't exactly stealing, since she always brought them back. And the rules forbidding her borrowing them were nonsensical and arbitrary. So, she gave herself the privileges others were allowed.

And when—if—she went back, it would just be more of the same. All she'd be able to think about was how cute Tov was and how kissable his lips looked.

Victory, she wanted to kiss him.

And she wanted him to kiss her back. Wanted him to never find out the truth about who she was and how she'd lied to him.

She'd told him she had a membership card. She hadn't just let him think she belonged, she'd said as much. She'd lied to his face. And it was a lie she wouldn't be able to keep up. He'd find out the truth and she'd lose him and the Library.

Not that he was really hers to lose.

But the Library wasn't hers to lose either.

She'd stolen it and in the back of her mind, somewhere deep inside, she always known it would come to an end eventually.

And that time had come. She couldn't go back to the Library. It was easier to end it like that than to face him again. She couldn't face him again.

But she'd sworn on her life—the highest vow a Liosi could make. Because she was stupid and impulsive and just said whatever popped into her head. She should have told him no.

She reached the apartment building, almost startled when she looked up and saw it there. She'd been so lost in thought her feet had brought her home while her mind had wandered elsewhere.

She sighed as she looked up at the weathered stone building she'd called home for most of her life. It wasn't a bad home and at least she'd gotten to stay in one place—a perk for no other reason than she got to stay across the hall from her best friend.

But as she looked at it, she couldn't help thinking how sad and sorry it looked. How badly the air stank as the heat made the smell all the viler. At how cramped and crowded and dirty it was when just across the river the Library sat in its glorious splendor.

And she thought of how Tov looked—clean and sleek and rich, like a storybook hero—while she looked far more like her sad, sorry apartment building.

She needed to stop those thoughts before they went too far, needed something else to fill her mind, and so she went to the one thing she knew well.

"*Yesterday, or perhaps long ago,*" she began, the traditional words for beginning a story falling off her tongue with ease. "There was a Mahsirian princess, Elisandra by name…"

Chapter 3

Amya Cole shut the door to her family's apartment with a heavy sigh, still able to hear the sounds of laughter, arguing, music, and life that came from the other side.

She pressed a finger to her throbbing temple as she ignored the twinge of guilt that fluttered within her for slipping away. But Norah and Alana were arguing about the best way to make bazzerals and Malaya and Dalen were supposed to be finishing their chores but were instead turning everything into a competition that always ended in a wrestling match of sorts. And in the midst of it were her parents, slow dancing to the decidedly not slow song that filtered through the radio.

Amya had attempted to focus on her mending but found it impossible. And all her siblings weren't even home.

She slipped across the hall to the Garrick residence where she rapped on the door and waited a moment before she knocked again. When no one answered she used her key to let herself in, grateful for Rinity's stepfather and his willingness to let the girl across the hall have a key to his apartment.

The shower was running as she stepped inside. She wasn't sure if it was Rinity or Mr. Garrick, but either way they'd want tea when they got out and Amya wasn't ready to go back to her own apartment yet.

She moved from the front room—with the threadbare sofa and stuffed chair with the hole in it and the nicked low table that Amya often spread her sewing projects out across when she was over there—and into the cramped kitchen. The Coles had taken down the wall that separated the kitchen and the front room so they had one room in their house their entire family fit in.

She set the water to boil and washed up the few dishes that were left out. Rinity usually did them but she had an interview and probably forgot or was too nervous.

The shower shut off as Amya settled at the table with a contented sigh, her fingers wrapped around the warm cup of tea.

She was halfway through it when Rinity padded down the hall, dressed in a plain lavender tee shirt and black shorts, her orange hair wet.

"Hey," Rinity said as she grabbed a cup and poured herself some tea.

"How'd the interview go?" Amya asked as her friend took a seat across from her.

Rinity looked dazed, as if she didn't know what Amya spoke of. Had she forgotten she had an interview or had she forgotten to go in the first place?

Rinity sighed and shrugged. "They said they'll get back to me. Which we both know means 'no thank you.'"

Amya had worked—taking in mending—since she was eleven. But Mr. Garrick didn't want to burden Rinity more than necessary. He always said there was plenty of time for her to work when she was older. But that time had come and there were few places that wanted to hire someone with no experience.

"I'm sorry, firefly."

Rinity shrugged again, her gaze on her mug.

"I'm surprised you're not at the Library." Amya wasn't exactly fond of her friend's habit. If Rinity was caught, she'd be banned from the library at best—which she already was, but it did no good—or jailed at worse, if they saw her as a threat. If they caught her stealing books she'd be tried for treason; it was a crime against the Crown to steal from the Royal Library.

But Rinity was never cautious, not when there were stories involved.

"I met someone," her friend blurted out.

Amya leaned forward, concern washed away and replaced by curiosity; it was the most interesting thing she'd heard all week. "Someone as in a romantic someone?"

"He's a Librarian." Rinity stared intently at the mug of tea before her like it was something worth watching.

"And?" Amya pressed as she rested her elbows on the table and her chin on her fists.

Rinity sucked in a breath. "I was trying to hide, and I might have let him believe I just happened to forget my membership card. And I might have injured him and then he still helped me sneak out even though he was bleeding."

There was so much to unpack in that but Amya started with the most important question first. "Is he cute?"

Rinity shook her head.

"He isn't cute?" Amya wrinkled up her nose, not sure why they were even having the conversation if he wasn't attractive.

"Of course, he's cute!"

It wasn't really a given, but Amya wasn't going to argue that point, not when there were more important things to discuss.

"But it doesn't matter," Rinity continued. "Because we're never going to see each other again."

"You injured him and he still helped you," Amya said with a roll of her eyes. "I think it's worth pursuing. It could be true love."

"He thinks I'm rich and connected. When he finds out I'm not, he's going to hate me." Rinity looked up and met her eyes. "Besides, who are you to talk about love—I thought all that mattered was how high up the social ladder you could climb?"

It was a low blow. Amya had to remind herself that Rinity'd had a bad day, she was disappointed about her interview, she was anxious about the Librarian she was clearly taken with. It wasn't personal, Rinity was just stressed and tired.

"You can have both though, with your Librarian. I never said I didn't want love. All I'm saying is if I had to choose between love and social standing, I'll climb the ladder any day. I'm not going to spend the rest of my life in a cramped apartment struggling to survive. Love doesn't pay the bills, firefly."

Amya loved her parents, she really did. And she knew what Mr. and Mrs. Cole had worked for them. But it didn't work for her. Nine kids were too many—far too many—for that tiny apartment. She knew how hard they worked to keep food on the table and the lights on and each child clothed. It all added up. And Amya just wanted to not have to worry about those kinds of things anymore.

"You're all talk," Rinity said with a shake of her head. "Some horrible rich man is going to propose and you're going to realize you can't go through with it."

Rinity really was a bad listener sometimes. "I never said I was going to marry someone horrible; he can be rich and still be decent. And he can be decent and I can still not love him. All I'm saying is I'll take stability over passion if it comes down to it."

"I'm not arguing this with you," Rinity said as she finished her tea and set the cup down in front of her.

She was the one who had started the whole debate but Amya didn't feel the need to point that out. "So, tell me what happened."

Rinity shook her head. "I told you, it doesn't matter. When he finds out the truth, he's going to hate me."

"You mean when he finds out you aren't rich?"

"I don't even know who my father is, My." Rinity's voice was soft and sad.

Rinity had always wondered about her father, a struggle Amya couldn't even pretend to understand. Her own father had always been present in her life—working hard to provide for them and then coming home at the end of each shift. He wasn't even one to go to the bar, eager to be home with his family.

"I'm sorry." Amya wasn't sure what else to say, not when she was at the Garrick apartment to escape her family when Rinity would do anything to have what she had.

Rinity shook her head and brushed a tear of her face. "It's fine."

Rinity had always been a sweetheart, far more than Amya could ever hope to live up to; not that she wanted to, but there were times she felt a little guilty about not being at least a little more like her friend.

It wasn't fair for Rinity to have to cry over a boy that way, over something as simple as circumstances she had no control over.

"It's not fair," Amya said with a shake of her head. Rinity deserved a chance with her cute Librarian. She did. Nothing as stupid as social convention ought to keep them apart. So what that Rinity wasn't rich or connected? She had a good heart and that's what mattered. "We're going to make those wishes come true."

"What?" Rinity's brow scrunched in deeper as she looked across the table at her friend.

Amya brought her palms down on the table as she pushed herself up, ready to spring into action.

"We're going to make your Librarian fall in love with you. And you're going to spend the rest of your days reading books and being far better than me."

Rinity shook her head as she opened her mouth to protest the comment about her being better than Amya, no doubt. But Amya wasn't about to hear it.

"No, it's true, you are better than me. It's fine, I like who I am. And I know what you deserve—and we're going to get it for you."

Rinity didn't know what Amya was talking about as her friend rose and started to pace. Amya spoke to herself in low mutters, whatever she said clearly more for her benefit than Rinity's.

Finally, Amya turned to her, a frown on her face. "First things first, we need a place for you two to interact that's a little less...well, no, rather gives you a little more of an opportunity for genuine connection."

They'd had a genuine connection already. Except, she'd been lying to him.

Rinity shook her head. "It'll never work."

It couldn't. And even if it could, regardless of what her friend said, she didn't deserve it. Not when she'd lied to him.

Amya frowned at her; she never did like being told what she could or couldn't do. "It's not right—there's no logical reason why you shouldn't be allowed in the Library and why your Librarian shouldn't be interested in you— you're funny and smart and have a better heart than the rest of us. We're going to make him see that."

Amya was both Liosi and Alisethian and having the dual heritage made it easier for her to distance herself from and be quicker to call out customs that didn't make sense to her, things she hadn't been indoctrinated with since birth. Rinity opened her mouth to protest but Amya kept talking.

"Field trip—you're going to sneak me into the Library too. I want to make sure he's worth it and see what exactly I'm working with. Then we'll go from there."

It would be hard to sneak two people into the Library. And it was a foolish plan. But...Amya was good at getting what she wanted and she did really seem to want that.

And maybe she was right—maybe Rinity did deserve a chance.

At the very least, Rinity would rather talk about that and pursue it than her failed job interview. No, it was interviews. Plural. Because it had been time and again that she'd struggled through it—awkward small talk and feigning interest in jobs that seemed mind-numbingly boring—because she wanted to get paid.

She didn't know how Amya did it, how she always seemed interested in everything when it clearly wasn't; Rinity had books to read, she didn't want to know that anecdote about the previous receptionist that she doubted would have been funny even if she had been there to witness it.

Rinity nodded. "Tonight?"

It wouldn't end well. But if Rinity refused, it would just make her friend approach it with all the more gusto. Better to ride it out and let it end disastrously so Amya could see for herself what a terrible plan it was.

"I have to help make dinner tonight." Amya's frown deepened as she glanced at the clock on the wall. "How late is the Library open?"

"We'll go tomorrow," Rinity said, because she didn't know if she could go back that night. Plus, Tov might not even be there; the medic probably sent him home.

Amya nodded in agreement. "Tomorrow it is then. All right, I don't have to be home for another hour at least, tell me everything—from start to finish."

What that really meant was she didn't want to go home. Rinity had a hard time understanding that—she'd have given anything for a family like Amya's. They were all so warm and close. And sure, they were a little loud, but that was life, filling their apartment and brimming over. And while she liked her own little family of just her and Will—though she missed her mother dearly—she'd have given anything for a sibling, especially an older brother, as they always seemed a decent thing to have.

Though, according to Amya, brothers were complete idiots and nothing to be coveted.

"We need more tea."

They settled into their usual easiness, the time passing as Rinity told Amya every detail of her adventure and Amya caught her up on the latest escapades—stupidity, as she called it—of her siblings.

The front door opened, interrupting the conversation.

"Hey, Will," Rinity called as her stepfather came through the door. His slate blue coveralls were covered in grease, as always.

A smile spread across his grimy face, brightening under the dirt and sweat. "Hey, kiddo," he said, reaching down to unlace his boots. "Amya."

"Hi, Mr. Garrick."

"Amya was just telling me a story," Rinity told him as he set his boots onto the mat by the door.

She looked at her friend and then back at Will. She really needed Amya to finish the story she was telling before it drove her mad. Not because it was particularly thrilling, but because it was already starting to itch, the way the words were left hanging there, untold, existing in a limbo of waiting. They deserved to be—needed to be—released.

Amya looked at the clock and Rinity remembered that she needed to get home to cook dinner.

"You two finish up," Will said, already headed down the hall to the bathroom to take a shower, like he always did at the end of a work shift.

"Can you stay another minute or two?" Rinity asked her friend.

Amya's smile softened. "Don't worry, I'll finish the story."

Rinity melted with relief.

It only took her another minute to tell the tale to its completion. Then she gave Rinity a hug—or, rather, she let Rinity give her a hug, because Amya hated hugs—before she left for her own apartment across the hall.

Chapter 4

"You're here."

Rinity closed the volume she'd been reading but didn't look up. She'd only talked to him once, but she knew the sound of that voice well already.

She drew in a shaky breath as she slipped the book back into place on the shelf and turned to the speaker. The blond-haired Librarian looked back at her with eyes wide, mouth slightly agape. A plaster bandage was taped across his hairline, on the left side of his forehead and stuck out from under his blond hair. The curls shone in the soft, overhead light; it created a glow that was akin to an Elassi prince.

"Hi," she started to say but he reached for her and his arm slipped around her waist to draw her to him. Before she knew what was happening, he placed a quick kiss on her lips.

Her first kiss.

It was over before she even truly knew it had begun and she was left breathless as a strange warmth filled her down to her toes. She rather liked the way it felt. And she understood why heroines in stories liked being kissed so much.

He drew back, with a violent shake of his head that made his curls dance. "I'm so sorry. I shouldn't have..."

"Oh."

She felt the breath knocked out of her; he regretted kissing her. Of course, he did. It was okay; she shouldn't want him to kiss her again anyway. She wasn't some beautiful heroine; she was just a girl who snuck into the Library that didn't want her and whose biggest life skill was failing job interviews.

"No!" he exclaimed as he reached a hand toward her before he drew it back again. "No. I—I didn't mean it that way."

Were there other ways to mean it? "Then how...?"

He let out a shaky sigh. "I don't even know you. I—I have a habit of doing that—of falling hard and moving too fast. I didn't even ask. You just met me. You probably didn't—"

"I liked it," she cut him off.

He stared at her, mouth open, saying nothing. But what was there to say? She was bold and had said the wrong thing. He hated her. He probably liked genteel, connected girls, who knew how to act around men, not civilian girls who wanted to be kissed and kissed and kissed by boys they'd just met and didn't know how to tell them that properly.

"I'm sorry," she said with a shake of her head, turning. "I ought to..."

His hand caught her wrist, not exactly holding her back; she could have easily slipped herself free. It was more a request for her to stay than a demand. She turned back.

"I liked it too."

She would have accused him of teasing her except his expression was so sincere. He stepped toward her and she let him, her back pressed against the bookshelf so she was tucked nearly between it and Tov. It was like every dream she'd never known to have—books and someone who wanted to kiss her and a feeling of safety, that she didn't need to be anything more than exactly who she was standing there.

"I was hoping you'd come back today."

"I come back most days." Yet, somehow, she'd never seen him before. But she did often avoid the Librarians, for fear they'd throw her out. "I come to read the books."

What else did someone come to a library for? Obviously, she came to read the books. Why did she always say stupid things?

"And to hide in vents," he reminded her.

She dropped her gaze. "Only when I don't have my membership card."

It wasn't strictly a lie. She never had a membership card on her. But it did imply she had one, she just forgot it.

So still a lie.

"What were you reading?"

She perked up at that, looking back up at him as a smile spread across her face. "*Ramsey's Myths*. I like her version of Verena and the Rahf better than other versions because Verena plays a more active role in her story. The kidnapping aspect of other versions always makes me uncomfortable, but in this one she stumbles upon the injured Rahf and chooses to stay with him to nurse him back to health."

She was rambling. To a Librarian. "Sorry, you probably know all of this because you've read it before."

"I actually haven't," he confessed. "It sounds fascinating."

"It's one of my favorites," she mumbled.

She looked away from him, at the space between them, at the books just behind him, anywhere but his eyes. Her gaze fell on the plaster bandage on his forehead. It nearly blended in with his skin tone, but she could see it faintly outlined in the dim library lighting. She ought to have asked about his head sooner but they'd been...busy...

"How's your head?"

"Spinning," he murmured as he stroked her cheek lightly.

"You ought to sit down." She started to push away. "Head wounds aren't something to mess with."

At least, it never seemed to end well for characters in stories when they got head wounds. Sir Callum, the Warrior of Samara, Lady Marin, Sir Duran, Lord Corrin, the Lady of Dix. They all died from head wounds.

He put a hand on her arm and the warmth against her bare skin, chilled from the air conditioning, sent a shiver through her. "I thought you meant from kissing you. I forgot you tried to kill me yesterday."

"I didn't try to kill you!" She fought to keep her words a hiss, keenly aware that they were in the Library and the books wouldn't like it if she yelled.

His brown eyes were warm and inviting—like the tea she and Amya often shared—and his mouth quirked in a faint, teasing smile. "If you say so."

She settled back into her space between him and the bookshelves.

"I like kissing you," he said, tracing his finger up and down her check in a way that made her shiver and warm all over at the same time.

At least he wasn't angry with her about his injury. He'd teased her about it and you didn't kiss someone like that, not when you were angry. It was too light, too pure, too decidedly not angry.

"And you said you liked kissing me," he said, looking at her with that earnest look again, searchingly, as if he were questioning it, doubting that she'd meant it.

A teasing smile pulled at her lips, a match for the one he'd given her. "I think I liked it."

"You think?"

His expression fell and he started to release her, to take a step back, but stopped when she said, "I think I might need you to kiss me again, just to be sure."

A grin spread across his face as his eyes lit up and he reached for her to do just exactly as she requested.

Chapter 5

Amya and Rinity had been at the Library all of ten minutes before Amya lost her friend completely.

It didn't surprise her. She had taken Rinity to the Library. Of course, she'd lose her to the books, she never stood a chance in that competition.

She tried to remember everything Rinity had said about her Librarian but all she came up with was that he had the same name as the Prince and a kind smile—neither of which would help her find the man. Oh, and he did have blond hair, that would help distinguish him from the other librarians.

Not that librarians wore uniforms or anything, so Amya really had no way of knowing who was a Librarian and who was a patron.

So, she was looking for a blond-haired boy with a cute smile. If she saw any, she'd just have to ask his name.

Everyone was dressed in blazers and button ups and pressed trousers in neutral colors. It reminded Amya once more just how much she didn't fit into that world in her long, flowing skirt with the floral pattern and her fitted, periwinkle high-necked crop top. She regretted not borrowing Alana's blazer, not only because it would have made her fit in a little better, but also because it was freezing there; why did they have the air conditioning cranked so high? Rich people—wasting perfectly good money on things like air.

It was too late to go home and change though.

She scanned the Library, searching every face for someone Rinity might give her heart to so easily. Her friend could be trusting, it was true, but she'd never fallen for a boy before. So, whoever he was, he must be very special.

Her gaze fell on a young man sitting at a table across the room, his own gaze also scanning over everything. There was something carefully schooled about his neutral expression that gave the impression that he worked hard to keep the emotions off his face.

He was just a bit older than her—mid-twenties perhaps, to her early twenties—thin and wiry and his dark, wispy hair stuck out in all directions, untamed, in sharp contrast to the complete order and control of his schooled expression and crisp white button-up.

Their eyes met across the Library and his scowl deepened.

Amya was okay with that; she didn't mind a challenge. He was cute enough—*victory*, he was cute—and he looked to have an air of affluence about him that only came with actually having money; it wasn't something you could put on without the money to back it up.

Besides, she would never seriously consider a relationship with someone she'd meet at the Library. They were either rich or had a military rank or were connected to someone who did or all of the above. Any flirting she did with him was just practice for someone she actually stood a chance with.

She crossed the room to him, weaving through the rows of tables, her long skirt swaying with each step. She let her hips sway too as she walked, a shy smile on her face as she approached.

The man's expression never changed. He kept scanning the room and came back to her from time to time but never fully settled on her.

She reached his table and slid out the chair next to him. "Is this seat taken?"

He looked at her, his brow furrowed in as he tapped his fingers on the table in front of him. "Why?"

"Because I want to sit in it," she said with a laugh.

His brows raised, a question in them. "And I'll just ask again—why? There's a whole library full of seats, surely you can find another that isn't occupied."

"Maybe I want to sit next to you."

He snorted at that and his mouth quirked up into something that resembled a smile; it was a very nice mouth, she did have to admit. He had shifted to one finger tapping rather than four, the single finger drumming rapidly on the table.

"And maybe I'm not interested in what you're offering."

"And what's that?" she asked with a laugh. "All I said was hello."

"Actually, you never offered a greeting," he replied, not looking at her as he continued to scan the room and he switched back to drumming all four of his fingers on the wooden table before him.

That was true and also a little rude of her. "I'm sorry. I suppose I should have started with hello. Should I start over?"

He looked at her, as if sizing her up. But his expression was so schooled she couldn't tell how she measured up. It left her imagination to fill in the blanks and it wasn't a flattering assessment. "I still wouldn't be interested in what you were offering."

"Who says I'm offering anything?" She laughed to cover the way the words stung; she knew she didn't belong, but he didn't need to remind her so bluntly. "Maybe I just want to sit next to you."

"So, you can flirt with me, though to what end I haven't decided yet," he replied, back to scanning the library. He rose. "But either way, I'm not interested."

She looked in the direction of his gaze and saw Rinity with a blond-haired young man.

Rinity's Librarian did have a rather nice smile, Amya had to admit.

Amya's attention gone from her failed flirting, she rose. She and the man stood side by side and he towered over her. *Victory*, he was tall.

Or, perhaps she was just short.

But she put that thought from her mind as she pushed past him so she could cross the room hastily, until she reached Rinity and the Librarian, Tov.

The man followed her though and she had the sinking realization that he intended to join the group, no doubt friends with Rinity's cute Librarian.

"We should go," she said as soon as she reached Rinity.

She didn't want the man to come over and judge Rinity, to size her up with the same critical eye with which he'd assessed Amya. Because his thoughts on her had been rude but warranted. No doubt he would see Rinity the same way when she didn't deserve that and Amya wouldn't subject her to it.

Rinity was sweet and kind and would never pursue someone based on looks and position alone. If she liked her Librarian it was because she saw something deeper in him and Amya was not going to let anyone—especially not that arrogant man, no matter how perfect his face and general appearance—make her feel insecure about those feelings.

"Now, Rin," she said as she dragged her protesting friend away. Rinity's fingers had been entwined with Tov's but they untangled as Amya pulled her away.

"Gibbs!" she heard Tov say as the man approached but Amya walked so fast, they were out of earshot before any reply could be heard.

So, his name was Gibbs. The wildly attractive, arrogant man.

Not that Amya found arrogance attractive. In fact, it made him all the less so. Then he gave her that little quirk of a smile and she was mush. Insufferable man! He had no right to be that attractive if he wasn't going to have the personality to accompany it.

"My, we can't just walk out the front door," Rinity hissed and it pulled Amya back to reality. That was exactly the direction they were headed as Amya stomped with purposeful strides.

She made eye contact with the doorman, the one who checked membership cards as people came in, and his eyes narrowed, no doubt trying to place whether or not he'd let in these two girls who clearly didn't belong there.

It was too late to back down. If they turned and ran, it would be an admittance that they didn't belong there. And they didn't. But Amya was sick of being reminded of that.

She raised her chin and straightened her back to pull herself to her full height. She shot him a glare through narrowed eyes that all but dared him to come over and question whether or not they were allowed there. He withered under the look and the thrill of it rushed through her.

Her deliberate strides sure, she stomped out of the Library and dragged Rinity down the steps. Warm air hit her cold skin and it sent a shiver up her spine. That was precisely why there was no good reason to waste perfectly good money on cold air when you'd just have to step back out into the humidity later.

She continued stomping down the street, waiting until they were a good ways away to finally give in and listen to her friend's pleas to slow down. Rinity ought to be able to keep up, since her legs were longer than Amya's. But Amya stopped all the same to turn and face Rinity, who looked at her with questioning eyes.

"Are you okay, My?"

Was she okay? Did she have any choice but to be anything else? Her encounter with the man called Gibbs had rattled her. It would complicate things if he and Rinity's Librarian were friends.

She didn't like complicated.

But she didn't have a choice, she never did. It was always complicated and she'd learned to adapt and move on.

"So, you saw him again?"

It wasn't about Amya. It was about Rinity. And she'd keep the focus there.

Rinity flushed at the mention of her Librarian. "He kissed me."

He what? They were kissing already? They'd only just met. But Rinity smiled that shy smile of hers and Amya couldn't judge her. It did feel nice to be kissed.

"Did you like it?" Of course, she did; it was written all over her face.

Amya linked her arm in Rinity's and her friend slipped her arm free to put her arm around Amya's waist and draw her closer. She rested her head on Amya's shoulder as they started toward home.

"He kissed me more than once."

"So, you must have liked it."

Rinity giggled. "I did. I liked it very much. Then he ruined it when he asked if I was going to be at the Library Dedication Ceremony—though I couldn't tell if he wanted me to be there or not, by the way he asked the question."

"The Library what now?" Amya asked; the Library had been around for generations, surely it had already been dedicated.

Rinity sighed. "The Library Dedication Ceremony. It's to celebrate the Library's anniversary and dedicate it to

Prince Tov before his coronation next month."

The Prince turned nineteen next month and even though he'd all but taken on the position as ruler, he still wasn't officially king. Technically the country was run by a Lord Regent and several advisors.

"Why would they dedicate the Library to the Prince?"

Why did the rich and ranked and connected insist on such endless frivolity all the time? As if there weren't far more important matters to see to, better have a party to dedicate the Library.

"It's tradition," Rinity explained. "Whenever a new king is crowned, they dedicate the Library to him, as a show of goodwill, in hopes that he'll continue to support them."

So, it was for funding. That made sense. They threw a big party and stuck his name on a plaque and in return the King made sure there was plenty of money for them in the government's budget. But she wasn't about to rant about how stupid that was—especially when once again, only the upper class benefitted from it—because it wouldn't do Rinity any good.

And besides, Rinity was still talking anyway. "There'll be dancing and readings of classic myths and probably the most divine food you've ever tasted."

"Why can't you go?" Amya asked.

Rinity snorted. "Because it's not something you sneak into, you have to have an invitation and they have real security and everything. The Prince will be there, they have to be cautious."

"So, we get you in." Amya said.

Rinity shook her head and sighed. "It's not that simple."

"We'll get you in," Amya promised. She'd find a way.

"What will I even wear?" Rinity said with a shake of her head, looking down at her tee shirt and ripped, faded denim leggings.

Amya grinned. "That's the easy part."

Chapter 6

Rinity had never been shopping with Amya before.

Shopping was Amya's sanctuary, her way to recharge, and the only place she felt truly herself—or so she claimed. She had also said, time and again, that she didn't want to expose Rinity to that side of her.

But Amya said she could make Rinity something divine to rival any dress at the Dedication Ceremony and dragged Rinity to the shop without waiting for confirmation.

They stepped through the doors of the secondhand shop and Amya's whole demeanor shifted. Something melted off her; Rinity watched it fall. It was as if the mask disappeared to show a side of Amya that Rinity didn't see even during conversations over tea.

Rinity didn't doubt her friend's sewing skills—she'd seen what Amya had done with her own wardrobe—but she doubted they'd rival anything so fine and fancy as someone who had a personal seamstress. Rinity didn't want to offend her friend by such a suggestion—Amya was her own personal seamstress in that instance. But what Amya had offered to do was different from the simple mending or modifications she did for a living; it was a serious project, one people spent years training for.

But Rinity saw the way Amya's whole body relaxed, the hard edge to her expression softened by the genuine smile that played at her lips. And Rinity wouldn't have contradicted her for all the books in the galaxy.

As Amya glided to a rack, she moved with a careful ease that was different than the confidence she usually moved with. There was nothing coy about Amya's movements there; they were unbridled but calculating and precise.

She took her time to look through each rack, each bin, each shelf, to not overlook or underestimate anything. She muttered to herself as she looked. The first few times, Rinity had inquired what had been said only to have Amya look at her in a daze, confused by the encounter. It was after the second or third time that Rinity caught on that nothing being said was meant for her.

Amya shoved dresses upon dresses into Rinity's arms until Rinity could barely see over the pile. But she dutifully trailed behind—partially out of concern and partially because she was curious to see how the matter played out.

They weren't all ball gowns and honestly, Rinity didn't want to put on the ones that were. They were several decades out of fashion with a ridiculous number of flounces and poofs and frills.

And several were shorter dresses, not something one wore to a high-class event like that. But she wasn't about to tell Amya that, because her friend was clearly in a daze, and also, she didn't want to remind Amya that the world she wished to sneak into wasn't one either of them belonged in.

She shouldn't go. Shouldn't get in any deeper with Tov. She'd betrayed him when she'd lied to him and she'd betrayed him again when she'd let him kiss her knowing she'd lied to him.

She ought to break it off before either of them got hurt.

Except it was too late for that.

Before either of them got hurt any more than they already would?

Amya grabbed Rinity's hand, somehow finding it buried under layers and layers of satin and tulle and lace, and marched in the direction of the fitting room.

"My, I don't think..." Rinity began as she was pushed into a fitting room. Amya came in behind her and shut the door. "I mean, I don't know if any of these..."

"I'll make it work," Amya said as she grabbed the dresses from Rinity one by one. She divided them out in what seemed to be some form of organization; some were hung on one hook, others on another hook, and more on the hooks on the opposite wall.

Once Rinity had been completely relieved of her burden, Amya took a step back and surveyed the scene before her. Finally, she pulled a green dress from the hook and handed it to her friend. "We'll start with this one."

It was an adorable little dress, perfect for a night out or an intimate gathering. But it was hardly appropriate for the Library Dedication Ceremony.

"My..."

Amya frowned at her, her brows pulled in, her lips pursed. She waved her hands around her at the walls of dresses hanging about them. "We have everything we need here to create you a dress fit for a Librarian's girlfriend."

"I'm not his girlfriend," Rinity protested.

"He kissed you," Amya stated. "Several times. He better have honorable intentions or he and I are going to have a very long chat about what one should and shouldn't be doing with good-natured girls in the dusty corners of the Library."

Rinity blushed, pleased at her friend's passion about her honor and embarrassed that she'd let a boy kiss her when she barely knew him and had no idea what his intentions were. He was probably leading her on. And she couldn't even be mad at him because she'd lied to and betrayed him too.

"I can't do this."

It was wrong.

"I'm not going to make you do this," Amya said, studying her with questioning eyes. "But I'm also not going to let fear hold you back. I thought you liked him."

"I do." She did. She really, truly did.

"And you seem to think he likes you."

He did. She thought. He had kissed her. And he'd seemed so happy when he'd seen her. And he'd even teased her about getting injured.

And he'd kissed her. Like she was the heroine in a legend.

"He does," she said. She shook her head. "But it doesn't matter."

He'd find out the truth about her and it'd be too much to forgive.

"You deserve this." Amya put a hand on either of her shoulders and looked up to meet Rinity's eyes. "You are more than good enough for him. And if we don't push back against these rules, who's to stop people from making more rules that are even worse? It's a stupid rule."

Rinity shook her head. Amya would try to fight the entire class system over that. But it wasn't that bad; she just wasn't allowed to read books.

Her chest squeezed at the thought of never reading another book again. She'd lose the Library. She'd lose her books. No matter how it ended, she'd lose.

Unless Amya was right.

Maybe Tov could forgive her. Maybe he'd understand. If he were a hero in a legend he'd understand and forgive. That's what heroes did. And Amya thought they had a chance at happiness; why shouldn't she go after it?

She could have a kindhearted Librarian with gentle kisses and a soft smile for the rest of her life. And books. So many books.

It was the life she'd always wanted—the books anyway; the Librarian and the kisses were a new desire, but rather strong all the same. Why shouldn't she be happy?

"Do you really think I have a chance?"

Amya laughed. "You're right that he has a very nice smile and I only saw him for a moment, but the smile was directed at you. He's fallen hard, perhaps even as hard as you've fallen for him. So yes, I think you stand a chance."

"I lied to him."

Amya frowned, the wrinkles on her forehead growing deeper. "What else were you supposed to do? You were driven to it by unjust laws. That's not a lie, it's merely self-preservation.

Rinity started to protest that she didn't in fact need books to survive but realized that wasn't true. She did need them. She always had. Surely a Librarian, of all people, would understand that.

Amya pulled another dress from a hanger—a champagne gown with bold glitter. "Let's try this one instead, I forgot, since you dyed your hair, I can't dress you in green anymore without you looking like a Liosi flag."

Chapter 7

Amya's eyes had burned for an hour or more but the longer she sewed the more the burning subsided, as if her eyes had come to terms with the fact that the burning, dry sensation was their reality.

It wasn't as if it were the first time she'd done it to them.

She only had a few days and between her work sewing and her project, it seemed every waking moment was spent with a needle in her hands. She probably would have dreamt about sewing and dress designs, except that she was so exhausted her sleep was nothing but a brief moment of darkness before morning came far too soon.

Not that she was complaining. She liked being able to contribute to her family and the dresses for the party were coming along beautifully. She'd worked hard on the designs—harder than she'd worked on anything in her life before.

But as she sat there in her family's apartment, bent over her project that she was nearly done with, her eyes squinting to see the tiny stitches in the dim light, the realization hit her.

They needed invitations.

She'd forgotten that. She'd put it from her mind when they'd been looking for dresses, because she'd determined to tackle the situation one problem at a time. Except she'd been so preoccupied with her sewing she'd forgotten about everything else.

She let the mound of fabric and lace fall from her hands, not caring that it fell to the floor, the needle lost in the mess. The thread would surely get knotted, but it didn't matter. Not anymore.

She'd spent three days on two dresses—cutting apart three different dresses for parts to salvage what she could. She'd used every piece and raided her scraps and notions as needed.

She'd sacrificed her sleep, pushing herself to stay up just a little longer and just a little longer after that until it had somehow slipped into that strange interval that wasn't quite morning yet but was also no longer exactly night. She barely managed to sneak in a few hours of sleep before she awoke again to sew her heart out once more.

Her poor family had learned not to disturb her, as she'd all but taken to hissing at them when they tried to engage with her. She'd been so fixed on her project, her attention focused solely on getting those dresses made.

They were gorgeous—her best work. Rinity's had a full skirt of a soft peach color, the bodice ivory, coming down and sewn into the skirt in such a way that the two flowed together, no longer looking like the two pieces of very different dresses that they had previously been. Her own was a mulberry miracle she'd managed to make from a single hideous dress that she'd trimmed down, reshaped, and embellished.

But it was for nothing.

She let out a frustrated sigh that came out more like a strangled scream.

"What's up?"

Amya jumped as she looked up and found her older brother, Bender. He towered over her—tall and muscular—and looked down with a frown. His arms were crossed over his broad chest, his muscles bulging under his shirt, the tip of his tattoo that wove around his bicep peeking out from the hem of his sleeve.

She hadn't realized she'd been heard above the usual noise of her family; six of her siblings were home and it made it easy to blend into the background or even be drowned out completely.

"It's fine," she said with a shake of her head. She wasn't going to explain it all to him.

He bent down and picked up the discarded dress. She didn't even wince as his calloused fingers touched her precious fabric; she would have bitten his head off if he'd touched them the day before but she was too exhausted, all her drive suddenly gone. "Doesn't seem like nothing. You worked pretty hard on this to just throw it on the floor."

She let out another frustrated squeal as he tried to hand it to her and attempted to push him away before he could set the dress on her lap; he was sturdier than her, so it was like pushing at a stone wall.

"It doesn't matter anymore." Her eyes burned as they begged her to give them reprieve and she cursed them as they started to water. She wasn't crying—she wasn't a crier—but sometimes her eyes betrayed her like that so it might seem like she was crying to an observer.

Dalen let out a shriek and a wet dishrag sailed through the air, coming toward them. Bender caught it and turned to their siblings. "You three need to settle, Mam and Da aren't going to be happy if I tell them you were causing trouble while they were gone."

Mam and Da weren't home? Amya hadn't even noticed they'd left, she'd been so caught up in her project.

Her siblings shrank back under Bender's scowl; Amya remembered being scared of her brother too when she was younger. She'd since learned there was a lot more bark than bite, at least when it came to his siblings.

Bender turned back to her. "So, what's the dress for?"

Amya shook her head. "Rinity and I were going to go to the Library Dedication Ceremony—Rinity really wants to go. But you need an invitation and obviously we aren't getting invitations and it's tomorrow and I forgot about that part. I was so caught up in the dresses I forgot that part."

Amya didn't forget stuff, not usually. But when it came to sewing projects, she just...got lost. She forgot everything when she was that invested in her sewing.

Why wouldn't her stupid eyes stop burning?

Bender snorted and she fixed him with a death glare that rivaled his own; they were related, after all. "Just because you think it's stupid, you don't have to tease me about it. I didn't want to tell you and you made me so just go away."

She wasn't in the mood for his scoffing; she was never in the mood.

"My, I can get you a stupid invitation."

She looked up, still scowling by default. "What?"

"This is your big brother you're talking to." A grin spread across his face. "I can call in a favor."

Amya wasn't entirely sure what it was her brother did. There was a strict 'don't ask' policy and in all honesty, she didn't want to know. But she knew it was less than legal and his scary features earned him his keep; they also helped earn the roof over her head.

Favors were a precious commodity to him; for him to trade one for her, it meant something. It wasn't an offer he made lightly.

She narrowed her eyes as she studied him. "What would you want in exchange for it?"

"Can't a guy just help his sister out?" Bender put a hand over his heart in exaggerated offense. "That's what brothers are for."

It was said by the same brother who just the week before had told her that if she so much as touched his leather jacket—she thought it might look nice with her floral skirt—he would kill her and make it look like an accident.

But she decided not to bring that up.

"If you're sure..."

He looked at her very solemnly. "Just promise me one thing."

"I knew it!" she exclaimed as she made a move to push him away again.

But she saw the way his eyes twinkled as a smile tugged at the corners of his serious expression. "Promise me you won't let the Prince fall in love with you, okay? I'm not going to call you 'your highness' or anything stupid like that."

She laughed. "I promise. I'd make a lousy queen anyway."

"Yeah, you would, actually."

"Hey!" She picked up a ball of fabric scraps and tossed them at him. "You don't have to sound so sure about it."

He let the scraps hit him as he stood and grinned down at her. "Just finish the dress. I'll take care of the rest."

"Thanks, Bender," she said as he walked away, but since he walked into the midst of Dalen and Malaya and Dominic as they finished the dishes—still arguing over whatever it was they were arguing about—she wasn't entirely sure he heard her.

Chapter 8

Rinity had always been one for ripped denim leggings and faded tee shirts but the moment she slipped into the dress Amya had made for her, something magical happened.

It was impossible to believe the dress had been made from thrifted pieces hobbled together. She knew her friend was talented, but she hadn't realized the extent of it until she stood there in the bathroom, dressed like a princess, in a dress that had been tailored to her like nothing she had ever worn before.

She'd always loved peach, but there was something about the shade, as if it had been dyed exactly to match her complexion and to compliment her orange hair rather than work against it. The way the fabric rustled when she moved. The way it hugged her body but felt like another skin, comfortable and flattering at the same time.

It was magic. There was no other explanation.

Amya herself looked amazing as well—her own mulberry dress hung off her shoulders in a way Rinity would never be comfortable wearing. Rinity appreciated that her friend had known her well enough to make her something that came up a little higher and rested a little more modestly on her frame.

Amya pushed another pin into her hair, her dark locks twisted into an elegant bun at the base of her neck, tendrils spilling down and framing her face.

Rinity's orange hair was down, one side braided to pull it back from her face, the plait dotted with tiny plastic gems stuck to bobby pins.

Rinity leaned over the sink as she applied a layer of lipstick.

Amya stepped back and surveyed her face in the mirror, her brow wrinkled. "I guess we're ready."

"You look amazing," Rinity told her.

"I know," Amya said, still frowning as she refused to look at Rinity.

"Are you nervous?"

Amya looked at her with a scowl. "What would I have to be nervous about? We have invitations to get us in, your Librarian is going to be dazzled by you, and it'll be great."

"And you'll be surrounded by girls who have everything you want and men who can give that to you," Rinity said. "Are you on the lookout for someone tonight too?"

Amya often insisted she had no intention of setting her sights too high—that a merchant's son was enough stability for her. But she'd never been afforded the opportunity to flirt with anyone else before.

"Tonight's about you." Amya offered her a small smile; she had a better fake, but she never used it on Rinity. They were friends and with that came the perk that even in something as small as the conversation they were having right then, Amya never lied to her.

"You have a lot to offer," Rinity told her. "Any guy would be lucky to have you in his life. A good guy will fall for you, My, he will."

Her friend snorted. "What a guy wants is a pretty girl on his arm and no drama, not someone with nine siblings and no money or station. I'm not looking tonight because I know better than to set my sights that high."

"What about Tov?" Rinity challenged. "He wants more than that, doesn't he? You said I stood a chance with him."

Amya rolled her eyes. "You're a good-natured sweetheart with no siblings and a hardworking stepfather. It's a little different."

"My..." Rinity said.

"It's fine," Amya told her. "Tonight will be good practice with no consequences. It's not like I'm going to see any of these guys again. Come on, we should go."

She took Rinity's arm and pulled her from the bathroom out into the front room where Will had just come in, dirty from work. He stepped aside in a hurry when he saw the girls, to avoid accidentally coming into contact with their dresses.

"What're you two up to tonight?"

"Just a party," Rinity told him, a little too quickly. She hadn't told Will about Tov or the Library. Another lie. That's all she seemed to do those days.

He frowned at them both, but his eyes came to settle on Amya. "You're not getting my girl in trouble, are you?"

His girl.

And how had she repaid him for that title?

"Of course not, Mr. Garrick," Amya assured him, her fake smile plastered in place. Her rules about lying didn't extend to Will; Rinity was probably the only person truly privy to Amya's full honesty.

"Have fun." He didn't sound all that convinced by Amya's declaration. But there wasn't time for anything more because Amya dragged her away again.

The trip to the Library was a strange one. They were far too fancy for the walk and Underground ride. Those they passed made no secret of their appreciation for the show they got as the girls walked past.

Amya shot withering glares at the men that brought silence from some and simply served to encourage others. The women who gave genuine compliments got smiles and thanks and those whose comments were sarcastic or biting got haughty replies. Rinity didn't know how it was that Amya was always so confident. Her friend never had any problem shooting down an enemy or making friends with anyone who smiled at her.

They reached their Underground stop, just on the other side of the river. All they had to do was cross over the bridge and they'd be in the Library district—one of the nicer sections of the city. It did nothing to help with the strangeness of the situation.

Everyone else rode in a vehicle; anyone dressed that fine ought to be able to afford a ride as well. Only an imposter would be dressed thus and walking.

"Yesterday or long ago," Rinity murmured as she drew in a breath.

"We're almost there," Amya said. "You might not want to start a story now since you won't have time to tell it all."

Her friend knew her well. Unfortunately, Rinity already had started the story by uttering the words and what was meant to be a means of calming her brought nothing but stress the longer the words sat there in the air, followed by nothingness.

"Go ahead." Amya offered a sympathetic smile.

Rinity breathed a sigh. "There was a girl—a common, ordinary girl who lived in the poorest part of the city. She made her living helping her father steal things. Pretty, expensive things she could never have for herself."

"Really?" Amya wrinkled her nose. "The story of Cosima?"

Rinity forgot Amya hated that one, but she'd started it so there was no taking it back. She let the words wash over her and she drew comfort from them as she and Amya crossed the bridge, the waters of the Englever River crashing far below, its power and might reminiscent of the strength of Liosa's ancestors and heritage.

She was only halfway through the story when the Library came into view. She shot a look to her friend and Amya gave her a smile.

"We'll stop here and you finish, firefly, it's okay," Amya said, offering her a reassuring smile as she pointed to an alleyway.

They stepped just inside as Rinity drew in another breath. She finished her story and turned to her friend. "Thank you."

"That's what I'm here for." She offered Rinity her arm.

Rinity linked her arm through her friend's as they stepped from the alleyway. "Is it going to be suspicious if we arrive on foot? I didn't even think about that."

"Because it wasn't yours to worry about, firefly," Amya told her with that smile she got when she was going to do something particularly bossy. Her green eyes sparkled and her whole face lit up. "Just trust me, I've already got this figured out."

She hastened her pace and dragged Rinity behind her.

"I can't believe we made it." She let out a giggle as she approached the guard dressed in a sharp green uniform. She put out a hand and rested it on the guard's arm. She let out a heavy breath. "Whoo, sorry about that. Our vehicle broke down three blocks back and, well, we weren't about to let that stop us from coming. Do forgive our unseemly display."

The guard had already been frowning when they approached, but he directed it at them. Digging in her purse, Amya pulled out the two invitations and handed them over. Rinity hadn't asked how she'd obtained them and Amya hadn't volunteered that information. The guard barely glanced at them. "Show them to the footman, not me."

"Sorry," Amya said in a sing-song voice. She dragged Rinity up the stairs of the library.

Rinity's heart skipped a beat. Her chest grew tight as her breathing came in forced breaths. She wished she could start another story, but that was foolish. Amya would have every right to be annoyed with her.

Not that Amya was often annoyed with her. In fact, Rinity felt her friend was far more patient with her than she ever deserved.

Her palms were sweaty, and she wiped them on the skirt of her dress. She regretted it as soon as she did, her damp hands coming away dotted with glitter.

Amya linked her arm in Rinity's and pulled her to the wide double doors being held open by footmen on either side. Rinity dug her heels in so Amya was forced to stop, her friend's brow furrowing in as she frowned her unspoken question.

"I want to savor this." She kept her voice low so no one but Amya would hear her.

She always went through the back door; it was the only way she was allowed in—her moments in the Library stolen. Thanks to Amya she could walk through those doors and no one would stop them.

Would they?

She looked around, studying the footmen and finding they weren't looking at her. The other guests that walked about around them and entered the Library, didn't even give them a second glance.

No one cared.

She could walk through those doors. She didn't have to sneak.

Amya flashed her invitation to the footmen as they stepped inside and once again Rinity had to freeze as they stepped inside.

The Library had been completely transformed. Twinkling lights, strung up across the ceiling, washed the place in a golden yellow haze. The tables down the aisle that ran the center of the room had been removed, leaving the space open. Orange and green Liosi flags along with streamers of orange and green were hung all about.

An orchestra was situated off at the far end of the room, playing soft music, barely heard over the chatter and laughter. To their right was a long table with refreshments and drink, waiters in dark livery working behind it and mingling among the guests.

The books weren't whispering that night; had the soft orchestra music put them to sleep or had they hidden away at the changes and overwhelming number of strangers in their space?

Amya stood beside her, eyes on the refreshment table. It was piled high with more confections than Rinity had ever seen in her entire life: bazzerals were piled high into towers, perfectly round balls fried to perfection and sprinkled with powdered sugar; soft cookies with colored dough shaped to look like cynders—Liosa's national flower—spread out on platters; a stack of flaky pastries filled with spiced custard.

Her mouth watered just looking at them.

But she realized Amya wasn't looking at the pastries at all, but at a man standing beside it, drink in hand and a dark scowl on his face.

The man had been at the Library the day Rinity and Amya had gone together. He'd spoken to the Librarian, Tov, but Rinity didn't think she'd seen him before. So, the man by the table was either not a Librarian or he was new. But she'd never seen Tov before the day they'd met either.

She didn't know why Amya was staring though. Maybe she was on the lookout for a man after all. Though it would mean she'd changed her mind, perhaps only when she'd seen the man, because her words earlier would have been true. Amya always told Rinity the truth.

"You came."

All thoughts of Amya flew from Rinity's head as she turned at the sound of Tov's voice. She offered him a shy smile and was about to greet him but stopped short at the sight of him.

Because standing before her was her Librarian, but there was one important detail that was different than the last time she'd seen him.

That night, Tov wore a crown.

Chapter 9

When Amya had graduated, two girls from her school had rented a hotel ballroom to celebrate. It was the fanciest event Amya had ever attended in her life, with live music and the most magical food.

But standing in the Library, surrounded by wealth and splendor, was unlike anything she'd ever seen before. And she knew she belonged in the world of hotel ballrooms, not high society Library Dedication ceremonies.

It smelled celestial—of sugar and flaky pastries, mingling with the soft scents of floral perfumes and darker, muskier colognes. And the dresses. So many dresses. The colors were bold and vibrant, made from fabrics Amya could only dream about working with; she would kill to get her hands on the fine silks and satins and taffetas. And the styles. She made a mental note of them all so she could sketch them later.

Her gaze wandered to the refreshment table piled with cookies, and bazzerals, and pastries, and her mouth watered. But she noticed the man named Gibbs standing beside it, his dark scowl resting on his perfect face. Did he ever smile? Why leave the house if you were so miserable every time you did? Her appetite fled instantly and Amya cursed it. The coward.

She shook her head to remind herself it didn't matter; he wasn't her concern. But she turned and found Rinity whisked away by a young man. Apparently, she was alone.

She turned her attention back to Gibbs and in a split-second decision, decided to take a shot. He was out of her league, but it would be fun. And at the very least, it'd be good practice.

Making her way around the room, she reached Gibbs and slid up beside him.

"I didn't expect to see you tonight."

He raised an eyebrow but kept his attention on the room before him. "I didn't actually think about you since the last time we met, so I didn't have any expectations."

Ouch.

"I don't mean to be harsh," he continued, as if he hadn't already said enough. His arms were crossed over his chest. One hand was tucked under his arm, so that the action was hidden, but standing beside him, Amya could see that his finger tapped against his side at the same frenzied pace it had at the Library. "I'm just not particularly interested in sustaining a conversation with a social-climber."

Amya knew what she was and she didn't care what he thought. So why did the words sting so?

She crossed her arms and returned his frown. "You say that like it's a bad thing."

She didn't have to continue the conversation. She could just walk away. But then the man would win, he'd know he'd rattled her, and if there was one thing Amya liked best in life it was winning.

He turned to look at her and she bit back the smug smile; she had his attention. "You don't think it's a bad thing?"

"Oh, it's a terrible thing." It wasn't as if she intended to marry the man—she hopefully would never see him again—so she might as well speak plainly. "It's terrible that society is set up in such a way that gives women little opportunity to get ahead outside of military service or marriage and then scorns them for taking advantage of those opportunities."

His scowl softened and she hated it. He pitied her and that wasn't what she'd intended.

"You don't have to worry though," she assured him. "I only intended to use you for practice until someone interesting came along."

The pity disappeared but his expression remained soft and the scowl didn't return. "I apologize. You're right that I have no right to judge you, Miss..."

Oh, he wanted to do introductions, did he?

"Amya," she told him with a smile, offering him her hand. He took it and made an exaggerated show of bringing it to his lips and kissing her fingers lightly.

"Advisor Carrigan Gibbs," he said, releasing her hand.

Advisor? As in a royal advisor?

She'd thought him perhaps the son of a general, maybe someone with a rank himself. But a royal advisor? That made him one of the most powerful and influential men on the planet.

"I must say, you're not very good at this social-climbing thing anyway."

His attention was back on the room but he smirked as he said the words. His hand was tucked away again and he resumed the tapping.

"Excuse me?" she demanded.

He nodded across the room. "Your friend, you let her have the Prince and settled for a royal advisor."

She followed his gaze to where Rinity was being led away by the blond-haired Librarian—

—who wore a crown.

"Prince?"

He turned to her, his brow furrowed. There was something oddly familiar about it. "You didn't know?"

Did she know she'd pushed her friend to pursue a relationship with the Crown Prince of Liosa? No. No, she didn't.

"Who did you think he was?"

She shook her head. "He told her he was a Librarian."

He'd lied. And she wanted to march over there and tell him off for that, but then Rinity's secret might be exposed. Or, at the very least, they might be kicked out of the Library for causing a scene. She was fairly certain telling off a prince—the crown prince, no less—was against the rules.

But he'd played Rinity. He'd kissed her while she was under the impression that he was simply a Librarian, someone she could see a future with. But the Crown Prince?

Rinity didn't stand a chance with him.

He was playing her and Amya might not be able to tell him off for it, but she was going to drag Rinity away from there before she got her heart broken.

Before she got her heart broken any more than it already would be. Because Amya knew Rinity well enough to know her friend had already fallen—hard—for her Librarian.

Or, rather, for that dirty, lying scum of a Crown Prince.

"Excuse me," she said, though it came out mumbled and she didn't really care if Advisor Gibbs heard it. She scanned the room for Rinity and Prince Tov but they had disappeared. She started in the direction she'd seen Prince Tov pulling Rinity.

"Where are you going?"

She glanced over her shoulder to find Advisor Gibbs behind her. She stopped so she could hiss out her words. "I'm going to tell my friend His Highness lied to her and is undoubtedly playing her."

She didn't consider herself well-versed in politics, but she'd heard stories of the late King. While obviously no one spoke directly against the sovereign, the whispers were still there—stories of his wandering eyes and handsy nature. Rinity deserved a cute Librarian, not a prince who didn't know how to keep a promise.

"I don't know where you got your information from, but His Highness isn't like that." Advisor Gibbs put his hand on her arm lightly, as if such a casual action were enough to stop her. Still, she gave him the courtesy of allowing him to say his piece. "He falls in love easily, but never lightly. If he told your friend he likes her, he's told the truth."

He frowned, his brow furrowed. "Though I don't know why I'm stopping you."

Music grew louder as the dancers took the floor and Amya stepped away so as not to get caught up in it; Advisor Gibbs followed. Amya pondered his words as they moved and by the time they reached the edge of the dance floor she returned his frown.

"Why would you just assume my friend isn't good enough for him?"

He had no right to make such an accusation, not against someone he'd never met before. She wanted to smack his perfect face. Amya had done her best to make sure she and Rinity looked the part—with extra care to

Rinity's appearance. She looked stunning. Surely no one could have any objections to her.

He raised an eyebrow and shrugged as he countered, "Why would you just assume His Highness was duplicitous in his attentions to her?"

Amya had no idea what that word meant but she was smart enough to make a guess based on context. "History."

His expression remained neutral, but Amya caught the glimmer of a wince that flickered across his schooled features. "That's a fair point, though one you probably shouldn't make in a room full of ranked and connected people."

Victory, she was stupid. He was a royal advisor, not some merchant's son who'd repeat whatever his father said in an attempt to impress her with his political knowledge. She couldn't make accusations against a monarch—living or dead—so freely.

"If you're so against the relationship why don't you stop it?" she asked as she took a step back only to find a bookshelf unyielding against her back.

"I never said I was against it, I just don't have enough information to be in favor of it." He'd turned his gaze from her again and looked out at the dancers who swept across the floor in time to the music. "And I'd hardly call it a relationship, given they've only met, what? Twice now?"

Amya snorted. "They have kissed though. Multiple times. Apparently, he's a very good kisser."

That drew Advisor Gibbs' attention back to her. He offered her a faint smile. "Not information I needed. And I didn't realize he was that serious about her."

"You really think he's serious?"

He sighed and ran a hand through his hair that only caused it to stand up all the more. "I've only seen him this serious about a girl once before and that ended in a proposal." He winced again and swore under his breath. "But that's a state secret, so let's forget I said that."

Amya filed the secret away, though she had a feeling he was at least partially teasing her about that—he couldn't truly be spilling state secrets to a girl he'd just met. "So, you think his intentions are honorable?"

"Yes," he said without hesitation. "Regardless of how fast he's moving, they're definitely honorable. *Rook di goo.*"

Amya was fairly certain when a royal advisor swore on his life, the words had to mean something.

"Fine," she conceded. "But if he proves false, I will kill you."

Advisor Gibbs took a step back and bumped into the end of the bookcase behind him. "Excuse me?"

Maybe she'd taken it just a step too far. But still she meant it. "I can't do anything to him, he's the Crown Prince, so I'm holding you responsible."

"While not nearly as grave an offense as threatening a sovereign, threatening a royal advisor is still..." He trailed off, as if searching for the right words.

Serious. She knew that.

Before he could say anything else, she grabbed his drink from his hand and downed it in gulp. She should have known it was alcohol, but still she hadn't been expecting it and it burned going down. She winced.

"We should dance before I make even more of a fool of myself," she told him.

He grinned at that, taking the glass from her and handing it a waiter who passed by.

"Thank you," she told the man who took the glass away. Advisor Gibbs held out his hand and she slipped her own hand into his and let him lead her out onto the dance floor.

She hadn't been joking when she'd said she was making a fool of herself. It was a good thing this was just practice—though she could hardly call it that anymore, that ship had taken off. If this were someone actually in her league, she'd have blown her chance with him entirely.

Chapter 10

Tov—His Highness Prince Tov, Crown Prince of Liosa—stood before Rinity with an earnest expression on his face.

No wonder he had looked like a prince of legend. Because he was an actual, literal prince. The crown looked so right on his head as the emeralds and amber sparkled against the gold. It contrasted his blond curls, which glowed in the Library light.

"I know I've no right to ask, but could I maybe speak with you in private?"

He'd lied to her—but she'd lied to him. And so, the crushing weight of his lie was far overshadowed by the reality that sunk in—he was already so far above her when he'd been a Librarian. But the Crown Prince? She might as well walk away.

But he was holding out his hand to her and his expression held a question when it could have made a demand. He'd lied to her. And yet, he was still the sweet, earnest Librarian who had kissed her, she could see that.

So, she took his hand and let him lead her away.

It was only once they were halfway across the Library that she glanced back to Amya; she probably ought to have said something to her. But her friend was already making her way across the room to the refreshments.

Tov—His Highness—led Rinity across the open floor and down a long row of bookshelves—the wildlife and nature section. Then he led her up the stairs until they reached the dark corner that housed the biographies. The books were quiet, which was eerie. Dead people, Rinity had found, were usually surprisingly chatty.

"I'm sorry I lied to you." He avoided her gaze as he ran a hand through his thick, blond hair, setting his crown askew. "It was inexcusable and I've no right to ask your forgiveness. I do apologize though and I want you to know I wasn't trying to be dishonorable. And I didn't lie about my interest in you. I do truly like you, Miss Rinity."

He looked up and his eyes met hers. Her heart fluttered.

"Why'd you lie?"

She knew why she had—why she still was, for she could have easily relieved his apology with a confession of her own. But she didn't understand why he had, if he meant what he said—that he truly liked her.

Victory, he'd said that he liked her.

It was probably just a pretty speech. Heroes in stories were always making speeches. But they usually meant them when they made those speeches. That's what made them the hero.

He rubbed the back of his neck as he looked away from her once more. "I was here for a meeting and you just assumed I was a Librarian and I just…let you think that. And then I came in hopes you'd be here again. I liked that you didn't know because it meant you were interested in me, not…not just in the Crown Prince."

He looked so young and Rinity remembered that he'd only just turned nineteen. How hard must it have been for him to have so much responsibility thrust upon him at such a young age? And to not know who you could trust? She couldn't imagine.

"I'm sorry."

She was still lying to him. She ought to tell him the truth, but while Amya was quick to call her a fool, she wasn't entirely oblivious; the moment she told him the truth what was felt between them would come to an end.

"I'm sorry," she said again as she stepped away.

"I understand," he said and she stopped.

Victory, he thought it was because of his lies. "No, it isn't you, I promise. I just..." She shook her head, unsure what to say. "I haven't been entirely upfront with you. I thought, perhaps, I might be able to find happiness with a Librarian, but you're the Prince and so far out of my league..."

She trailed off again as she turned to go, to find Amya, to tell her friend they were wrong to come and should just leave. Perhaps Amya was right—perhaps Rinity was, in fact, a fool.

He caught her wrist, lightly, and she turned back to him. Their eyes met.

He reached for her, a question in his expression, and she didn't draw back as he took another step toward her and took her face in his hand. His warm fingertips brushed against her cheek and it sent tingles through her as he touched her cool skin.

She leaned into the touch as her heart beat faster.

"I don't care who you are—I mean, I do—I do care. And that's all that matters—I want to know you and nothing else matters. I'm not out of your league."

She shook her head as she pulled back and he let her go. "I can't...if you knew..."

She couldn't tell him. She couldn't. She ought to just walk away from it and let it lie. And if he wasn't a Librarian maybe she could let him go and keep the Library. She couldn't have them both but why did she have to lose them both?

"So, don't tell me."

She looked up at him. "What?"

"Don't tell me," he said again as he reached for her once more. His hands slipped to her waist and she leaned in when she should have leaned away. "Whatever secret you're keeping, you'll tell me eventually. And in the meantime, it doesn't matter."

It did matter. He'd find out and he'd hate her.

But he didn't have to find out yet. And his hands were on her and she wanted nothing more than for him to kiss her. She felt like a heroine in his arms, someone worth being seen and loved and kissed.

Surely a kiss couldn't hurt?

It was wrong, she knew that. But she wanted it and so she didn't protest as he bent his head so his lips met hers.

Amya shouldn't have been surprised that Advisor Gibbs was a wonderful dancer.

She didn't have much experience with those sorts of dances, but her father had taught her—and all her siblings—several Alisethian dances, to share their heritage with them. And she found the practice helped.

But somehow, she guessed that even if she wasn't good all she'd have to do was follow Advisor Gibbs' lead and it would have been just as smooth.

The song came to an end and he put a hand to her elbow as they stopped dancing. "You're a marvelous dancer."

He guided her off the dance floor as she laughed. "You flatter me. We both know you carried that dance. I could have been unconscious and it would have gone much the same."

"You do yourself a disservice in discounting your company," he said and Amya pushed down the warmth that filled her. He was flattering her, she knew that.

Before she could come up with an equally flirtatious reply, a woman at her left said, "I don't believe we've been introduced."

Amya turned to find a dark-haired woman beside her in an electric yellow dress that didn't work with her complexion at all. It also had ruffles that worked against her figure rather than with it. The fabric was exquisite though and Amya silently cursed the designer who wasted such a treasure on such a hideous dress.

Advisor Gibbs stepped to insert himself into the conversation. "Please, allow me, Miss Siphone Fredricks, may I present Miss Amya..." He trailed off, his brow furrowed as he looked at her with a question.

"Cole," she supplied.

Miss Fredricks laughed as she gave a good-natured disapproving shake of her head. "Do you not know your companion's name, Lord Advisor?"

Advisor Gibbs' lip quirked in a smile, as if that were humorous to him for some reason. "We've only just been acquainted."

"Well, can I beg your leave to drag her away from you?" Miss Fredricks offered the Advisor a warm smile.

"She's not mine to make such a request of," Advisor Gibbs said with a dip of her head. "I believe that would be a question for the lady herself. Though, I think they're about to start the readings."

Miss Fredricks rolled her eyes. "No one actually listens to the readings."

It was a good thing Rinity wasn't there to hear the woman say so. She'd gushed to Amya about the readings so much so that Amya guessed she was more excited about that than seeing her Librarian—no, her Prince. *Victory*, what a thought.

Miss Fredricks turned to Amya. "I hope you don't think me too forward in insisting on an introduction but I absolutely need you to pass my card along to your designer. And I've some other girls who'd love to meet you and pass their cards along as well."

"Excuse me?" Surely Amya hadn't heard the woman correctly.

The woman withdrew a card from her purse and held it out to Amya. "I'd love to work with your designer if they're accepting clients. Your dress is celestial."

Amya took the card, a little confused. She understood the concept—that was how designers found new clients, their current clients collected the calling cards from those interested in purchasing—but she wore a dress she'd made from piecing together dresses from a secondhand shop.

She wasn't a designer.

"I don't..."

"Please," the woman said, her mouth twisting into something that resembled a pout. "I'm a respectable client and I'm willing to pay top dollar."

That got Amya's attention.

She'd managed to make something for herself and Rinity from discarded dresses leftover from another era; if she had the resources to purchase actual materials, she could only imagine the wonders she could create.

"I'll be sure to pass it along." She offered the woman a smile as she tucked the card into her purse.

"And you'll come meet the other girls?" Miss Fredricks pressed as she looped her arm in Amya's. Amya stiffened at the touch; why was it considered rude to push her away but not rude for the woman to grab her in the first place? "They're ever so eager to be presented and I promise they'll be nice. You'll miss out on the legend readings, but honestly, they're an absolute bore."

Amya didn't want to be dragged away by anyone. She told herself it was because only Rinity was allowed to loop her arm with Amya's that way, it was simply because of the touch.

It couldn't be because she didn't want to walk away from Advisor Gibbs.

Could it?

The focus of the room shifted to the far end of the Library where an older man dressed in a long, rich yellow robe mounted the podium, presumably, to read the legends Amya had heard so much about.

"Please, do say you'll come," Miss Fredricks begged in a low hiss.

Amya had to go, it was the only practical option. Staying to chat with a man who she never stood a chance with when there was money to be had, it would be foolish.

"Thank you for the dance," she said to the Advisor, her tone low, so as not to be too out of place in the quieting Library.

His attention had been on the man in yellow, but he turned it back to her. His expression softened as their eyes met. "If you aren't opposed, I'd welcome another, later."

She hadn't noticed before how warm and rich his brown eyes were. But as he looked at her, she found she was happy to stand and look right back.

Except she had already made enough of a fool of herself tonight.

"Of course, should the night permit."

He dipped his head in acknowledgement. "Until then, My Lady."

"Lord Advisor."

Chapter 11

Miss Fredricks dragged Amya away from Advisor Gibbs, to the small group of ladies standing off to one side of the room in a little cluster, like a bouquet of ill-attired wallflowers. Three wore dresses that suited them a little better than Miss Fredricks did and the other wore a formal green uniform.

"Miss Cole, might I please present to you First Lieutenant Hawthorne, Second Lieutenant Thornton, and the Misses Rosier and Branwell. Ladies, Miss Amya Cole. She's happy to collect cards for anyone who wishes theirs passed along." She spoke low, so the other ladies had to lean in conspiratorially. None of them seemed to mind that they were missing the readings.

Not that Amya blamed them; the man's voice was terribly droll so that it droned on and on in a monotone that would have put Amya to sleep, even standing there in the crowded Library.

Miss Fredricks leaned in to speak to Amya, as if it were an aside, though the other women clearly heard her; they were all huddled up in a way that would make it impossible not to be overheard. "Though I do hope you'll give my card priority, as I was the one to introduce you."

It seemed a fair exchange to Amya and one she was willing to accept. "Of course."

The ladies hastened to open their clutches and pass their cards Amya's way, which she happily accepted and tucked into her own bag. She was surprised two of them had ranks, as only one wore a uniform. But it wasn't as if it were a military function.

Though, wasn't everything a military function on Liosa?

"Is this your first time out, Miss Cole?" one of the ladies asked—Amya didn't remember her name, she'd been introduced to them so quickly and Miss Fredricks had only really vaguely waved in their direction as she'd rattled off their names.

But honestly Amya was less concerned with the woman's name than with answering her confusing question. "No, I've been allowed out of the house before."

"Oh, you're too funny, Miss Cole," the lady who had asked the question replied as the other women giggled. "But I haven't seen you before, so surely this is your first time at such an event. Have you been kept in or are you new to town?"

'Kept in'? Did those with rank and connection keep their girls locked away from the public?

But going on a tirade would do little good; they were potential clients, she didn't want to tick them off and damage their future relationship.

So, she smiled and she laughed and said, "My father has never been big on such events but I couldn't miss such an important one."

Amya didn't have any trouble lying, but the first part of her statement was in fact true—her father hated such events with their useless displays of wealth, and he'd instilled more of that into his daughter than she liked. Part of the reason she'd never set her sights that high was because she wasn't sure she even wanted to be a part of that world.

That was another reason why she was looking for a stable, middle class man; not only was it practical, it was far more comfortable than whatever it was she endured in that moment.

"Your father?" one of the other ladies asked. "I don't believe..."

"Comina, look!" the woman in uniform elbowed the woman who spoke as she nodded across the room to where a tall young man in a dark blazer stood scanning the guests with an appraising look.

What was the point of having a legend reading if no one was going to pay attention? Amya scanned the room to see if Rinity was upset about it—she'd no doubt be livid at stories not given the gravity they deserved. But Amya couldn't find Rinity anywhere. Was she off kissing her Librarian—Prince—still?

Miss Comina watched the man with clear interest as her breath hitched and her gaze followed the man as he moved across the room.

"Maybe he'll ask you to dance tonight," Miss Fredricks said, patting Miss Comina's arm; apparently, she needlessly touched everyone, not just Amya.

Miss Comina shook her head. "He doesn't even know I exist."

"Have you talked to him?" Amya asked.

Miss Comina rolled her eyes while the other girls laughed.

"I'm serious," Amya said. Why did it seem such a strange concept to these women?

"We haven't been introduced," Miss Comina said with a shake of her head.

"So?"

Miss Fredricks put her hand on Amya's arm—again with the touching—and Amya pulled away. "That's not how things are done, not in polite society."

The man stepped down from the podium and the orchestra struck a note, the reading clearly over. Rinity had played it up to be something to look forward to, but frankly, Amya wasn't impressed; Rinity told the same stories far better. Amya actually cared to listen when Rinity told them.

"So why can't someone introduce you?" It wasn't Amya's business, not really. But she saw the look in Miss Comina's eyes, longing and desperate, and no matter how foolish Amya thought her, she couldn't just walk away.

"None of us have been introduced," one of the other ladies explained.

That was ridiculous.

"But you're still interested in this..." She hadn't caught his name, perhaps it hadn't been said.

"Major Favager," Miss Comina supplied. She ducked her head. "And yes."

It was Amya's turn for the touching, as she reached out and took Miss Comina's hand.

"Where are we going?" the lady demanded.

"To introduce you." Amya all but dragged the girl across the room; though it didn't take much effort as the woman didn't offer any resistance.

"It's not proper," Miss Comina told her.

"It'll be fine," Amya assured her. They reached Major Favager and Miss Comina shrank back.

"Major Favager!" Amya exclaimed, pulling Miss Comina in before she retreated from the scene altogether. "So good to see you tonight."

The man's brows furrowed as he no doubt tried to remember how he knew Amya. She felt bad to put him in that situation, but it was a silly rule that a person couldn't talk to who they wished when they were perfectly capable of introducing themselves.

And it gave her a new appreciation for Advisor Gibbs, as well; he hadn't seemed fazed at all by her breaking social convention. In fact, he'd been quite comfortable simply introducing himself to her.

"Miss Cole?" she supplied. "We met..." She trailed off as she waved her hand dismissively. "Well, who can tell these functions apart anyway? Clearly it didn't make an impression on you."

"Please, forgive me, Miss Cole..."

"Not at all," Amya said, cutting him off, which wasn't how one accepted an apology and she realized it as soon as she said it. "That is, it's fine. I just wanted to introduce my close friend, Miss Comina..."

She hadn't actually caught the lady's last name. She wasn't one with a rank, was she? That would make the blunder all the more obvious.

"Rosier," Miss Comina supplied. "General Rosier's daughter. It's a pleasure, sir."

Major Favager took Miss Comina's hand in his, bringing her fingers to his lips. "The pleasure is all mine, My Lady."

"If you'll excuse me," Amya said as she stepped away, but she didn't need to; Miss Comina and Major Favager were focused solely on each other.

She turned and found Advisor Gibbs behind her.

"My Lady."

"Lord Advisor."

His mouth turned up in a slight quirk. "Would now be a good time to ask you for another dance or do you have more matches to make?"

Amya ducked her head, not sure why she was embarrassed that he'd seen that. "You noticed that, did you?"

"It was kind of you to put them out of their misery." His words were warm with humor and she looked up to find a smile in his rich brown eyes. "They've been pining after each other for weeks. I'd have introduced them myself, but I've never met the lady."

She gave a small shrug. "I'd never met the gentleman before, but something needed done."

"You've never met...of course you hadn't." He chuckled, a change from his usually serious expression and she found she liked that—not just the smile, but that she'd been the one to inspire the action when it was a rare one. "About that dance..."

"It'd be an honor, sir."

Chapter 12

Rinity and Tov had started kissing and somehow ended up on a bench under one of the library windows. Eventually they pulled apart, though Tov kept his arm around her waist, the fingers of his other hand entwined in hers.

"I'm going to have to go make a speech soon," he told her, not sounding pleased by that. "And I'll have to make an appearance or I'll never hear the end of it."

"I suppose it is expected," Rinity agreed. She ought to go soon anyway, she had a job interview in the morning. But he hadn't pulled away so neither did she.

"And that's my job, to do what's expected of me," he muttered with a shake of his head. He looked up and met her eyes. "Sorry, I shouldn't complain. It's an honor to serve my people."

Rinity remembered what he'd said earlier about not being seen as more than the Prince when people found out. How hard must it be, to be seen as nothing more than a crown? When was the last time someone saw him for himself?

Even she had seen him as a Lord Nash or prince of legend. It was hard not to, with the way his curls glowed in the light, or the way his brown eyes just begged to get lost in as if they were a jungle or vast library. But he didn't want to be seen that way. He wanted to be seen as Tov, not the Librarian or the Prince or the hero of legend.

And Rinity didn't understand it, not really—not when she wanted more than anything to have a legacy to embrace, to be seen as more than simply Rinity, the girl with nothing else to be said about her. But she didn't have to understand to accept his words. She'd heard what he said and she could sympathize with him all the same.

"Still, it must be hard, that's a lot of pressure."

He sighed and it was so heavy. Just how much did the burden on his shoulders weigh? "I don't know that I'm cut out for this, but I don't have a choice—it's an honor to have been given the position but...I'm not exactly...good at it."

"I'm sure that's not true."

At the very least, he was certainly better than his father, he had to be. Rinity had heard the rumors about the late King, about his affairs and disregard for his people. He loved wealth and comfort and while he wasn't a cruel king, he hadn't been a caring one and he'd been known to make choices based on what benefitted his purse rather than his people.

The fact that Tov cared, that he considered it an honor to serve his people, it already made him better than his father, in her eyes.

He shook his head again, tossing his blond curls as he did and Rinity tried not to get distracted by how beautiful they looked. "It's just that I have a legacy to live up to..."

"Are you sure you want to live up to it?" Rinity asked before thinking. She had been thinking about the late King and the words had just come out without her bidding them to. "I'm sorry. I shouldn't have...that was rude." He looked at her and she stood. "I should go."

He was still holding her hand and he made no move to let her go. "Should I not wish to live up to it? He was considered a great king."

"I'm sure he was."

"Rinity?" The word was a plea, soft and earnest and she couldn't help meeting his eyes. "Please, everyone thinks I can't handle the truth about things, but if I'm to be a good king, I need to know. I can handle it. I promise."

She shook her head. "I like you. And I can hardly show you that by speaking against your own father—our late sovereign no less."

"Please?"

She sighed as she sat back down next to him. "He wasn't a bad king, he just...wasn't exactly great..." She shook her head. "I'm sorry, I shouldn't..."

"There has to be a reason," he insisted. "I want to avoid his mistakes, I want to be a good king."

She didn't want to have that conversation. She really did like Tov, quite a bit, and it felt wrong to speak against his father that way. But he'd asked for the truth, when he hadn't asked for it before, when he'd allowed her to keep her secret. It wasn't fair to deny him the request, especially when it was made so earnestly, especially when he hadn't made it before.

She sucked in a breath. "Your grandfather unified the planet, after the revolution."

"I know that." There was a hint of irritation in Tov's voice.

"But he gave priority to certain people—as a way of rewarding those who had supported him."

It was how those with rank and connection had been formed—those who had joined what had been the losing side of the revolution at the time were given privilege and opportunities others weren't afforded. It was a thank you for their good faith.

"Then when your father rose to power, it shifted from those who had showed support to those who he could best profit off of, at the expense of the rest of his people."

It was how the rich had been added to the list of those with influence and power. You no longer had to have military prowess or connections to someone with such. You just needed to have enough money.

"They don't even let—" She cut herself off before she said 'us,' before she gave herself away. "—anyone but the rich and ranked and connected into the Library. And that's not the only place the civilians are restricted from."

There were so many jobs they weren't allowed to hold, properties they weren't allowed to own or rent, extra taxes placed on them for things the ranked and connected enjoyed without the hindrance.

She felt like Amya all of a sudden. She hadn't realized she'd cared about more than the Library, but sitting there talking about it...

"Do the civilians even want to read the books in the Library?"

Rinity couldn't believe she had kissed the mouth those words had just come out of. "Excuse me?"

Tov pulled back and she could see it in his eyes that he regretted his words. But it was too late for that.

"You say you want to be a good king to your people—perhaps you might start by treating them as such. Just because books are a luxury for the civilians and not as readily available as they've been for you your whole life, that doesn't mean you get to justify your privilege like that."

She shook as she spoke.

It wasn't fair. She liked Tov, she liked kissing him, and he was easier to talk to than Amya even. But as she sat among books she could only read illegally, she couldn't just overlook what he'd said.

And she found she didn't want to talk to him about it anymore.

She stood and pulled her hand from his, not even giving him the chance to ask her to let him continue to hold it.

"Rinity, please."

She turned back but didn't meet his eyes. "If you want your people to love you, stop seeing them as 'the civilians.'"

"Rinity, I never meant—"

"I know." She did, she did know it. But it just proved that despite the lies she told herself, whatever it was between them couldn't continue.

"Rinity, please," he said. "I was wrong and I need you to tell me that—you're right, there's so much I don't know. I want to be a good king. Everything I do, I'm just so scared I'm failing. I'm going to end up being just like him."

She didn't have to ask who he was talking about to know he meant his father. "The fact that you want to be better than him already makes you so."

"Can you forgive me?" He ran a hand through his blond curls.

She sighed. "I shouldn't have snapped but..."

"I clearly struck a nerve," he said. "And I was wrong. I do see my subjects as people—all of them. I never want to imply otherwise. I just...want to make sure I prioritize the things people are actually passionate about—which the Library is clearly one. I'll speak to my advisors about it and see what can be done. And I'll look into the other things too. I don't like that—that idea of people getting priority just because of who they're related to or how much money they have. It's not right."

It was that simple? He'd make books accessible to people like her, just like that?

She'd have books, without having to sneak, without having to steal, without having Amya lecture her about how it was treason and constantly reminding her of the consequences if she was caught.

"Thank you."

She was still the girl without any connections, a nobody, she reminded herself, but her heart soared. She realized it was because as the hope rose in her at the idea of her books becoming accessible, so did the hope of the Prince becoming accessible as well.

As if a civilian could end up with a prince—soon to be a king.

Princes didn't marry civilians. Even Lord Nash didn't marry the women he rescued; it wasn't about the romance, it was about helping others.

"I should go."

"Aren't you going to stay for my speech?" he asked. "It's a really boring one my advisors wrote for me—pretty sure they just dusted off the one my father gave when they dedicated the Library to him. You'll be missing so much."

She laughed. "I have...an obligation tomorrow. I need to be up early."

She'd miss the readings too. She'd heard they were to be glorious. She'd wanted to hear them. But if she was out of it for her interview, she'd have less chance of getting the job.

And her chances were already so low she had no desire to stack the odds even farther out of her favor.

"Of course." He nodded. "I wouldn't dream of keeping you. But...there's another ball at the end of the week—will you be there?"

She shook her head. "I can't—"

"Please?"

She wanted to say yes; oh, how she wanted to say yes. "I didn't receive an invitation..."

"Gibbs can take care of that," he said. "Just promise me you'll come?"

She couldn't tell him no, not when he looked at her with those light brown eyes of his—like the leather of one of her favorite books—and not with the way he'd kissed her earlier. "Okay."

"We should find Gibbs."

His hand in hers, Tov dragged Rinity away, back to the dance floor. All eyes were on them and Rinity pressed closer to Tov out of instinct. She scanned the room for Amya, for someone familiar and comfortable to focus on.

Finally, she found her beside the man from earlier, the one from beside the pastry table. Amya had a pastry in her hand and she laughed as she took a bite. Her eyes were bright, her smile wide as she looked at the man.

"There he is." Tov started again, in the direction of Amya and the man, pulling Rinity with him.

The man called Gibbs said something to Amya and she brushed at her cheek before she replied with a teasing smile. He returned her smile with one of his own, though it was more guarded than Amya's.

"Gibbs!"

They'd come close enough for Tov to call out to them and both Gibbs and Amya turned. Amya's eyes lit up as she saw Rinity, and her teasing smile turned into the warm smile she always gave her friend.

Tov kept his hand in hers as they reached the others. Rinity was keenly aware that every eye in the Library was focused on the group. "Gibbs, this is Rinity. Rinity, this is my Royal Advisor, Gibbs."

A royal advisor? Amya had said she wouldn't even flirt with someone with a rank and she'd spent the evening with one of the most powerful men on the planet.

But then, so had Rinity.

Gibbs dipped his head in acknowledgement. "Miss Rinity."

"She needs an invitation to the other ball this week," Tov explained. Amya smiled at that, her eyebrow going up in question. Rinity ducked her head.

"Did you not receive one?" Gibbs' voice was low and suspicious.

Rinity shook her head. Her mind raced for an explanation at the same speed as her rapidly beating heart.

"An oversight, I'm sure," Gibbs conceded. Rinity looked up and met his eyes but his expression was unreadable. "If you have just a moment to wait, I'll see it's sorted."

"She has to go soon," Tov explained.

"Then I'll be quick." He turned to Amya and dipped his head. "If you'll excuse me, My Lady."

Amya smiled softly at his words as he walked away, his strides long and purposeful. She shook it off quickly though, turning her attention back to Rinity. "Have you tried the pastries? Because you absolutely need to try this, you've never had anything this celestial in your entire life."

Chapter 13

Rinity's alarm blared far too early the next morning and she groaned and rolled over before she remembered.

It didn't matter that she'd stayed out too late and hadn't wanted to go to sleep, instead lying awake replaying the night before over and over again in her mind. What did matter was she had a job interview and if she was late, there'd be no second chance.

She rolled out of bed and padded to the bathroom to stare at her tired face in the mirror. There were bags under her eyes—or maybe that was remnants of the makeup she'd hastily washed off the night before, too tired to do a thorough job. Her orange hair stuck out in all directions and she patted it down before she gave up almost immediately.

A glance at the clock told her she had enough time for a quick shower, which she took and relished. Then she dragged herself from the hot water and dried off. She dressed in her one good outfit—a long skirt with a floral pattern and a flowing tank top that scooped at the neckline but didn't show off too much. Not that Rinity had much to show off.

Hair still damp, she went to the kitchen and made a cup of tea, too nervous to actually eat anything. She could hear Will's voice in her head, telling her to take care of herself, to breathe, that she just had to be herself and she'd do great.

But it was important it went well. She needed the job. Needed it desperately, if for no other reason than to prove to herself that she could do it. All the other girls she'd grown up with had gotten jobs years ago, but Will had insisted she wait until she was out of school. He'd meant well, and she did appreciate having the extra time to study and recharge, but not having a work history had hurt her in the end.

As ready as she'd ever be, she left the apartment, closing and locking the door behind her. She sucked in a breath and reminded herself that she could do it. She'd never waited tables before, but she was a quick learner, she was confident in that.

She could do it.

She had to.

Champion Diner was just a few blocks from the apartment building and Rinity reached it before she was even supposed to be there, she'd been in such a rush and had left earlier than she'd needed.

She sucked in a deep breath as she pulled open the glass door. Immediately, she was assailed with a burst of cold air, the air conditioning blasted as she stepped inside.

The room was filled with booths and tables, as well as a long counter straight ahead, with stools on one side and a display case of baked goods and bazzerals on the other. The smells of slow roasted meat, and peppers, and yeasty dough filled the air, mingling with the sweeter scents of spice and buttery pastries, and chocolate.

"You must be Rinity," a woman addressed her as she came through a swinging door in the back. She was tall and thin, more angles and bone than anything else, with dark hair with streaks of gray striped through it. She smiled warmly at Rinity and the girl liked her instantly.

Maybe the job wouldn't be so bad.

"Yes, ma'am," Rinity told her. "Rinity Garrick."

"Twila Setki," the woman said, coming around the counter and offering Rinity her hand. Rinity shook it, trying to remember to be firm; Amya had told her once that her handshake was too weak and Rinity had been self-conscious about it ever since.

"Thank you for coming in," Twila said. "Why don't we have a seat and you can tell me a little about yourself and past work experience and I can tell you a little about the Champion Diner."

Past work experience.

Which Rinity didn't have.

But she'd also asked Rinity to tell her about herself so maybe, just maybe, that would be enough.

But the only times Rinity didn't feel like she wasn't enough was when she felt like she was too much. She'd never quite learned the balance between the two and she doubted that would be the day the balance magically made sense to her.

Rinity walked back to the apartment with a heavy heart. She didn't have to ask, she knew how the interview had gone.

Twila was nice and seemed willing to give Rinity a chance. But the truth was, she had other prospective candidates and if someone with more experience applied, the woman would be a fool not to hire the more experienced worker.

So, it was another dead-end.

She made it back to the apartment building, not paying attention to where she was going—why should she? She'd walked through those doors and up the stairs to her floor so many times, there wasn't exactly anything to pay attention to.

"Hold the door!"

Rinity stopped and turned to catch the door just in time, so that the man on the other side could come through. A man with a dark scowl towered over her, though his frame was limber and lean.

"Rinity Garrick?"

She scowled back at him. "Who wants to know?"

His expression somehow darkened, unimpressed; not that Rinity cared, she wasn't exactly impressed with him either. She'd been having a pity party and she didn't appreciate that being interrupted by a stranger who knew her name for some reason.

"You ought to learn to curb your tongue," he told her. "That's no way to talk to your uncle."

She took a step back. "Excuse me?"

He was crazy, he had to be. But he'd known her name. He wasn't just some raving fool speaking delusions. He knew her and that was the only reason she didn't flee the lobby and leave him there.

She tried to see the resemblance to her mother but it wasn't there. Besides, her mother didn't have any siblings. Which meant if he were her uncle, he was related to her father.

"I've spent a long time searching for you," he told her as he looked her up and down with an appraising eye. He wrinkled up his nose as if perhaps he didn't much like what he saw.

He was finely dressed, in pressed black trousers, a rust-colored blazer, and a white button up. The outfit screamed of wealth and influence. Even in her interview outfit that Rinity had picked out so carefully, she didn't come close to giving off such an air.

"Might we step over here, to speak in some semblance of privacy?" he requested, nodding to a small room with the mail boxes, connected to the apartment lobby. There was no door so they wouldn't be completely closed off from everyone.

They stepped into the deserted room. Rinity allowed the man—her uncle?—to go first so that as she stepped inside, she was closer to the doorway, though her back was to it.

"Are you my father's brother?" It made the most sense, if she was figuring correctly, but she needed to ask, to be sure.

"His older brother," the man confirmed, his voice low, so that it wouldn't carry beyond the room. "Isaias—well, then, I can't tell you my last name, can I? That would be telling. And from what I understand, you know nothing of my brother—your father."

She ducked her head. "I don't even know his name. But, you—"

"We'll get there," the man—Isaias—interrupted curtly as he held up a hand, as if the motion could silence her. Which, it did, she supposed. He dug into his pocket and pulled out something small, holding it out to her. It took her a minute to realize it was a small silver ring. "This belonged to him."

She reached for it slowly, not entirely sure that's what the man intended. But when he didn't draw his hand away again, she took the ring from him and turned it around in her fingers to inspect it. It was a simple band of silver, engraved with a delicate design—a crescent moon with a thin strand of ivy around it, the leaves almost shaped like stars.

"I hear you often frequent the Royal Library."

Rinity looked up to meet the man's dark brown eyes. She shook her head. "No, that's...I don't...I'm not allowed."

"Please," the man called Isaias interrupted as he held up his hand again. "I take no issue with it and I'd never stop you—a book's very purpose is to be read, after all. Why should they not be read by you?"

She ducked her head again and looked down at the floor, at the tips of her toes sticking out from beneath her skirt. "I mean no harm."

"I believe you. And as I said, I see no harm in it. In fact, I think it could prove useful."

She looked up and frowned at him. "Sir?"

"I'd like to offer you an exchange—you wish to know more about your father and those are answers I can easily give. I have something I wish retrieved from the Library, which I believe you can accomplish rather easily." He gave a nonchalant shrug. "The exchange seems a fair one."

She took a step backward. "You want me to steal something for you?"

Surely, she misunderstood him. Surely, he wasn't asking for something so grave in such an easy manner. Amya had a habit of calling her foolish and, in some ways, it was true, but she was not so exceedingly stupid as to commit treason.

Not that she didn't commit it every time she borrowed a book but...she always took them back. What the man asked was different.

"Keep your voice down," Isaias hissed.

She shook her head. "I'm sorry, sir, I need to go."

She turned to leave but his words stopped her in her tracks. "I'll need to ask you for the ring back."

She turned back, the ring held fast in her hand.

He said it belonged to her father. The polished silver was clearly real, the engraving too fine a workmanship to come from anyone but a man of means. And it was her one tie to the man who made up half of her, to the man whose blood ran through her veins.

Her mother had been taken from her too soon—a long, lingering illness that Rinity pushed away as the memories arose. Her father had never been hers to have. Her mother hadn't told her anything about him before she'd died, though Rinity had asked. His name was no doubt one that meant something. She just wanted to know if he was someone worth knowing.

"What do you want—" What word had he used? "—retrieved?"

It couldn't hurt to hear the man out.

Chapter 14

Amya didn't get butterflies often but they definitely fluttered in her stomach as she stepped up to the beautiful greenstone house and mounted the stairs.

She sucked in a breath for courage. She was Liosi, so she didn't run because something terrified her. She was Alisethian, so she was adaptive and resilient. She had the blood of her ancestors pumping through her veins and their strength and virtue whispering in her ear.

So, she rang the bell beside the door and stepped back.

"Name and business, please," came a voice from the bell. Amya took another step back; she forgot the nicer neighborhoods had such technology.

She cleared her throat. "Miss Amya Cole, I've come to call on Miss Siphone Fredricks, she gave me her card."

"Please wait."

So, Amya stood on the greenstone steps and waited.

Several minutes ticked by and she wondered how long she was supposed to wait. They were coming back to her, were they not? Surely, they wouldn't leave her waiting on the steps there forever.

The door swung open and a stern-faced butler in sharp livery stood on the other side. "Miss Siphone will see you in the parlor."

He moved back so Amya could enter and as she stepped in her breath was taken away.

The Library had looked beautiful the night before, but it was the Liosi Royal Library. But where she stood was simply the hall of a house people lived in.

Ornately carved stone and wood embellished the walls and ceiling, rich and dark and magical. It was like something out of one of Rinity's stories, not someone's home.

Did people truly live that way?

"This way," the butler said, holding out a hand toward a set of ornately carved doors so that Amya could precede him, which made little sense, as she didn't know where she was going. But it was inappropriate for him to walk in front of someone above him in station.

Perhaps she ought to tell him the truth, that she wasn't any better than him at all.

He stepped in front of her as they approached the doors and drew them open so she could step through them. Rich people, she couldn't help thinking, made everything far more complicated than it needed to be.

Miss Fredricks jumped up from the settee she'd been sitting on as Amya entered. She was dressed in a sundress a sickly shade of green and Amya tried not to wrinkle her nose at the sight of it. Miss Fredricks was beautiful, but someone was either giving her terrible advice on shades and styles that suited her or else providing her with no advice at all.

The young woman practically threw herself at Amya. Amya tried not to shrink back at the touch. What was it with her insistence on so much unnecessary touching?

"Miss Cole! I expected your designer, not you." She drew back. "Forgive me, please, do sit, I've ordered tea."

Amya took the seat on the settee that Miss Fredricks indicated. Miss Fredricks perched on the other end. "I know it hasn't even been a day, but did you perhaps have a chance to pass my card along to your designer? I'd love to know if she's available to make me something in time for the ball."

"She is," Amya confirmed and the butterflies returned as she drew in a breath for courage. "I'm actually the one who designed the dress. And I'd love to design something for you."

"Oh!" Miss Fredricks said as understanding lit her face. She'd assumed Amya had connections and with Amya's words the assumption had changed to that Amya was rich. Working rich.

Amya didn't see any reason to correct her. You could get in serious trouble for impersonating military personnel, but there was no rule against pretending to be rich.

She held up the book she'd brought with her. It was full of fabric samples from a very reputable fabric shop and Amya had dipped into her savings to purchase it that morning. It was an investment, she told herself.

"I thought we might discuss fabrics and styles—are you set on what you like or are you open to suggestions?"

The young woman worried her lip. "My dress last night was dreadful, wasn't it? Orphah said it was. She told me last party that I needed a new designer." She shook her head and her soft brown curls bobbed. "I'd thought it looked good, but then, I'm very muddled when it comes to such things."

She buried her face in her hands. "And to think, I spoke to Colonel Anson dressed like that. It's a wonder he wishes to ever speak to me again. I'll have to do better if I wish to be his wife."

Amya had some distinct judgments against Miss Fredricks' fashion choices, but she bristled at the idea of a man not wishing to marry her over them. "He hardly sounds the type of man whose opinion ought to matter to you."

She cringed as soon as the words were out of her mouth; she was there for business and she didn't know Miss Fredricks nearly well enough to speak to her that way. "Forgive me—"

"No, no, he's not like that!" Miss Fredricks hastened to assure her. "He's lovely, *rook di goo*, and he does adore me. But his family is very respectable, you see—he's a colonel, after all, and my father is only a major. He does have to take their thoughts into consideration. I do so wish to impress them, you see." She buried her face in her hands.

Amya still wasn't convinced she much liked the man but she patted Miss Fredrick's arm awkwardly all the same. "Well, we'll make sure this next ball you're dressed so perfectly no one will dare speak a word against you."

Miss Fredricks pried her hands away from her face. "Thank you, Amya..." She ducked her head and gave that shy smile of hers. "May I call you Amya? It's fine if not, I don't wish to be too forward."

"Of course," Amya assured her. Civilians didn't use the same formalities those with money and connection did so it was strange to Amya to do so. So, if the woman wished to drop the formalities, Amya had no objections.

Miss Fredricks smiled at her. "You shall have to call me Siphone. Now, please, do show me your samples. I wish to know what you think will most suit me."

By the time Amya left Siphone, she had taken the young woman's measurements, found several colors that suited her complexion, mocked up some sketches of designs she thought would suit her body type well, and consumed a copious amount of tea.

As she left, she couldn't help thinking how much she liked the young woman. Siphone was sweet and earnest and a little too careless with her touch but Amya was grateful to have made the connection.

Siphone was also willing to pay Amya handsomely for the dress she'd ordered. The sum she'd quoted as her previous designer's price was more than Amya made in a month of mending. And it would only take her a couple days to make the dress. If she was able to maintain even a few such orders a month, she'd make more than a modest income.

She'd never considered such a career before. But just like that, Amya was a businesswoman. A designer.

She practically skipped to the bank with her sample book tucked under her arm, and a check for the first installment of payment tucked securely in her pocket. She held her head high as she plopped the check down on the counter. She withdrew some in bills and deposited the rest. Then she went to the fabric shop and purchased what she needed for Siphone's new dress.

Hugging the sample book and parcel of fabric to her, she made her way home. Rinity had a job interview. She ought to check in on her and see how that went. And they needed to discuss their gowns for the ball; they'd have to go thrifting again.

As she was going in a sharply dressed man stepped out. He brushed past her and scowled, as if she'd had the nerve to get in his way.

"Excuse me," she mumbled as she passed. She slipped inside to find Rinity in the lobby, headed toward the stairs.

"Rin, wait up!" Amya called and her friend turned. Rinity didn't smile when she saw Amya and Amya's heart sank; her interview must have gone poorly.

Chapter 15

Rinity hadn't expected to see Amya so soon.

She'd hoped to have more time to think, more time to process, before discussing with her friend what had happened.

Not that there was anything to discuss, not really.

Isaias wanted her to steal a book from the Liosi Royal Library. He told her it was just a dusty, forgotten volume that the Library was only holding onto due to tradition. It had all but been forgotten. All she had to do was sneak it out and he'd tell her everything she wanted to know.

It was that simple.

She'd told him she didn't know, she wasn't sure. She didn't want to steal, it was crossing a line she'd never crossed before. Will had raised her better than that and it seemed poor repayment for all he'd done for her. And she'd be betraying the Library and her beloved books. And Tov. She didn't want to betray Tov.

Would that make her the villain? It was treason, after all. But it didn't hurt anyone, Isaias had promised that. You couldn't be the villain if you didn't hurt anyone.

And she could find out who her father was. For the first time in her entire life, that knowledge was within her grasp.

The man had been understanding—kind, even. He'd told her to think it over, to keep the ring for the time being and take some time to consider. All he asked in return was that she tell no one about the encounter.

And she'd sworn, on her life, to keep silent. *Rook di goo*. The vow of her ancestors.

So even if she'd wanted to, there was nothing to discuss with Amya. She'd read enough stories to know the consequences of breaking a vow like that.

"How are you doing?" There was concern in Amya's voice and Rinity started to ask her why—Amya didn't know about Isaias—when she remembered.

The interview.

"It was okay," Rinity said with a shrug as the emotions from that flooded back and drained her all over again. "She was really nice and I've got a chance, but I doubt I'll get it."

"I'm so sorry, firefly." Amya's face was soft and wrinkled with concern. Her clear, green eyes shone like the emeralds in Tov's crown the night before.

Tov.

He'd be so sad if she betrayed him.

But he didn't ever have to know. Did he?

Rinity shrugged again because Amya awaited an answer and Rinity just didn't have one. When she'd left the diner, she'd wanted nothing more than to discuss it with Amya over a cup of tea. She'd been ready to cry and rage and vent to her friend but standing there in the lobby with Amya looking on earnestly...

The ring weighed heavy on her hand, though it was just a thin, simple band. She ran the pad of her finger over the band.

"Did you go shopping?" she asked as she noticed the book and package tucked under Amya's arm, grateful for something to change the subject to.

Amya shook her head. "I can tell you about it later, if you want to talk."

"I don't really," Rinity told her. What was there to say? She had no skills and no experience so no one wanted to hire her and she was going to be worse than a villain—she'd be a burden.

She ran her finger over the ring band again and thought about what Isaias had said.

It was just a book. One simple book. She could know who she was. She'd know whether she could walk through those Library doors and whether she belonged at parties like the dance the night before.

She'd have her answers and maybe those answers would turn into solutions.

It could take her from a nobody to a hero. It could be her origin story.

"I was commissioned to sew a dress," Amya said.

That pulled Rinity out of her thoughts and back to the dingy apartment lobby. "What? By whom?"

"One of the women I met last night. And I collected several other cards."

All other thoughts flew from her mind at that. "My, that's amazing."

Her friend had been taking in mending and alterations since she was twelve and she'd turned it into quite the business, but she enjoyed making her own clothes even more. She'd just never had the chance before. And to have it given to her, with such prestigious clients...

"I'm so proud of you," she told Amya, pulling her into a hug. "That's amazing."

The dresses Amya had made them for the ball were beyond a dream. She deserved to get to work with real fabrics and her own designs. She had the skills, Rinity would never doubt that again.

"Thanks."

Rinity slipped her arm into Amya's. "You'll have to tell me all about it over tea."

"Actually..." Amya gave her an apologetic smile. "I should really get started on this if I'm going to get it finished before this weekend and also have time to make you something as well. I'm sorry."

Rinity ran her finger over the silver band. She'd looked forward to a distraction from her decision. She never liked making decisions, but even less so when they were as grave as the one before her. There was no right decision, no clear path, and those were the worst decisions of all.

But she couldn't tell Amya no. She couldn't tell Amya she needed her. Not without her words leaving the need for follow-up questions. And besides, Rinity didn't want to be a burden. She was already too much of a burden as it was. There was no need to add to it.

She shook her head as they started up the stairs together. "No, it's fine. Really. You should go sew."

"You're a legend," Amya told her. They reached Rinity's door first. "I promise I'll make time for tea. I will."

"It's fine," Rinity assured her with a warm smile.

But the smile disappeared as soon as she shut the door behind her and was left alone.

It took all of Rinity's energy to drag herself to the kitchen to put tea water on to boil. She ought to eat something too, she supposed, so she dug around in the cupboard until she came out with a box of crackers. She didn't have energy to make anything and so she nibbled on a cracker while she waited for the tea water.

She couldn't be mad at Amya, not really. Rinity really was proud of her for getting a client to commission a dress from her. That was huge. And Amya was kind enough to make Rinity another dress on such short notice. She didn't have to do that.

She probably shouldn't.

It was foolish of Rinity to go back. She ought to just stay home and forget all about it. She wasn't the hero of a story. Tov would find out the truth soon enough. He'd been sweet to let her keep her secret, but he'd find out the truth eventually.

Or, at the very least, it would all come to an end. He would be crowned king and she'd...well, she didn't know what she was going to do. That was the problem—no one wanted to hire her and she had no purpose in her life. She couldn't just keep reading books and pretend reality didn't exist.

The truth was, she was a girl from the streets who loved something useless. Stories, as much as they were a part of her, meant nothing.

They'd never pay Will back for all he'd done for her. They'd never help her to be less of a burden to him than she already was.

And they'd never give her a chance with anyone—least of all a kind prince with soft kisses and earnest eyes.

She rubbed the ring on her finger again, the smooth metal cool and comforting.

It was foolish. It was wrong. She shouldn't even entertain the idea. But if she knew who her father was, it would change things. Even if she didn't stand a chance with Tov still, she could get a job at the Library. Her father's name could do as much for her as the work history she desperately wished she had.

But it meant stealing. It meant betraying Will and Tov and the Library she loved so much.

She couldn't do it.

She wouldn't.

Not yet, anyway.

Amya regretted telling Rinity she didn't have time for tea. Perhaps if she'd made the time, she'd be over in the Garrick apartment and could cut the dress out in peace rather than...whatever that racket was that was exploding within the Cole apartment.

She was fairly certain from the amount of screaming, that her two youngest siblings were torturing each other as war criminals.

Her head started to pound as doubts swirled in her mind. She smoothed the expensive fabric out over the table—which she'd scrubbed thoroughly and ran her hand over the length four or five times to be certain there were no splinters that the fabric could snag on.

It would take her several days to create and that was assuming it needed no alterations. She doubted Siphone would be a demanding client, so there was that to be grateful for, but it would still need adjustments to be fitted to her perfectly.

And she'd promised Rinity she'd make her another dress and Amya herself would need one.

And on top of that, there was her growing pile of mending. She shouldn't get behind with that, it wasn't fair to her clients, many of whom had been faithful patrons for years.

Perhaps she should just let Rinity go to the ball on her own. Rinity seemed to not need Amya and Siphone could collect cards from anyone who wished for a dress; it wouldn't hurt her to stay home. She had no reason to go.

She pushed back the image of the stern-faced Advisor that sprang to her mind, unbidden. He had no right popping into her thoughts that way.

She let out a frustrated huff as she laid out her pattern over the fabric smoothed out across the table. She'd enjoyed dancing with him. More than she should have.

Maybe she ought to see if Sari was doing anything. Amya was closer to Rinity but Sari was who she went to when she wanted to have a good time. Sari was more likely to introduce her to guys she might actually have a chance with.

But if she wasn't going to the dance, she would do better to stay home and sew. She didn't know if she wanted to go to a party and flirt with a guy who—

—wasn't Gibbs.

She shook the thought from her head as she began pinning the pattern. It was dangerous to think things like that. And besides, it wasn't what she wanted—to have her heart broken by a guy who'd lose all interest when he found out she came with nothing but a small mending business and a family that was far too large.

Not that she regretted any of her siblings.

Except maybe the two who wouldn't stop screeching.

"*Rook di goo,* if you two don't stop..." she screamed, but trailed off as she found herself too tired to come up with a creative threat. Her parents had banned 'I'm going to kill you' and it made venting her frustration a lot more difficult.

She turned back to find her twelve-year-old sister, Norah, standing beside the table and reaching for the fabric.

"If you touch that, you're dead." That had also been banned but she meant it. The fabric was far too dear and replacing it would cost more than she would make on the creation.

Norah drew her hand back sharply and looked up at Amya with wide hazel eyes.

Amya sighed. "Did you need something?"

It wasn't Amya's turn to make dinner and she was technically the oldest home, but Mam usually let Alana in charge over Amya.

"If you're going to be doing sewing projects, are you going to get your mending done?"

Amya rolled her eyes. She was already stressed enough about that without her sister having to pester her about it too. "I'll get to it."

"I could do it." Norah ducked her head and worried her lip.

Amya thought it over. After herself, Norah was the best seamstress in the family and she was the same age Amya had been when she'd first started taking in mending.

"On two conditions." She held her fingers up as she counted them off. "I have to sign off on everything before it gets delivered and if you have a problem, you come to me, you don't try to hide it or fix it yourself."

It was her business and her reputation. She couldn't afford to discard those clients just because she was hopeful that her new venture would lead to something more stable and profitable.

Norah nodded in agreement.

"Good," Amya said. "I'll give you fifty percent of the take."

She and Norah shook on it and as they broke away Norah grinned at her. "I would have taken twenty-five percent."

Amya grinned back at her. "I would have given you seventy-five."

Norah frowned and Amya laughed but her sister didn't argue as she skipped over to Amya's mending trunk. She lifted the lid and pulled out the client folder.

"Leave Cora's dress, I'll work on that myself," Amya told her as she turned her attention back to the fabric laid across the table. Cora lived three floors up and she and Amya and Rinity had gone to school together. She'd bought her wedding dress second-hand and had asked Amya to alter it for her and it felt wrong to Amya to hand that over to her sister.

Amya and Cora had never been close and Amya had often wondered if the other girl disliked her. Amya had taken Cora's request as a sign of friendship. Even if it wasn't a serious friendship—or even anything more than the dress alterations—it still meant there was no animosity between them. And Amya would like to keep it that way.

Norah hummed under her breath and Amya turned to ask—yell at her—to please be quiet but stopped short at the sight of her sister curled up in the chair Amya herself often occupied, carefully undoing stitches with the seam ripper.

Her dark hair was pulled back into a braid but a few stray tendrils fell across her face and she kept pushing them back. Her lips were pursed in concentration as her brow furrowed in.

"You're going to get a headache if you keep your face scrunched up that way," Amya said gently. Their oldest sister, Bina, had told Amya that same thing when she'd taught Amya to sew so many years ago.

Norah looked up and relaxed her face. She offered her sister a sheepish smile before she ducked her head again and returned to her work.

Amya wondered if that's how she had looked ten years ago, sitting cross-legged in that same chair, hair done the same way, those same hazel eyes staring intently on their work with that same expression on her face.

Norah had only been two at the time. When had she gotten so old?

Amya shook the thought away as she turned back to her project. She'd given her sister the mending so she could focus on Siphone's dress, not reminisce about the past.

What mattered was what was to come.

Chapter 16

Rinity had to drag Amya along with her, but she managed to get her to come to the next dance, despite her protests.

She'd pieced together two new dresses and Rinity didn't know how she'd managed, not along with the dress she'd been commissioned to make as well.

The only downside was, with all the work she was doing, Rinity hadn't seen Amya much at all in those few days. Amya had kept her promise about the tea, but she didn't bring her mending over and stay for a while like she usually did. Instead, she just popped over for an hour before she hurried back to her apartment to work again.

Not that Rinity didn't understand, because she did—she knew how important it was to Amya, and she didn't want to take for granted the hard work she'd put into Rinity's dress.

But it had given Rinity entirely too much time alone to think—about Tov, about her failed job search, about the man's proposition.

She rubbed the pad of her finger over the smooth metal band; Amya hadn't asked about it, but there'd hardly been an opportunity.

"It's just here," Amya said as she pointed to a beautiful greenstone house, nestled between two others.

"And this is...?"

"Siphone," Amya reminded her. She was the one that Amya had made the dress for—Amya had told her their vehicle had broken down and begged a ride with the lady so they wouldn't have to arrive at the palace on foot.

Rinity tried to focus on the fact that Amya had lied to the woman when she never lied to Rinity rather than the fact that Amya had spent more time with Siphone than she had with Rinity that week. It was because Siphone was a client, Rinity knew that. She shouldn't be jealous and yet...

Amya rang the bell and the door opened to reveal a stern-faced butler in sharp livery. "Miss Siphone says you may go straight up."

Amya stepped inside like she knew the place well and Rinity pushed back the pang of jealousy again. Amya had always had other friends, ones that Rinity didn't know. They were so different, Rinity and Amya, that while they got along well, Rinity had never quite fit in with Amya's other friends.

Amya knew Rinity's friends well, though Rinity had always suspected that was more because Amya made the effort than because she was actually interested.

It was also different because all Rinity's friends were fictional.

Several of them sprang to her mind but she pushed them back. There was no time to start a story—or rather, there was no time to finish one. She doubted Amya would stop halfway up the stairs so Rinity could finish a tale she had—as Amya would no doubt put it—foolishly started.

So, instead, she sucked in a breath and hoped that was enough.

Amya stopped so Rinity could take the three steps to close the gap between them and then Amya slipped her arm through Rinity's.

"You can tell me a story on the way home, if you'd like."

The guilt swallowed Rinity. She had known Amya for fourteen years—for so long, she didn't even remember the meeting. Amya had always been there for her; she'd no right to doubt her loyalty just because good things had come her way.

"I'd like that," she replied, laying her head against Amya's shoulder.

"Come on," Amya said as she slipped her hand into Rinity's and pulled her friend up the stairs. "Wait until you see Siphone's chambers—they're absolutely stunning. Like something out of one of your stories."

The whole house was stunning—carved stone and wood, with intricately woven carpets and tapestries. Rinity had never seen anything so fine in all her life and she understood all of a sudden why Amya often said she wanted more out of life.

For Rinity, it was books she chased—the stories and the space they filled in her life. For Amya, it would seem, it was things that shone and glittered.

They reached the first door at the top of the stairs and Amya rapped lightly before pushing the door open. They stepped into a room far brighter than the hall and staircase. The carved wood was lighter, the tapestries and rugs and furniture all brightly colored. There was no rhyme or reason to the patterns—just constant pops of different colors strewn about the richly furnished room, and none of them particularly complimentary to the others.

It wasn't even a bedroom they'd stepped into, as Rinity had expected. Instead, it was a living room with a desk and two chairs, a settee and low table, and a whole wall of bookshelves.

So many books.

"Isn't it beautiful?" Amya breathed as the door on the far side of the room opened and in swooped a young woman in a cobalt blue dress. Rinity had seen Amya's sketchbooks enough to know it as one of Amya's designs.

The neckline was a simple vee and there were no embellishments on the fitted bodice—a delicate sheer lined with a solid fabric underneath. The skirt was two parts. The overskirt was shorter in the front and trailed down in the back, an extension of the bodice and made of the same gossamer sheer. The underskirt was of the solid fabric, falling all the way to the floor, the fabric flowing from the waist like an elegant waterfall.

Miss Siphone wasn't a particularly curvy woman, but the dress highlighted the ones she had, drawing out her shape. The color highlighted her skin tone and drew out the color in her eyes, making them all the brighter.

"I've never looked this beautiful before," Miss Siphone squealed as she skipped into the room. She gave a twirl along with a little laugh.

She was right, she was gorgeous, with her bouncing curls and smooth skin. Rinity instinctively put a hand to her own orange hair. Amya had fumed when Rinity had dyed it and declared she could never wear green again without looking like a Liosi flag. Rinity had suspected there were other reasons as well that Amya didn't like it, though her friend was too kind to come right out and say that.

But as she stood there and watched Siphone twirl, Rinity couldn't help regretting, once again, the hair choice.

Siphone stopped herself short and stumbled forward before she caught herself and ducked her head. "Sorry, that was rude of me. I'm Miss Siphone Fredricks. You must be Miss Rinity, Amya has spoken so highly of you."

Rinity looked to Amya with question but Amya was looking at Siphone.

Amya had told Siphone about her? And not just told Siphone about her, but spoken highly of her.

Until that moment, Rinity had imagined she wasn't a friend Amya discussed with her other friends and if she was, well, Rinity imagined it wasn't flattering what was said.

But apparently Amya had nice things to say about her, though what, Rinity couldn't imagine.

Perhaps the insecurity lay less with her friendship with Amya and more simply with herself...

Amya nudged her and Rinity realized she'd lost herself completely in thought and Siphone was staring at her. Rinity wasn't entirely sure what had last been said so she replied to the last thing she had heard.

"It's a pleasure to meet you. And so kind of you to let me be part of your entourage."

She looked to Amya to make sure her friend wasn't giving her a weird look, in case she'd accidentally missed something important and had replied completely wrong. But Amya's face was about the same as it always was, so Rinity assumed she'd replied correctly.

Siphone's smile widened and Rinity wondered if it wasn't just the color of the dress that brightened her eyes, but her smile that also played a part. "Please, it's the least I can do after all Amya has done for me. You're fortunate to have her for a best friend."

Amya had called Rinity her best friend? Rinity knew, objectively, that she was, but it felt nice to hear that Amya told other people too.

"But enough about me," Amya said. "Can we appreciate how beautiful you look?"

Siphone laughed. "Because of a dress you made. Did she make your dress as well?"

"She did." Rinity smoothed her hand over the sparkling fabric of her dusty pink dress. She'd fallen in love with the color the moment Amya had shown it to her.

"Anyway," Amya said with a roll of her eyes. "We should get going. We don't want to be late."

Siphone moved across the room, the action one could only describe as a bounce, and slipped her arm into Rinity's. "I have a colonel to dance with and I hear you've got yourself a prince."

She'd heard that? Rinity looked to Amya who shook her head, so Rinity assumed her friend hadn't told the woman. But of course, there was talk. A woman no one knew had shown up and had stolen all the Prince's attention.

At least she was proving entertaining. And how much more entertaining would she prove to be when they discovered the truth about her?

She'd be the talk of Liosa.

Chapter 17

Amya wished she had let Rinity stop to tell a story. Perhaps then she wouldn't have looked so gloomy on the ride to the event.

Or perhaps it was just because she was uncomfortable around other people. Rinity had never been one for new acquaintances the way Amya was. Amya didn't understand what there was to be afraid of; they were just people.

But Rinity much preferred her friends to be fictional.

Siphone talked the entire way. She tried to engage Rinity in conversation and Rinity tried to keep up. She hadn't known the woman long enough to know more often than not, it was impossible to always follow what was being said.

Still, Amya liked Siphone. She was earnest and genuine, and Amya would rather those things coupled with a tongue that moved at the speed of a meteor than silence coupled with falseness and unfeeling.

Unsurprising, Amya was abandoned as soon as they arrived—her companions deserting her for the Colonel and the Prince eagerly awaiting their arrival.

Amya scanned the room, looking for someone as well—a certain Royal Advisor she had no business being on the lookout for.

She ducked her head, telling herself it didn't matter. She was here for Rinity, not for—

"My Lady."

She whirled around as she fought to keep in the grin that threatened to spread across her face. "Lord Advisor."

He was dressed sharply as always, in a dark blazer and trousers, a crisp button up shirt and vest underneath the jacket, his tie tight at his throat. But, best of all, tugging at the corners of his mouth was a smile.

It was nothing. It was just a smile. But Amya's heart soared at the sight; he was as happy to see her as she was to see him.

"I'd hoped to see you tonight," he said. His hands rested easily in the pockets of his blazer, but she could see the slight movement of his finger tapping underneath the fabric. His shoulders were tense, and his gaze flicked from her to scan the room before he looked back at her again.

"Are we on guard for something in particular?" she asked as she moved to stand beside him so she could scan the room as he did. She'd rather discuss something interesting than consider what it meant that he'd been thinking about her.

He shifted to look her way, which she thought was rude after she'd just moved to stand beside him. She'd have to move again if she wanted to see what he was looking at.

But he wasn't scanning the room anymore, he was looking at her. Her heart skipped as heat crept up her neck and spread across her face. Even with the air conditioning, the room was hot from so many people.

"My apologies," he said with a dip of his head. "Old habits that come from being a Security Officer."

That was far more interesting than the way her heart danced. She found it a little easier to breathe at the distraction. "You were a Security Officer? How does one go from Security Officer to Royal Advisor?"

She'd thought he seemed young for the position of Advisor. But even more so, if that wasn't even his first career choice.

He tugged at the collar of his blazer, smoothing it down as if it weren't already perfectly in place like everything about him; except his wispy hair but even that was perfect in its own perfectly imperfect way. She didn't doubt it drove him to distraction though, as he seemed more the put-together type than the type to go for curated imperfection.

"One helps save the life of one's crown prince," he replied. "And through the generous commendation of a good friend."

Victory, that was much more interesting than she'd even dreamed. "Were you part of what happened on Philosanthron? When they caught that traitor?"

Amya wasn't one for politics, but it'd been a big deal, the deserter who'd assassinated a royal advisor on Philosanthron and had tried to assassinate the Prince. It'd been all the guys wanted to talk about at parties for weeks, and she'd gotten an old hand at having the same conver-sation about it over and over again with each new guy she met.

Advisor Gibbs shifted uncomfortably; for someone so arrogant, he never seemed at ease when he talked about himself. "I was part of that, yes."

"Well?" she said. "What happened?"

"Unfortunately, that's classified," he said, his eyes off her again as he scanned the room once more and his finger continued to tap, out of time with the music.

"Boo," she said as she crossed her arms and frowned. "That's no fun. Surely you can tell me something about it."

He looked back at her. His rich, brown eyes sent all kinds of warmth through her as he took her in. His voice was low and husky as he leaned toward her. "There is one thing I can tell you."

She leaned in to hear him better, her own voice a breathless whisper. "What's that?"

"That it's classified."

He shifted back from her as a grin spread across his face, his expression smug, and looking far too pleased with himself.

She drew back with a huff, but had to fight to keep her own smile off her face.

"You look lovely tonight, by the way."

She looked down at the cream-colored dress she'd barely had time to finish—and had hoped to use as an excuse not to come. "It's hardly my best work."

"You don't strike me as the humble type," he said with a snort.

Was that an insult or an observation? "I'm not being humble—my hem's horribly uneven—see, when I shift, it drags on the ground here, but then here, you can see my toes." She wiggled her toes, though you could only barely see the movement through the small hole in her open-toed heels. "You shouldn't be able to see only one foot. Dresses aren't made like that."

Her dress wasn't made like that, anyway.

She shifted her attention from her foot to her abdomen. "Also, there's boning in here and whoever put it in did it incorrectly; let me tell you, it's killing me. But if I took it out, it'd have no shape at all." She poked her side. "So, I let it keep poking me even though I'll probably have bruises tomorrow."

She shook her head. "Sorry, you don't care about any of that."

"No, I'm learning so much." There was a smile on his lips, soft and teasing, and she ducked her head.

"I get excited about dresses," she mumbled.

"I noticed," he said. "And in your defense, I did start the conversation."

She lifted her head to meet his eyes as she rolled her own. "You said I looked nice, I could have just said thank you, I didn't have to ramble about..."

She trailed off as she realized she was coming dangerously close to rambling again.

"Actually, I said you look lovely," he corrected. "But next time I'll be sure to check your hem before I pay you such a compliment."

Victory, how she wished she could melt into the floor. The heat crept across her face but her heart skipped a beat at the same time as he looked at her with that little teasing grin. His gaze took in the hem of her dress and then slowly climbed higher until it met her face.

He held out his hand. "Shall we dance before one of us makes an even bigger fool of ourselves?"

As if he were making a fool of himself at all.

But he'd lost that serious expression and he'd kept his attention on her that whole time, not breaking his gaze to scan the room even once. And while she knew it meant nothing, Amya couldn't help feeling a little rush of pleasure that she'd been the one to do that.

"My Lady?" he prompted.

She took his hand. "Lord Advisor."

Tov's arm about her waist did little to settle Rinity's thoughts.

It was like one of her stories. No matter how many times she opened it up and reread the good bits, over and over and over again, she still eventually always reached the end. It was inevitable.

And while most of her books ended with a customary "and so we come to the conclusion of our tale—or perhaps the beginning," she knew that the tale she lived offered no such hope or promise. It would all come to an end. It had to. And she might spend the rest of her life opening the tale again and again to relive her favorite parts, but the end would always still come crashing down on her.

"Are you all right?" Tov asked as he brushed a strand of hair from her face.

She shook her head, then realized that would only bring more questions. She smiled instead. "I'm fine."

"Okay..." he said, though he seemed unconvinced, his expression wrinkled with concern.

She didn't want his pity. "Are you making any speeches tonight?"

"Always," he said with a sigh. "Gibbs will probably track me down soon to make sure I'm prepared. He's good at schedules and making sure everything runs smoothly. Although, he is a little distracted tonight."

Rinity followed his gaze across the room to where Gibbs stood next to Amya. She hadn't said anything to Rinity about him—they'd hardly had the time—but perhaps she'd discussed it with Siphone instead.

Amya deserved to be happy and could hardly do better for herself than the Prince's Royal Advisor. And she deserved the best. Rinity only hoped he was the best in more ways than monetary and prestige ones.

"What kind of man is your Advisor?" she asked.

Tov raised an eyebrow. "He's one of the best men I know. Why?"

"That's my friend he's flirting with," she explained. "And I just wanted to make sure he is...decent..."

"I've never known Gibbs to take anything lightly," Tov told her. "I've never seen him taken with a girl before, but I imagine he'd apply that same level of dedication and concern."

Rinity nodded; there was little she could do about it anyway. It'd have to be enough.

Tov held out a hand to her. "Shall we dance? Or we could..."

She hesitated. Would kissing Tov improve her mood? And which would create more fodder for gossip—if they danced where everyone would see them or snuck off away from everyone?

Taking initiative, Tov took her hand in his and pulled her away from the group. He walked with purpose, like a hero in a story—like the Prince he was—and she allowed herself to be led off to a secluded alcove.

"I don't think kissing you is a good idea right now," she said as she plopped down on the bench.

Tov sat beside her. "I wasn't going to kiss you."

"You weren't?" She looked up and met his light brown eyes, surprised by his words. If he wasn't going to kiss her, why had he brought to a secluded corner?

"It seems like something's bothering you," he said. "And I thought maybe you'd want to talk about it?"

Why was he always so earnest and sincere when he spoke to her? And why did his words make her want to cry?

"Is everything okay, Rinity?"

She should just tell him everything. It would be better that way, to get it out there and over with. But once it was said, that would be that. She would lose Tov forever.

She couldn't let him go.

She'd known it the moment he'd climbed up and spoken to her in that vent in the Library. And a little later as he'd stood there bleeding and begged her to come back, she'd lost herself in his light brown eyes that looked like sunlight.

She didn't ever want her story to end. All her life she'd wanted nothing more than to escape into one of her stories. It had been a foolish fantasy, one she knew could never come true. But it had. And she didn't think she could let it go. Deep in her heart of hearts, she knew that for as long as she lived, she would never find another story she liked better. The story of her and Tov would forever be her favorite.

But it was foolish to expect a story to last forever. Their very nature was to eventually come to an end.

"I need to tell a story," she mumbled.

"I beg your pardon?"

She looked up and remembered Tov still sat there beside her and awaited an answer. She ducked her head. "When I get worked up like this, telling a story sometimes makes me feel better."

"So, tell me a story."

She shook her head. "It's foolish."

"Rinity." He put his hand on hers, his fingers soft and warm. "Tell me a story? Please?"

She looked into his soft brown eyes. They were earnest and almost desperate, as if she'd be doing him a favor to tell him a tale.

She couldn't say no to him, no matter how hard she tried. And besides, she wanted to tell a story so wretchedly, the words itched to come out since the idea had been planted in her head.

So, she sucked in a breath and began. "Yesterday, or perhaps long ago..."

Chapter 18

"Your Highness?"

Rinity looked up, her eyes wide, as she found Amya and the Advisor named Gibbs standing before them.

It wasn't that she minded her friend or the Royal Advisor being there so much as she minded that Gibbs had interrupted her story.

"Sorry to interrupt," he said, though he looked at Tov, as if he'd been the one who was interrupted. "We'll need to get you ready for your speech, Your Highness."

"But we have time for Rinity to finish her story first," Amya said gently before Rinity could fully start to panic over the alternative.

"I mean, we—"

"—have plenty of time for Rinity to finish her story," Amya repeated, her tone firmer. Then her voice softened once more as she said, "Just make it quick, okay, Rin?"

Rinity nodded and began where she had left off, feeling self-conscious to have so many people listening—all of whom wanted her to be done with her story and fast. She hurried through it as quickly as she could. Though, not too fast, so as to disrespect the words.

"So, their children are forced to wander the stars, no longer part of either world they were born into. And so, we come to the end of our tale—or perhaps the beginning."

There was a moment of silence. Rinity kept her head ducked, mortified that she'd told the whole thing and the inconvenience she'd caused. But she felt Tov squeeze her hand lightly before he used his fingers to trace the back of her hand.

"Thanks...Rin?"

She warmed at his use of her nickname and her heart skipped a beat; he must have noted when Amya called her Rin.

"If we're done..." Gibbs broke in, though his tone wasn't unkind. Rinity remembered what Tov had said about how he always kept things on track and running smoothly. Had she put them terribly behind with her story? It had only taken a few minutes to finish but still.

Tov rose. "Right. Better get this over with. Will I see you afterwards?"

Rinity looked to Amya, who shrugged, so Rinity assumed the decision was up to her. "Yes? Probably?"

"Good." Tov offered her a smile that made her heart skip faster and a warm, giddy feeling well inside of her.

Gibbs nodded to Amya. "My Lady."

"Lord Advisor."

Amya definitely liked him, Rinity noted as Gibbs and Tov walked away. The corners of Amya's mouth strained against the smile that threatened to form as she watched the Royal Advisor walk away.

"So, it's serious?" Rinity asked.

Her friend whirled to face her. "What?"

"Gibbs. You like him." Her words were a statement, not a question.

Amya snorted. "What? No." She shook her head. "We're just friends. Not even friends. We barely know each other."

"That's weird," Rinity noted as Amya plopped onto the bench beside her. "Because I've never seen you smile like that about someone you barely know."

Amya's face hardened as she crossed her arms across her chest. "It can't be anything, Rin."

"You always said you wanted to marry rich," Rinity argued. "And Tov says he's a good man."

Amya didn't smile about boys, not like that. She'd gone on dates before and always shrugged them off and told Rinity the kissing was nice but the boy was wrong. She'd gotten giddy over a few boys when they were younger too, but Rinity knew her friend well. And even just from the brief interaction she could tell two very important things. The first was that Amya liked the man. A good deal too.

And the second was that the Royal Advisor liked her back.

"He's a good man until he finds out I'm a poor civilian from a huge family," Amya said. "What's he going to say when he finds that out? 'Why thanks, I'd love to be burdened with your large family.' And also, I'm both Liosi and Alisethian. A merchant's son might not care, but a royal advisor sure as fury will."

"You don't know that he'd feel that way," Rinity protested.

Amya glared at her. "It's just a bit of fun, that's all it is. And then I'll find myself a nice merchant's son who appreciates that I have a good head for figures and know how to charm a customer. I'm okay with that, Rin, you can stop pitying me."

Rinity hadn't realized that she was, but Amya was right. Rinity did pity her. Because Amya was the most amazing person Rinity knew, and she deserved to have someone see more than her head for numbers or way with customers. She deserved someone who made her smile the way the Royal Advisor did.

"It's just not fair."

"Life rarely is, firefly," Amya said, her voice heavy.

"But how come you told me Tov shouldn't care if he was the right one?" she pressed. Amya didn't have the monopoly on caring, Rinity could give as good as Amya gave. "Don't you deserve the same?"

Amya shook her head. "It's different. He's just flirting with me. We haven't made each other any promises and it's not as if we've even kissed or anything. I think I'll be fine."

But Rinity had made promises. And she had kissed Tov. And despite what Amya said, he would mind when he found out the truth.

She ran her thumb over the silver ring on her finger.

"There you are!"

Rinity looked up to find Siphone standing before her and Amya, tears streaming down her face.

"Siphone?" Amya jumped up. "What's the matter?"

The young woman shook her head as she sucked in a shaky breath. "I need to go home. I'm so sorry to put you in such a situation but—"

"We can go," Amya said. She looked to Rinity for confirmation.

Rinity rose. "Of course."

She hadn't promised Tov that she'd stay, not really. And she wasn't sure she wanted to.

It didn't matter what Amya said, he was a prince and she...well, she was a nobody. She knew that. It was wrong of her to have ever pretended otherwise.

Princes didn't marry civilians. She'd read enough stories to know they married princesses and brave, clever girls who were far, far better than her.

Siphone swallowed hard, choking back her tears. "I—I can't—if I walk through there now, they'll all see me crying."

"Let them." Amya put her hands on Siphone's shoulders and looked her straight in the eyes. She had to look up to meet her gaze, but she had a lot of practice since Rinity was taller than her.

Rinity knew the action well, it meant an Amya pep talk was on the way.

"If anyone out there sees you cry and their instinct isn't concern, if they want to use that to ridicule or belittle you, that's on them, not you. You don't want to associate with that sort of a person anyway."

Rinity had seen Amya cry three times in the fourteen years she had known her best friend. And Amya had spent the entire time she'd cried apologizing for it. She hated when people saw her cry and never let anyone—not even Rinity—see her tears if she could avoid it.

But that was what Amya did—she gave you advice she didn't know how to follow herself. Because the low opinion she had of herself didn't extend to her friends.

Rinity felt a twinge of guilt for her jealousy earlier and the pangs that wanted to eat at her as she saw Amya calming Siphone.

Amya had been her friend for fourteen years. And while Rinity often struggled to see what it was Amya saw in her, Amya never had that same struggle. She always saw the best in Rinity, no matter how hard it was for Rinity to see it herself.

"Come on now," Amya said. "Rinity and I are going to be by your side the whole way and if anyone so much as blinks at you wrong, I promise we'll give them our best death glares, *rook di goo*."

Siphone gave a little laugh that came out strangled amid her tears. "I don't know why you're being so kind to me."

"It's what she does," Rinity said as she moved to slip her arm into Siphone's. "She's a good friend like that."

True to her word, Amya cast her most withering glares at everyone as they walked through the crowded room and people started to stare. To her credit, Siphone held her head high and Amya was proud of her for that.

It wasn't right, people shouldn't take entertainment from a friend's misfortune. But how many of those people were truly friends of Siphone's and how many were merely acquaintances?

Siphone had opened up to Amya some in the time Amya had spent working on her dress—it wasn't hard, since the young woman was naturally inclined to chatter once she got comfortable. And in that time Amya had learned that while Siphone could—and would—talk to anyone, there were few she felt truly close to.

Scanning the room, Amya's gaze fell on Gibbs. He was bent forward as he spoke to Prince Tov but he looked up and their eyes met. A smile came involuntarily to her mouth and she lifted her hand to offer a little wave before she caught herself and looked away.

She acted the fool when she was with him, but she'd meant what she'd told Rinity—no matter how she acted, she wasn't a fool, not really. She knew her place and it wasn't—and never could be—by his side.

When they got outside, Amya instructed a footman to have Siphone's vehicle brought around. The young woman started sniffling again and the sniffling turned to more tears and Amya patted her absently on the shoulder as they waited.

She ought to offer some words of comfort. It would be polite. But what was there to say? Mindless platitudes would offer no solutions.

The vehicle rattled up and Rinity, Amya, and Siphone climbed inside.

"What happened?" Amya asked as the vehicle lurched forward and they set off.

Siphone shook her head, her dark curls bouncing as she did.

"Did something happen with Colonel Anson?" Rinity asked, rubbing the young woman's arm soothingly.

Siphone drew in a sharp breath and Amya knew Rinity had hit on the root of the problem. Siphone began to sob softly again.

"Did he do something untoward?" Amya asked. There was a harshness in her voice she didn't mean—because it wasn't directed at Siphone. She meant her anger; if Colonel Anson had done anything to her friend, Amya would kill him.

"No!" Siphone protested with another shake of her head. "That is...not...intentionally."

"What does that even mean?" Amya sucked in a breath. It did no good to be cross with Siphone, the lady was distressed enough. "I'm sorry. I only meant, if he did something to offend you, his intentions mean little, not if he distressed you like this."

Siphone drew in a ragged breath then let it out slowly. "His only offense is being a colonel."

"So?" Amya looked to Rinity. Rinity read books so she knew things; Amya herself had no idea how any of that worked. Wasn't being a colonel a good thing?

Rinity shook her head, looking as confused as Amya. "Is that a bad thing?"

"Apparently my father's rank of major and modest fortune aren't good enough for him." Siphone threw herself back against the vehicle's seat and let out a heavy sigh. "I liked him too. I thought he was sweet."

"I'm sorry," Rinity said, rubbing the young woman's arm while Amya patted her other shoulder awkwardly. "It's not right."

"I just don't understand what's wrong with me."

"There's nothing wrong with you," Amya scoffed. "He's an idiot and he should be ashamed of himself. You'll find someone far more worthy of your attention and be glad this came to nothing."

Siphone let out another sigh. "Father thinks I should join the military and find my own honor instead of waiting for a man to bestow his affections on me."

Amya tried to picture Siphone with a gun in her hands but she had a hard time conjuring the image.

"Do you think that's a good fit for you?" Rinity asked, her nose wrinkled up, clearly having as much trouble as Amya imagining that.

Siphone shrugged. "What other options do I have? And I'm stronger than I look. Maybe they'll send me to Taras and I'll earn enough prestige that people will stop seeing the girl in the pretty dress when I walk into the room. I'm tired of being underestimated."

"I'm sorry." What else was there to say? She'd made plenty of pretty promises to Rinity but it was clear her words were hollow and empty.

"Don't do anything rash you might regret later," Rinity cautioned, which Amya thought humorous, coming from the girl who stole books from the Royal Library on a regular basis.

"I'm running out of time. If I wait too long, I'll be too old to join—they'll still take me, but I won't have as much of a chance of working my way into as high or prestigious a position." The vehicle pulled to a stop outside of Siphone's greenstone house and the young woman sat up straight, squaring her shoulders. "My driver will take you home."

"We couldn't—" Amya started to protest but Siphone interrupted her.

"I insist. I'm sorry to have dragged you away so suddenly and to have burdened you with my troubles."

"Would you like some company?" Amya asked. It felt wrong to just let her go inside. But Amya didn't blame her for wanting to be alone. She just wanted it to be Siphone's choice.

Siphone hesitated a moment before shaking her head. "I won't keep you."

"It's no problem, that's why I offered," Amya insisted.

Siphone shook her head once more. "Good night, Amya. It was lovely to meet you, Rinity. I'm sorry again."

She exited the vehicle before Amya could protest any further or Rinity could respond. They watched her walk up the walk, a cobalt blue cloud that bounced in the moonlight.

Amya's heart bled for her. It wasn't right. She shouldn't have to sell herself—to a man or to her planet—in exchange for respect.

"Where to, ladies?" the driver asked.

Amya hesitated before she gave him their address. What did it matter anymore? So what if Siphone discovered the truth, it wasn't as if they could keep the charade up any longer.

"It's not fair," Rinity said.

Amya sighed. "It rarely is, firefly."

"It's not right."

"No one said it was."

"How can you just give up?" Rinity demanded.

Amya sank back against the seat. "What do you want me to do? March up to the man and demand he give Siphone his attention? Tell you both that men don't care about that sort of thing? You've been telling me all along it was foolish, well fine, I'm admitting it. You want a prince? Find yourself a fortune or some connections."

Rinity gasped but Amya didn't look in her direction. She didn't care, she couldn't. She didn't want to hurt her best friend, but it was the truth.

If colonels didn't fall in love with majors' daughters, then princes didn't fall for civilians.

And a royal advisor could never fall in love with a Liosi-Alisethian girl with too many siblings and nothing else to her name.

She'd known better—it'd just been a bit of fun. She'd never meant to get her heart involved. And she hadn't, she reminded herself. She didn't feel anything for him; she didn't feel anything much for anyone. She'd gotten over how many boys in her lifetime? She could get over another one.

She pushed back the little voice that told her that boy was different—for one thing, he was a man, not a boy.

She ought to apologize to Rinity, she knew that, but she didn't have it in her. Rinity would want to talk it through and Amya just didn't want to do that. She didn't want Rinity's soft words of comfort when they weren't deserved. She'd say nice things meant to make Amya feel better but they'd do no good.

Because the truth of the matter was, Amya had been a fool. And she'd gotten not only her own heartbroken but the heart of her best friend as well. And if there was one thing Amya wanted more than anything else, it was to protect Rinity's heart. She'd had one job, just the one, and she'd failed.

Just because Rinity deserved a prince with soft eyes and a good heart, it didn't mean she'd get one. It didn't mean that was the way the galaxy worked.

She'd meant it when she'd said life was rarely fair. And she should have kept hold of that long before any of that had happened.

The vehicle lurched to a stop as they pulled up in front of their apartment building. Amya slipped outside, Rinity right behind.

"Come on, let's go up and I'll make you some tea." Rinity slipped her arm into Amya's.

Tea would set things right with them, it always did. Because Rinity was too pure to hold a grudge for long.

But it wouldn't fix everything swirling through Amya's mind. It wouldn't fix the cracks in her heart. And she knew if she went up for tea, she'd end up sobbing on Rinity's bedroom floor. And that time, it wouldn't just be because a boy had hurt her. It would be because she failed Rinity, really and truly.

And she wasn't ready to face that, not yet.

She sighed. "You know I love you."

Rinity leaned in and put her head on Amya's shoulder. "Always."

"Would you mind if I went for a walk instead? I need to clear my head. I just...I don't know anymore."

"Of course."

Rinity drew Amya in for a hug. Amya had been mean to her, had said things she didn't mean, and Rinity returned the favor with kindness and understanding.

It was true life wasn't fair and Amya was grateful for that. Because if it were, a horrible person like Amya would never be friends with someone as good as Rinity.

Chapter 19

Rinity watched Amya walk away, as her words from earlier rang in her ears.

You want a prince? Find yourself a fortune or some connections.

Amya had said it out of bitterness, out of anger, but Rinity firmly believed that no one said anything they didn't really mean, deep down.

And deep down Rinity knew it was the truth. She hadn't wanted to admit it and hearing Amya say it stung far more than she expected it to. Of course, Tov wouldn't look at her the same when he found out about her. She knew that. She'd always known that. But hearing it said out loud?

She turned to the apartment building, though she didn't have the energy to drag herself inside. She could hardly stay outside though. It was too hot, for one thing, and it wasn't as if they lived in the best neighborhood.

So, she let out a sigh and pulled the door open.

"Miss Garrick."

A shiver ran down Rinity's spine as she saw the silver haired man who called himself Isaias, a scowl resting on his face. It reminded her of someone but she couldn't place who. She was just tired, she told herself. She was just remembering her encounter from the other day.

"Excuse me, sir, I need to get home."

He stepped in front of her. She could have stepped around him but that would mean moving and her legs felt like jelly.

"I merely thought to stop by and see if you had reconsidered my proposal."

The one where she betrayed her books. Her beloved books. And Will and everything he stood for. "I told you before, I can't."

"Were you at a party tonight?" He looked her up and down, at the dress Amya had so tirelessly worked on and for what? She'd wasted her time and Amya's talents.

"I don't see how that's any of your business."

The door behind them opened and Rinity looked over her shoulder to see Nant Corry slip inside. The woman furrowed her brow at the man. "Everything okay, Rin?"

Nant lived on the floor above Rinity and usually had at least three of her grandchildren with her. It was odd to see her without even one of them.

"I'm fine." Rinity nodded.

The woman studied her a moment before she nodded once. "All right then. You take care now."

She slipped past to the stairs and disappeared.

Rinity turned back to the man. "I should go."

"By all means." Isaias stepped aside with an exaggerated show of getting out of her way.

Her skirt rustled as she moved around him, each step agony. Should she shower when she got upstairs or just throw herself into bed?

"It doesn't have to be your last party."

Rinity stopped and turned slowly to the man. "I beg your pardon?"

"The party you attended tonight, it doesn't have to be your last." He adjusted the cuff of his jacket rather than looking at her. "You'd have access to the Library too."

Her heart jumped. She would?

But it meant betraying her books. Betraying Will. It was wrong. She couldn't.

Could she?

She ran the pad of her thumb over the ring on her finger, the smooth metal cold against her skin. She could find her answers.

She wouldn't be enough to impress a prince. But maybe, if she knew, she'd find someone willing to write another love story with her—maybe not as good as the one her heart tried to write about her and Tov, but close.

"It's just one book?" she clarified.

One book wouldn't hurt. There were thousands at the Royal Library. Would anyone even notice if one was gone? She had three up in her room at that moment; she doubted they were missed.

And he'd as good as told her it would be worth it. She wasn't a nobody; she'd have connections—either through wealth or rank—he'd promised her as much.

"Just one book," he confirmed with a small nod of acknowledgment.

"And you'll tell me everything?"

He nodded again.

"Swear it," she pressed.

"*Rook di goo.*" He held out his hand. She shook it and the deal was sealed.

Rinity had never been in the Library after dark.

Usually when she snuck in, she left before closing, but after a torturous day of fretting and second-guessing, Rinity snuck into the Library the night after she made the deal with Isaias and stayed until the lights were off and the place was locked up tightly.

She hadn't seen Amya, though she'd considered going over to see her. But Amya would have noticed something was wrong and Rinity would have had to tell her. And Rinity wasn't ready to tell her anything. Not yet.

Maybe not ever.

Everything felt wrong as she walked down the rows, the books slumbering in shadows, all dark save where the beam of her flashlight fell. Her booted feet made soft footfalls on the carpeted floor, masking the sound of her pounding heart.

The books didn't whisper, didn't let her in on their secret conversations as they normally did. They let her walk in silence, their judgement thick in the air.

She rubbed her thumb over the silver ring, the only reason she was there at all. She'd earn the answers she so desperately needed and that would be that.

It was wrong what she was doing, she knew that. It ate at her, deep inside. And she shouldn't care. She shouldn't.

And it wasn't fair to repay Will that way, not after all he'd done to be a better father to her than whoever's blood poured through her veins.

But no one cared about what a decent man her stepfather was. They only cared about whether he had money or a rank or connections to someone else with those things.

She froze, sinking back into the shadows, against the bookshelf, as she flicked off her light, listening.

Convinced whatever she'd heard was just her ears playing tricks on her—or else just a normal sound the building made at night—she flicked her light back on.

She'd never stolen anything before and even as she considered it, she knew the books judged her for her betrayal of them. She'd remove one of their friends from its home and take it without care or regard.

They might never forgive her.

It wasn't like the books she borrowed and returned. She wasn't so foolish—no matter what Amya said—that she didn't know that was stealing too, but it was different. Those were books kept from her for no legitimate reason—even Tov agreed with her on that. And she always returned them. Always. The volume she planned to steal would never be returned and that made it different than anything she'd done before.

Her heart pounded and she felt herself slipping away, the panic settling in. Drawing in a breath, she rubbed her thumb over the ring once more as she began, "Yesterday, or perhaps long ago, there lived a princess, Allomina by name, far more beautiful than any this galaxy has seen or will see for another millennium or more. But far brighter shone her inner beauty, possessing good will for all she encountered and a lively spirit of grace and warmth."

It was the story she'd told Tov the night before. She hadn't meant to tell the same story, not when it reminded her of him. But it had been started and she couldn't take it back.

"But humanity was far less beautiful than the princess and her highness soon found herself so surrounded by the ugliness of human nature that she was unable to remain among it any longer. One night, she found herself staring out into the dark expanse of space, pondering the depravity of mankind. Overwhelmed and unable to bear the sorrow her heart carried any longer, she opened the airlock and flung herself into space."

She ought to keep quiet, though she knew the guard wouldn't be making his rounds anytime soon. If he made them at all. Isaias had said he tended to skip them and it didn't surprise Rinity, given her experience with him.

"But as her lifeless body flew through space the Prince of the Elassi saw her and fell instantly in love with her. She was so unlike anything he had ever seen before, with her dark complexion and raven hair, with eyes that shone like river-washed stones. The Elassi prince took the princess home with him and there he breathed life back into her cold body. She awoke in his arms and in an instant was in love with him too, her very breath taken away once more by his radiating beauty."

Rinity was at the stairs then and ascended them carefully, her footfalls seeming to ring in the silence.

"There were wed immediately, by Elassi traditions, and bound together as one. Using his magic, the prince made it so his princess could breathe among the stars and he lost no time in showing her all the wonders of space she had so longed to explore."

She reached the hall with the offices and slipped down the corridor. She moved past the door to the office she'd hidden in the day she'd met Tov and her heart pounded at the remembrance.

The way she'd felt when he'd smiled at her, the way his voice had touched her, and she knew she'd fallen in love with him in that moment. Her heart was his, bound to him as if she was the heroine in one of her stories. Like he was an Elassi prince or adventure hero.

And, like the heroine in a story, she knew she'd never love anyone else for as long as lived.

"Before long, she found herself with child, a joyous occasion among the Elassi. And then another child was born and then another. The prince and princess reveled in their growing family and were happy."

She slipped into the office at the far end of the corridor. The man had told her exactly where the book was located—in the far office, tucked away in storage, on the topmost shelf. Thankfully she was wiry and not afraid of climbing.

"But as the children grew the prince and princess started to see their sorrow and discontentment, their listlessness for the world Princess Allomina had come to love so dearly. And one by one, as they came of age, their children left them for the people of dust."

She found the box the man had told her to look for. The cardboard lid was simple to ease off and she rummaged around until she found it. The book was small, the cover soft under her hands.

"But there too they found themselves not quite content in the world around them. They belonged to this world no more than the one they had been born into. So, the children set out across the galaxy, a restlessness in their hearts, looking for a place to call home."

Was that a sound she heard? She froze, listening. Voices perhaps? She couldn't look for the book—and certainly not come down from her hiding spot—without making too much noise, drawing attention to herself. She'd just stay there and hope the darkness obscured her enough if she remained still and silent.

But she hadn't finished the story. It itched, the way the words were left hanging there, untold, existing in a limbo of waiting. They deserved to be—needed to be—released or she'd go mad.

She breathed in and out, slowly, deliberately, as she told herself she could get through it. She could make an exception just the once.

It lasted all of two seconds before the words spilled forth and she fought to keep her voice as low as possible as she concluded, "They were called the Mahsirian—the wanderers—as they still, to this day, find themselves the nomads of the stars, never settling, never finding roots, still searching for their place in this vast galaxy. And so, we come to the conclusion of our tale—or perhaps the beginning."

She fell silent again, straining her ears to listen for the sound she had heard before.

It must have been the building again. One as old as the Library creaked from time to time.

Or perhaps the books had started to whisper again. Maybe they just hadn't been used to her presence so late at night. They must not have recognized her.

And she would betray them still. The book in her hand weighed heavy and she hastened to tuck it into her satchel so she might not have to look at it or feel the burden in her hands.

She climbed down with ease, the shelves creaking under her weight. When her feet were back on the floor once more, she breathed a sigh of relief.

She made her way back through the Library, the same way she had come, finding her way back to the restroom to settle for the night. There was a lounge couch which she spread herself out on and began the long wait for morning when she could sneak back out again.

Chapter 20

Amya batted Colin Jamison's hand away as he tried yet again to slip it around her waist. He'd been doing it ever since she'd arrived at Henning's party and nothing seemed to be getting the message across—not her withering glares or the way she kept pushing his hand firmly away.

She wanted to tell him off but Henning's living room was crowded with eligible middle-class men and she wasn't about to brand herself as the crazy girl who flew off the handle. That was a good way to make every single one of them decidedly not interested in her. So, she just batted Colin's hand away yet again and shifted a little farther away on the couch to put some distance between them.

"Excuse me, Amya, isn't it?"

Amya looked up and met the brown eyes of the tall man who stood before her, an easy smile on his face.

"Have we met?"

She didn't recognize him and she was sure she'd remember a face as handsome as his. But there was something about those brown eyes, not as deep and rich as they could be, and his easy smile, not the self-assured smirk she wanted smiling back at her.

"Steward Newton," he introduced himself as he held out his hand. "Can I get you a drink?"

She took the offered hand to shake it but he used it to pull her up instead. She was propelled forward and stopped just short of bumping into his broad chest.

She gave a laugh as she forced a smile to her face that her heart wasn't in. "A drink would be lovely."

He offered her his arm and she took it even as she missed another arm, another such interaction.

"Sorry if I pulled you away from something important," he said, his voice low in her ear as they walked toward the long table on the other side of the room. "You didn't seem too keen on the conversation you were having."

She snorted. "It was hardly a conversation. And I appreciate the rescue, Steward. I've been waiting for someone to come save me all night."

She could have just walked away. And in truth, Colin wasn't bad. A little handsy and bad at taking hints, but she'd dealt with worse. But the way Steward straightened with pride at her words, she knew she'd said what he wanted to hear.

They reached the table with drinks—a long table with everything laid out with an array of bottles. Steward looked at Amya with a questioning eye.

"Surprise me," she said with a teasing wink.

He raised an eyebrow as his mouth quirked into a smile, the expression so familiar and yet so foreign as it came from a stranger. He selected a bottle from the table and poured her a drink.

She sniffed it suspiciously and wrinkled her nose as the alcoholic smell hit her. She never understood the appeal—probably her Alisethian heritage—but nothing got one branded a prude faster than a distaste for alcohol.

She took a sip and bit back the grimace that threatened to overtake her face. It sank lower and manifested in a shiver that ran all the way down her body.

"You all right?" he asked.

She set her drink down. "Want to dance?"

The room was crowded but the living room furniture had been pushed off to the side to leave a small space for that exact purpose.

"Love to."

He slipped his hand around her waist and she recoiled at the touch. Not because he did anything wrong—his touch was light and respectful—but his wasn't the hand she wished about her. He wasn't the one she wanted to dance with. She didn't want to look into his brown eyes or return his easy smile because she wanted to look into different eyes, return a different smile.

But they belong to someone she could never dance with again.

It was time to move on.

So, she let him pull her closer.

"What business are you in, Steward?"

He laughed. "What's a pretty girl like you care about business?"

She wanted to ask how a pretty girl like her could afford to not care about business. But no doubt he expected her to be nothing more than a pretty smile to come home to at the end of the day.

Ideally, she wanted someone who needed her not just at home but at work as well. Someone who needed a secretary or a clerk. Having customers to charm was her dream; she liked interacting with people and the idea of spending her days at home all day scared her a little.

She thought about the mountain of cards she had stuffed in her bag at home, the ones she'd collected at the last two parties, and she idly wondered if they were worth pursuing. Would it be worth her energy to start something she'd only have to stop once she was married?

Surely it wouldn't be profitable enough for her to consider it in lieu of marriage.

She realized Steward had asked her a question and she'd gotten lost in thought. She let out a little laugh and said, "Sorry, what was that?" She put a finger to her ear. "I didn't hear you?"

It was a believable lie with the music and chatter around them.

He leaned in close so that his breath tickled her ear. "I said you were beautiful."

"That doesn't answer my question." The words came out before she could hold them back. She meant it though; she'd asked a question and his first response had been a deflection of that. Simply telling her she was beautiful was mindless flirting and not even very original at that.

All of a sudden, she remembered someone else telling her she looked lovely and she wished she were there, making a fool of herself as she rattled on about hems and boning, instead of whatever was happening right then. What would he think of her out of a party dress and in her crop top and skirt instead?

She started to draw away, because she'd said the wrong thing and men were testy, but Steward just laughed.

"Fair point," he conceded. "I apologize. My father owns a hardware business on the East Side."

That was a nice neighborhood with classy shops. She knew nothing about hardware but surely it wouldn't be that hard to learn. "Is there a learning curve to that business?"

"Are you interested in hardware, Amya?" he asked with a laugh. There was a twinkle in his eyes that she should like, but found herself uninterested in.

"I'm interested in you, Steward," she replied as she returned his smile.

He leaned in close so that he might speak in her ear once more. "I assure you, there's much more to me than hardware."

His breath tickled her ear. The room was sweltering but it sent a shiver through her.

She let out a laugh. "I apologize for implying there wasn't. Do tell me, what is it that makes Steward Newton so special?"

"I'd much rather hear about what it is that makes Amya Cole so special."

She didn't want to talk about herself; she wanted to go home.

"I think I'm going to need another drink," she said.

Chapter 21

Rinity met the man called Isaias in the alleyway behind the Declaration Hotel.

It was on the East Side—the nicer part of the merchant section of the city. Amya had once attended a party at the hotel, after they'd graduated from school, and had said it was the fanciest establishment she'd ever been in.

Still, it was a strange place for a rendezvous. But Rinity didn't care as long as he held up his end of the deal.

"Do you have it?" he asked, his dark, familiar scowl gracing his face as he crossed his arms over his chest.

Rinity crossed her own arms and returned the scowl. It hardly had the desired effect, as she stood beside a garbage can overflowing with trash. "Information first."

He narrowed his eyes at her. "Do you have it?"

"Yes," she said, her back straight and her chin up in the hope that it made her appear a little taller. She wasn't short, but he was a good foot taller than her. "Information."

She should have requested a more public meeting place. But she'd been afraid of being caught. After all, she was in possession of property of the Liosi Royal Library. She'd be jailed for treason if she was caught.

She knew that. And she'd done it anyway.

Tov came unbidden to her mind and she pushed him back. Her heart squeezed. If he ever found out the truth—not even about the book, just about who she was—she wasn't afraid he would hate her or resent her.

No, she was afraid of something far worse—that he'd forget her entirely.

"Information," she said again, her teeth gritted.

Isaias dipped his head in acknowledgement. "It seems we are at an impasse here. Good day, Miss Garrick."

He turned and started down the alleyway, stepping around a stray can that lay abandoned on the concrete. Her breath came in short gasps as her heart pounded. "Wait!"

He turned back and she knew he was playing her. But she also knew he had the upper hand and if he walked away, she'd never get her answers.

He'd all but promised she was somebody. She needed to know who that was.

"The book, Miss Garrick." He held out his hand.

"Then you'll give me the information?" She looked him straight in the eyes; in stories you could always see a person's true nature in their eyes. All she saw were two brown eyes. "*Rook di goo?*"

He nodded. "*Rook di goo.*"

She dug into her satchel and pulled out the little leather book. She'd had hours to spend at the Library, as she'd waited for it to open that morning so she could slip out. The best way to pass the time was to read and she thought she'd see what it was Isaias wanted so desperately. But it had been too dark and she'd been afraid to turn her flashlight on. She'd been too afraid after she'd left the Library to pull it out and be caught with it.

She was always too afraid.

He reached for it but she drew it back. She could see it better in the light of day, a small old-fashioned oil lamp embossed onto the cover, in what she guessed had once been a bright gold but had since dulled and faded with age. "You'll tell me what I want to know?"

"The book, Miss Garrick." He waved his fingers at her, the action a demand for her to hand it over.

"What could possibly be inside this that you want so badly?" she asked, taking a step back as she flipped it open.

Isaias let out a growl but she didn't know why, for inside the pages were blank. She looked up at him with a puzzled frown.

"Why would you want a blank book?"

"That, Miss Garrick, is my business," he said, his words a throaty rumble. "Now hand it over if you know what's good for you."

Why would the Library have a blank book? And what could Isaias possibly want with it?

Her mind raced, trying to make sense of it, but no matter how she puzzled it, the conclusion never made sense. She didn't even protest when he stepped toward her to take the book from her hands, she was so lost in her confusion.

She did notice, however, the smile that curled at the corners of his lips as he tucked the volume away, the expression having a particularly dark bent. A shiver ran up her spine, though the morning sun beat down unrelenting.

"Now my information." The blank book didn't matter. None of it mattered. She just needed her answers. The man's smile twisted into something sinister and Rinity's heart raced as she wiped her damp hands on her leggings. "You promised."

"Consider this lesson your payment, Miss Garrick—people lie."

"You swore!" She jumped for him but he was taller than her, and no matter how she tried to reach for the book, he just held it out of her reach.

He'd sworn. Sworn it on his very life. It was a vow of honor—words one didn't speak unless they meant them. Even if one wasn't superstitious and didn't believe that breaking such a vow would incur the wrath of the Elassi or bring you the dishonor of your ancestors, it still wasn't something to be taken lightly.

She'd trusted him when he'd made the vow. And look what good it had done her.

He walked down the alleyway and she gave chase, pulling desperately at his arm but to no avail.

"Do you even know who my father is?" she demanded. It too was most assuredly a lie, one she had fallen for like a fool. Amya always told her she was too trusting for her own good and it was no more evident than in that very moment.

"I've given you all you need to know, I promised you no more."

"You promised me answers," she shrieked.

He shook her off and she fell backwards, hard against the concrete. Her world rocked as she was shaken to her core, pain exploding through her body.

He climbed into his vehicle. She jumped up, lunging at it, but too late. The door slammed closed as the engine roared to life. She beat on the window, crying out curses that she knew fell on deaf ears.

The vehicle rocked and lurched forward and she jumped back to avoid injury. It sped away and she cursed her self-preservation.

She watched it go through tear-filled eyes, waiting until it disappeared from view to rub at the tears with the pads of her hands. She was a fool.

A fool for sneaking into the Library, for stealing books, for trusting people, for always trying to see the good. She was a blind and utter fool.

She stood there in the alleyway and cried. And cried. And cried.

Because she'd betrayed everyone—Will and her books and Tov and Amya even.

She ought to talk to Amya, it was the only natural course of action, but she didn't know if she could face her. How did one tell their best friend they weren't the hero, but the villain, after all?

Yesterday or Long Ago

In the last several days she'd lied, stolen, hidden things she shouldn't, fought with her best friend; when has she gotten so comfortable with such a life?

And worse, what would Will say if he ever found out?

Chapter 22

Amya woke with a raging headache and a whole lot of regret.

She'd only had the one drink—but even that was more than she wanted—so she wasn't hung-over. But she had stayed up too late, and it was far too early. She could hear her siblings fighting already, and Alana was singing an Alisethian ballad at a rather annoying volume.

Steward was nice enough, and he was exactly the sort of man she'd been interested in marrying. He was handsome, respectful, and worked at a family-owned business where she'd be useful. But she'd struggled to talk to him.

She kept comparing everything he did to Gibbs. And he kept coming up short.

It wasn't fair to Steward, she knew that. But it didn't stop her.

She rolled over and stretched out, enjoying all the room in the large bed because her sisters were all already up. The far wall fluttered—made of a worn quilt, hung up to create two rooms where there'd only been one.

"Oh, good, you're up!"

Amya groaned and rolled back over, pulling a pillow over her head. "I'm still sleeping."

The bed jostled as Norah climbed up beside Amya. Her sister pried the pillow from her hands and pulled it off her head.

"Go away," Amya groaned.

"Mrs. Washe wants to make an appointment—she has pants she needs hemmed," Norah said. Amya reached for the pillow, but Norah just tossed it off the bed. "I told her I'd talk to you about scheduling something."

Amya groaned and rolled over to face her sister. She hated hemming pants and it was too early for such a conversation. "What time is it?"

"Almost ten."

Amya sat up. "Who let me sleep in this late?"

"You would have murdered us all if we'd woken you up any sooner." Norah laughed. "You came in so late. Exciting night?"

"Nothing to message home about." Amya flopped onto her back.

"What's his name?"

Amya's future flashed before her eyes—introducing Steward Newton to her family, marrying him, working at his family's hardware store. Her family would all love him and she was a catch so obviously his family would adore her.

And for the first time in Amya's life, it wasn't what she wanted.

"My?"

Amya sighed. "Do you want to schedule an appointment with Mrs. Washe?"

"Just let me know when," Norah agreed.

Amya looked over at her little sister; Norah was still growing into herself but she was not the little girl Amya remembered. She was becoming a young woman. "No, do you want to take the job? I have some other clients to focus on and I need to talk to Rinity."

She and Rinity needed to work things out. She was sure things were good between them, they always were, but they needed to talk and Amya needed to give her friend a true apology. Rinity deserved at least that much.

And then she needed to take advantage of all the cards she'd been given. Even if she never went to another party, she had enough cards already to start a nice network. With the prices she could reasonably charge, there was a chance she could turn it onto something profitable. She'd need space to work and there'd be other costs too...

"I need my notebook," she muttered as she shifted past her sister to grab the sketch book she used to design dresses from the cluttered bedside table.

"Do you mean it?" Norah asked and Amya realized she hadn't actually gotten a response from her sister. "You think I can handle it?"

Amya raised an eyebrow in question. "Do you think you can?"

"Yes," Norah said. She drew in a sharp breath and sat up a little straighter. "But if I'm doing the appointment, I think I should get seventy-five percent."

Pride swelled in Amya at her little sister speaking up for herself and taking advantage of the situation. She had the leverage, and while she needed to work on her confidence, she'd negotiated. "You can have all the profits."

Norah's mouth dropped open. "Are—are you serious?"

Amya opened her sketch book and flipped to the end, the matter already settled in her mind as she turned her attention to her endeavor. "Can you get me my purse? The black one?"

Norah hopped up and returned with the requested item a minute later. "What are you working on?"

Amya explained to her as she took notes and sorted through the cards and her sister sat and ate up every word, asking questions, making suggestions. And when Amya started to get stressed, Norah brought her tea.

"You're literally the best sister ever," Amya told her.

Norah retook her seat beside Amya, a sewing project in her hands. "I know."

"Don't let it go to your head," Amya said with a laugh.

Norah grinned back. "Too late."

Amya worked a little longer, her sister working on some sewing beside her as they settled into something comfortable. Finally, Amya closed her notebook and sighed. "I should go talk to Rinity."

"You should eat something first," Norah suggested.

Amya sighed; food was so inconvenient. "It is lunch time, isn't it?"

"Just about and it smells like Alana might be cooking." Norah wrinkled her nose. "That means I'll have to do the dishes."

Amya pushed herself up off the bed. "You've got to make an appointment with Mrs. Washe too."

"I won't forget," Norah promised.

"Good." Amya moved to the door.

"My?"

Amya turned. "Yeah?"

"You think I can really do this? Like you do?"

Amya offered her sister a soft smile. "I do, but you'll get a lot farther if you do it your own way. You've got what it takes."

"You mean it?"

"*Rook di goo,* firefly."

Rinity woke confused.

Light streamed through her window and her brain was a fog as to what day it was and why she was in bed so late.

Her head pounded and she rolled over with a groan. She gave a sharp gasp of pain as she rolled onto her hand.

It came back, the memories all a rush like the Englever River, as the tears sprung to her eyes at the remembrance.

The shame of what she'd done filled her even as the rage came at what the man had done. The scene in the alleyway played in her mind over and over again. The words exchanged, her actions—her foolish, foolish actions—and the nagging question as to why Isaias wanted—and why the Library would even have—a blank book.

She'd made it all the way home before she had broken down, where she'd managed to crawl into bed and sob herself to sleep, too tired to do anything else.

The front door opened and Rinity sat up quickly. Will would have left for work hours ago so it could only be one person.

Amya.

"Rin?"

Rinity groaned and rolled over to face the wall, pulling the pillow over her head. Amya's footsteps rang in the hall, coming closer, until they stopped just outside the bedroom door. The door creaked open. "Rin?"

Rinity was a coward. She knew that. She needed to roll over and talk to her friend. She needed to tell her.

But maybe if she just laid there it would all go away. Maybe she'd go numb, like she did sometimes, and just forget it all. Maybe no one even needed to know. Maybe she didn't have to tell Amya. Or anyone.

It was just a blank book. It couldn't do any harm. Words had to exist to be dangerous.

The door creaked shut and Amya's footsteps receded down the hallway. Rinity didn't hear the front door though, and she wondered if Amya had stayed. She'd probably brought some sewing and had settled herself in the living room to work, as she often did.

Rinity let out a sigh as she rolled onto her back. She'd have to face Amya eventually. If for no other reason than that Rinity was terrible at keeping secrets; she told Amya everything.

She wasn't ready yet though. Dragging herself out of bed, she grabbed a pair of lounge pants and a tee-shirt. Then she slipped across the hall to the bathroom to hop in the shower.

Fifteen minutes of hot water later and she felt about the same as she had before. But she couldn't stay there forever. So, she climbed out and got dressed. She left her hair wrapped in a towel as she padded barefoot down the hall to find, sure enough, Amya was still there.

She was in the kitchen, making tea, and she smiled when Rinity walked into the room.

"Hey, firefly."

"Hey."

Rinity moved past her to rummage in the cupboard a minute and came back a moment later with a box of crackers. She took a seat at the table as she stuffed a cracker into her mouth.

She ought to say something. But the words wouldn't come. They sat in her chest, like a hiccup that had gotten stuck.

Amya rose and turned on the tea kettle. Then she pulled out a cup from the cupboard and set it on the table beside her own. It sat next to a sketchbook that lay open, but instead of her usual sketches, there were words scribbling in Amya's delicate illegible scrawl.

"What're you working on?" Rinity asked. Maybe they didn't need to talk about what had happened. She and Amya often left things unsaid between them. Did that have to be any different?

Amya flipped the book closed. "Just brainstorming. Thinking about taking on some more serious clients."

"You mean like...starting a dressmaking business?" Rinity clarified. It was a crazy idea but if anyone could do it, Amya could—she had the talent and the drive.

Amya shook her head.

"Then what?" Rinity pressed.

Amya sighed. "No, I am—I just—we need to talk—about what happened."

Rinity felt her breath squeezing out of her as her heart pounded. She wiped her hands on the legs of her pants. How did she know? How did Amya always know everything? That was why she couldn't keep secrets from her—because she always seemed to know everything always. And Rinity always spilled.

"How do you know about that?"

Amya frowned at her and it hit Rinity in a rush. Amya wasn't talking about the book and Isaias and the alleyway. She was talking about their fight.

"Rin, what happened?"

Rinity shook her head as the tears came. She needed to tell her, she knew that. But the words wouldn't come. They always failed her when she needed them most.

"Rin." Amya moved to Rinity's side and rubbed her back as Rinity buried her face in her hands and wept. "Rin, what's going on?"

Rinity sucked in a breath as Amya moved away again. Peeking at her through her fingers, she saw Amya at the stove removing the kettle and pouring water into the cup she'd gotten out. Amya picked up her own cup of tea—that she'd made before Rinity had come to the kitchen—and handed it to Rinity.

"Take a drink."

Rinity took the mug and tentatively sipped. The sweet liquid coated her tongue and ran down her throat. Warmth filled her as she swallowed, and she let out a shaky sigh. It didn't fix everything, but it made it better. Tea always made everything a little better.

"What happened?"

Rinity took a deep breath. "You asked about the ring—I never told you how I got it."

There'd been no time for Isaias to take it back—it probably wasn't even really worth anything. She guessed it was real silver, but she doubted it meant anything. It didn't belong to Isaias or her father.

"Did His Highness ask you to marry him?" Amya's mouth dropped open and she stared at Rinity with wide eyes. Rinity couldn't read her expression—was it excitement or concern that graced it? Or perhaps it was a bit of both.

But it didn't matter because Tov hadn't asked her to marry him. And he never would, not when he found out. Because if heroes didn't marry civilians, they certainly didn't marry villains.

Rinity shook her head as she gazed into the half-drunk cup of tea. "See, it all started when a man in the lobby claimed to know who my father was."

Rinity appreciated that Amya never pretended to understand her struggle. But Rinity also knew that meant

Amya didn't understand the gravity of it. She could be more objective in those situations.

But Rinity? Well, she just couldn't.

"And?" was all Amya said by way of reply and Rinity tried to read into the word—was that judgment or pity in her tone? And which was worse? Rinity didn't much want either of them.

Rinity didn't look up from the ring as she played with it. It took everything in her to force the words out. "He said he'd tell me if I helped him with a job. I couldn't say no."

Rinity was well aware that she was a human with free will and she was in fact quite capable of saying no. And she was sure Amya was thinking it too. But 'no' had never come easily to her.

"So, I said yes, and last night I..." She trailed off at the remembrance. She'd betrayed her beloved books, and they would quite possibly never forgive her; and she hadn't even gotten the information she wanted. "I stole a book from the Library last night."

Amya inhaled sharply and Rinity cringed.

"I know. I know how stupid it was, but I didn't know what else to do. And I had given my word."

It was a weak excuse, especially since keeping her word meant betraying the people—and the books—she loved.

But it was true that Rinity wasn't someone who backed out once she'd given her word. She hated breaking a promise.

She laid her forehead on the table as tears welled in her eyes. "I just want to know who I am."

Amya rubbed her back. "You know who you are, firefly."

Rinity raised her head to look at her friend. "I know you think I'm stupid for wanting to know—"

"Excuse me?" Amya interrupted. She drew back and narrowed her eyes at Rinity. "I never said you were stupid."

"But you're thinking it, and it's okay, I know you are," Rinity said, her words a strangled cry around the tears.

"Firefly, no," Amya said with a shake of her head. "No. I don't think you're stupid—I disagree with you sometimes, but I disagree with everyone sometimes. That's life. But I never—ever—think you're stupid. You're an amazing woman who wears her heart on her sleeve and always stays true to herself, and that's beautiful. So, then what happened?"

Amya was going to retract her words about not thinking Rinity was stupid in a minute. But still, it meant a lot to hear Amya say what she had, even if Rinity wasn't sure she believed it.

"When I went to give him the book, he didn't tell me anything." The tears poured freely at the remembrance. "He took the book, and left and I couldn't stop him, and now I'm a thief, and I don't even know..." She trailed off in a sob, not even sure what else to say.

Amya sucked in a breath, and Rinity looked at her again.

"See, you think I'm stupid."

"No, I think committing treason is a stupid thing to do, which is completely different than thinking you're stupid," Amya said. "I think you're an incredibly smart young woman who knows better than to do incredibly stupid things like that."

"I didn't think it would hurt anything."

Amya raised an eyebrow and Rinity knew she didn't buy her words for a second. "That may be what you're telling yourself, but we both know you know better than that. What book was it?"

"It didn't have a title," Rinity told her with a shake of her head. "And it was blank inside. I don't even know why the Library would have a blank book. It's not as if that'd be of any use to anyone."

"But it's clearly of use to...whoever this man is. So, we figure out what the book is and then we can assess how much damage has been done."

Amya's face set in determination, an expression Rinity had seen so many times over the years—Amya wouldn't rest until the problem was solved. Unfortunately, Rinity didn't even know if hers was a problem that could be solved.

But if anyone could solve it, Amya could. And Rinity was going to let her try. So, she pushed back the tears to ask, "Where do we start?"

Chapter 23

"Let me get this straight," Amya hissed, as she sat beside Rinity at a Library table. "You can just look up what the book is in this catalogue, and you didn't think to do that first?"

She loved Rinity, she really did, but what she'd done was far graver than borrowing books. They'd throw her in prison for sure.

Amya would never see her friend again if they were caught.

No. She would. Because Amya knew about it she'd be charged as an accomplice. They'd be thrown in prison together.

Victory. She was going to prison.

She didn't tell Rinity that, since her friend would just freak out and regret telling her. But Amya didn't regret it.

She was glad Rinity had told her. And, if she was going to be tried for treason, she'd rather it was because she helped a friend.

But she wasn't going to let Rinity off easy.

"It's not in here," Rinity said as she looked up from the giant volume before her and met Amya's level gaze. Her brow was furrowed in, and it reminded her of something—of someone—but Amya couldn't place it.

She shook the thought away; she'd known Rinity since they were children. If anything, someone else would remind her of Rinity, not the other way around.

"What do you mean it's not in there?"

Rinity looked at her with a dead expression, as if Amya had asked a ridiculous question. The expression was weakened however, by the redness and swollenness of her eyes from all her crying. "I mean, there's no record of the book in question here in the catalogue, the book does not exist if we go by these records, there is no entry to be found indicating that such a book ever existed."

Amya frowned back at her. "She's got jokes, everyone."

Rinity smirked at that, and Amya smiled back, and all was right between them. It still bothered Amya that Rinity had said what she did about Amya thinking she was stupid. There were definitely things the girls disagreed on, but

Amya loved her best friend and respected her greatly. And there was never a reason to call a friend stupid.

Even if she did make an incredibly stupid life choice that was going to get them both thrown in prison for life.

But the smile between them eased the tension as only happened when such an expression passed between best friends.

"So, what now?" Amya asked. "We can't exactly go ask about a book there's no record of."

"History of the Library," Rinity said as she stood.

"What?" Amya hissed as she followed after her friend. Rinity made a beeline for a shelf of books toward the front of the Library. They weren't exactly in a place of honor, but were clearly kept close at hand for their importance.

Rinity ran her finger along the spines, and Amya caught a glimpse of some of the titles—*The History of the Liosi Royal Library, A Look at the Library, Liosi Libraries Through Time, A Brief History of the Liosi Royal Library*—before Rinity pulled a volume off the shelf and handed it to Amya. Then she handed her another, and another.

Once Amya had a stack of books, Rinity dragged her back to the table they'd occupied before and spread the books out. She took her seat and began flipping through them. Amya sat back down beside her and let her work.

She would have helped, but she wasn't entirely sure what they were looking for.

And she'd never been a strong reader. She appreciated the books she'd read for school, and she loved when Rinity told her stories, but the truth was, not having books readily available to her, it was hard to focus on volumes when they were placed before her.

She could get by fine with everyday things—signs, and accounts, and those things. But to sit and stare at what looked like a very boring history book, Amya wasn't sure she'd even be of any use.

She envied Rinity, who had a desire for books so strong that she was willing to risk anything to satisfy it. It meant she had the practice Amya didn't.

"Huh..."

It was just one word but it sounded promising. "Find something?"

"I don't know..." Rinity frowned at her, and it was there again, that feeling that it reminded Amya of something but she couldn't quite place what. She shook it off; it made no sense and it wasn't the time.

Rinity rose, and Amya debated whether she ought to just stay there and wait for Rinity to return with more books. But she'd probably need someone to help her carry them, so Amya followed.

They reached a dusty corner of the Library, and Rinity ran her fingers along the spines once more, pulling out a thick volume.

Amya held out her hands to take it but Rinity was already flipping it open as she slid to the floor. She settled cross-legged with the book spread out in front of her, her elbows resting on her knees and her chin resting on her fists.

She leaned forward to flip the pages before settling back again to read more. Her brow was furrowed up in that frown and Amya wished she could place what it reminded her of. It was right there at the front of her mind.

Rinity looked up, a concerned look on her face. "Do we believe in magic?"

Amya snorted before she realized Rinity had her serious face on, and her question was in earnest. Amya watched her best friend shrink at the snort. Rinity shook her head as she ducked down and turned her attention back to the book in front of her.

Guilt filled Amya as she took a seat beside her friend. "I don't know—do we believe in magic?"

Magic was one of those things you learned about as a child, heard in stories and the tales of your ancestors, and you believed it. You even looked for it, in the dusty nooks and crannies of the world, sure you'd find it around the next corner. But there came a point when you'd never seen it yourself, when you started to believe it didn't exist, that maybe it was just something from stories after all.

Amya didn't know if she believed in it. She supposed she would if she saw it, but in all her looking, she'd never found it, so she didn't have a reason to ask the question she'd been presented with.

"I think so," Rinity said in a small voice. She pointed to a picture in the book spread before it. It was a sketch of a book with an old-fashioned lamp on the front. "And that looks exactly like the book I stole."

Amya doubted it looked exactly like the book, since it was such a crude rendering, but she didn't argue; she knew what Rinity meant, and she was still bothered that Rinity had said what she did about Amya thinking her stupid. She wanted to be extra careful with her teasing and sarcasm at least until they sorted through that.

Though she knew part of that was due to Rinity's own guilt over what she'd done, so Amya tried not to take it too personally.

"Tried" was the key word in that sentence.

"So, what's this magic book?" They needed to focus on the task at hand, not dwell on things that couldn't be addressed, at least not at that moment.

Rinity tucked her hair behind her ear. "They say it has the power to divine heritage—if you write your name inside, it can trace your ancestry and tell you exactly who you are."

There was a wistfulness to Rinity's voice and Amya knew what she was thinking—she wished she'd known that before she'd handed the book over. She would have used it for herself. She'd only stolen the book in the first place to find out who she was; how sad to learn she'd held the key to those answers in her hands only to have them stolen from her.

"What could the man want with it?" Amya asked.

Rinity shook her head. "Perhaps he needs to prove his identity to someone?"

Amya closed her eyes and concentrated. "Tell me everything we know about this book."

"*Bequeathed to—*"

"No," Amya interrupted with a little shudder. Reading a textbook was bad enough, listening to someone else read it and have to try to process the words without seeing them, that was even worse. "Your words, firefly, so I can understand it."

"Right, sorry," Rinity mumbled. "It's said to have been gifted to King Kinnick just as he rose to power."

"Which one is he?" Amya tried to recall all those history classes she'd sat through but came up empty.

"The first one," Rinity clarified. "He settled Liosa."

Amya nodded, her eyes closed as she started to put it all into place. "Oh, right, okay. Continue."

"There was a prophecy included when the book was gifted that stated that one day the true heir would disappear and his bloodline would be lost."

Amya opened her eyes and frowned at Rinity. "That's just rude to tell someone who just became king something like that."

Rinity raised an eyebrow. "I don't think prophecies are really concerned with being polite."

"Still rude," Amya muttered. "So, what happened after this supposed prophecy?"

"You scoff, but that did happen," Rinity pointed out. "When the Philosathrians invaded, we lost that bloodline completely. Alaric the Pendragon—and then King Isambard, Tov's grandfather—aren't related to the original bloodline."

Even Amya knew that much about their history—about how Liosa had been under Philosanthrian rule until the fight for independence. It was kind of a key moment in Liosi history, even she couldn't miss the significance of something that important.

She'd never really thought about what it meant about the royal family though. It was true though, she realized as she thought about it, that Alaric the Pendragon had been a nobody before the revolution. Tov's grandfather—King Isambard—had been Alaric's right hand and best friend, but he'd had no royal blood that anyone knew of.

Ranks had been handed out during the revolution and the military had been formed from that. And it wasn't that they didn't deserve honor. But in two generations, it had changed from bestowing honor to a popularity contest of who was connected to those people, and then it became who had the most money.

Amya's father had immigrated to Liosa after the war. He'd done so much to help rebuild Liosa to what it was and it was through his blood, sweat, and sacrifice that the Liosa she lived in—the Liosa those with connections so greatly enjoyed—was what it was. Mr. Garrick had worked hard too, just as Amya's father had. How had Rinity's father done less for the planet than Tov's?

And what more had Gibbs' father done for Liosa than Amya's had?

But that didn't matter. Because no one would care for her pretty speeches of righteous indignation in light of what Rinity had done. It was still treason. And they needed to figure out the gravity of it.

"Sorry." She shook her head as she pulled herself back to the present. Rinity wasn't shaking as she normally did when interrupted in a story, and Amya supposed her history lesson didn't count. "You were telling me about the book. So, the Elassi gifted it to King Kinnick, along with the prophecy and then the prophecy came true?"

"*Victory!*" Rinity exclaimed, her voice a low squeal as she clearly held herself back; they were in a Library. "That's it!"

Amya shook her head, not following Rinity's train of thought; that was a usual occurrence though, as Rinity's mind worked a lot differently than Amya's. "What's it?"

"The true heir," Rinity said. "Maybe that's whose identity the man wants to prove. He wants to bring the true heir back to the throne, and the book is his key to doing that."

Amya still wasn't sure she believed in magic, but she supposed it made sense. And Rinity knew more about that stuff than Amya did. And it was all they had to go on.

Besides, if they saw it through and it turned out to be a worthless book, that was better than them letting it go because Amya didn't believe in magic only to have it turn out to be true.

"My?" Rinity said, her voice small. "If he brings back the true heir, that means Tov's going to lose his throne."

Chapter 24

All Rinity had wanted to do was find out who her father was. She wanted to know whose blood pumped through her veins.

And she'd let herself foolishly believe that if she found that out, maybe—just maybe—she'd be worthy of being loved by someone like Tov.

She knew no matter what answers she found, she'd never be good enough for Tov. He was a prince, about to be crowned king. He wouldn't love someone so far beneath him.

But maybe there was a chance someone could love her. Someone who liked books as much as she did and said superstitious phrases when she sneezed. Someone who touched both her mind and her body. With soft kisses and a softer heart.

But deep down she knew that wasn't true. Because she loved Tov, like the love in her stories—pure and deep, and the kind that lasted a lifetime and beyond. Her heart could never replace him with someone else.

And she had ruined everything. Not so much for them—because they had never really stood a chance together—but he was going to lose his throne, and it would be her fault. Just because they couldn't be together, it didn't mean she wanted him hurt. She wanted him to be the best king Liosa had ever seen.

She buried her face in her hands and wept.

Amya rubbed her back as the tears came, and Rinity choked them back as she sat among the books she had betrayed. She hadn't heard their whispers since she'd come in, and she suspected they were still mad at her.

But not nearly as mad as Tov would be.

There was never a chance of them being together, but he might have forgiven her for being no one of any significance. But to expect him to forgive treason, especially when it would cost him everything?

He could have been the kind of king they wrote stories about—about his goodness, and the way he wanted to do what was right, and how he cared for his people.

"I've ruined everything," she whispered in a choked sob, more to herself than to her friend beside her.

"We can fix this, firefly," Amya said, because that's what she always said. She always tried to fix everything. But maybe what Rinity had done was beyond repair.

She should have listened all those times Amya had told her to stay home, to stop sneaking into the Library, to stop stealing books. Rinity had told herself it was okay, that it would be fine, but it wasn't. And deep down, she had always known it wouldn't be.

Rinity had betrayed everyone who had ever loved her—Amya, Tov, Will, her books—for the one person who probably never would. Why did she think knowing who her father was would change anything? It wasn't as if he'd suddenly want her after not wanting her for so many years.

"You can't fix everything, My." They weren't talking about some bruised feelings or a dress hem. They were talking about treason that would cause their entire planet to crumble. And it would be all Rinity's fault.

They'd write about her in books she'd never be allowed to read.

"I can try," Amya said, and there was a conviction in her voice that shook Rinity to her core. Where had that fiery fighter been the other night when they'd argued? And if that girl had been beside her that night, would Rinity have made the choices she did?

She pushed the thought from her mind. She couldn't blame Amya for her choices.

"This isn't a cute Librarian or a new dress." Rinity didn't mean the words to come out harshly. She was just so tired, she didn't know how to make Amya see there was nothing they could do. Rinity had messed up, and there was no way to fix it. "This is far worse. I don't think even you can fix it."

Amya's frown morphed into her determined, problem-solving face. "You're right, I don't think I can." It didn't feel as good as Rinity thought it would to hear Amya admit it; probably because the fate of the planet was still at stake. "But I think I know who can help us."

Chapter 25

Amya had done a lot of crazy things in her life—she liked to think of herself as at least somewhat courageous—but nothing had ever been quite as scary, or felt quite as brave, as the moment she marched Rinity to the nicest district of the city and pounded on the door of a certain Royal Advisor.

They'd gone to Siphone's first, to ask his address, though Amya had felt guilty for disturbing her in her grief. But the young woman had seemed genuinely excited to provide the information. Amya was certain Siphone thought she sought to pursue the Advisor, and she let the young woman think that; she obviously couldn't know the true nature of their call.

It was getting late, and the sun had just begun to set. The sky shone a bright shade of pink with delicate, wispy clouds that any other day Amya might have admired and pondered how she could replicate the look on a dress.

But instead, she was too focused on the hot summer air that blew around them and caused her to sweat. At least, she told herself that's why she was sweating.

She didn't know who else to turn to. Rinity was right, she had messed up royally. And who better to fix it than a royal advisor?

She stepped forward and rang the bell again. Footsteps sounded on the other side of the door and she cringed; he'd probably already been on his way, and she'd gone and made it seem like she was impatient.

Except she was impatient, the fate of the planet was at stake. Why did the man fluster her so? Anyone else and she'd feel nothing but confidence but when it came to—

The door opened and Advisor Gibbs stood there on the other side, his face pulled into a scowl.

It struck her then, the placement of all her thoughts of familiarity toward Rinity when she made that same face. Because that's exactly who it had reminded Amya of.

But she didn't have time to dwell on it because Advisor Gibbs was saying, "My Lady?"

"Amya Cole." She drew in a breath and let it out slowly before she added, "My father's a pipe layer."

Amya didn't know what his father did, but it was surely something more prestigious than Mr. Cole's blue-collar work. And to a Liosi royal advisor, something like heritage and connections were important.

His expression didn't change though, and she was struck with a thought, that maybe he had known all along. It changed things, somehow, but she wasn't sure exactly what it meant.

"Can we come in?" She didn't have time to puzzle over his reaction. It didn't matter if he'd been about to get down on one knee and propose, he'd never look at her the same again once she said what she'd come to say.

He stepped aside to make room for them to pass. "Please, come in."

She crossed the threshold and dragged Rinity with her. A wave of emotions threatened to come up, but she pushed them back; she didn't have time to feel things.

"Is there somewhere we could talk privately?" Amya requested, once they'd stepped inside and Advisor Gibbs had closed the door behind them.

He frowned at her. She'd brought her friend and then requested to speak to him out of her presence. But Amya needed to make some things clear first, and she knew Rinity was a bad negotiator. Her friend would crack too soon and give everything away before they'd had a chance to make a deal.

And Amya had every intention of keeping Rinity out of prison, if it could be avoided.

"Of course," was all Advisor Gibbs said. He showed Rinity to a little parlor and told her to make herself comfortable. Amya only caught a glimpse of the room before he closed the door and shut Rinity off from the two of them.

He turned before she'd had a chance to take a step back and all of a sudden, he was so close—too close—her nose almost bumping into his broad chest. His crisp white button up stretched across it, he looked so strong, and she felt so small and insignificant as she stood there with her heart racing.

She swallowed hard as she stepped back, her gaze downward.

"You have a cat," she noted as the creature wandered down the hall toward them. Amya squatted and held out her hand, grateful to have something to distract her a minute while she regained her wits. She wouldn't let him unnerve her. She couldn't.

"She doesn't like to be touched," he warned as the cat hissed at Amya.

She had come close enough for Amya to see her better. Even in the dim light it was clear she had once been white but was now a dull, dingy gray color. She had matted fur and a few balding spots in random places. One of her ears was nicked, and her tail seemed short—as if perhaps part of it had been lost. She was exactly the opposite of the type of cat Amya would expect the put-together Advisor Gibbs to have. And yet, somehow, it made sense.

"That makes two of us," Amya said, feeling a kinsmanship with the battered creature who didn't like to be touched. "What's her name?"

"I—uh—haven't named her yet…"

Amya looked up at him in surprise; how did one live with a creature and not have a name for it? How long had he had her that he hadn't gotten around to naming her yet? "That's ridiculous. Her name is clearly General Chunky."

As soon as the words were out of her mouth, she felt the heat rise to her cheeks. She hastened to her feet as she remembered she was there to discuss the treason her best friend had committed, not give a ridiculous name to a cat she would probably never see again—because the cat belonged to a man she could never see again.

Why did he do that to her? She was so smooth, so sure of herself, when she talked to other people. But when she was with him, she forgot herself completely.

And yet, she'd never felt more herself than when she talked to Advisor Gibbs.

"We need to talk." She needed to focus on the matter at hand and not the way he made her heart flutter and her thoughts race. There wasn't time for that.

"Would you be terribly offended if we spoke in the kitchen?" he asked, his expression earnest. Why was he always so sweet to her?

Especially because he'd been kind enough to show her friend to the sitting room when he could have easily left Rinity in the hall.

"The kitchen's fine," she said, going down the hall. It could only be in the one direction, because the only other ways were back to the front door or else up the stairs. She doubted his kitchen was upstairs.

Sure enough, she found the kitchen a moment later, though she wasn't prepared for it as she stepped inside.

It was homey and inviting, with a window along the far wall that washed the room in the warm evening light. In front of the window was a multi-tiered shelf full of little succulents in uniform pots, the rich greens and purples and oranges like a sunset on a shelf.

Everything in the kitchen was in its place—a shelf of mugs all facing the same direction, clearly marked containers with tea, and sugar, and flour, and other staples. The pots and pan were hung just so on another wall—it was exactly how she'd expect Advisor Gibbs' kitchen to look, and yet it was so personal stepping inside, giving her a glimpse of him that she hadn't seen before.

It was so domestic and that made it intimate. And Amya didn't want to be intimate with Advisor Gibbs.

Or rather, she wanted it too much and she couldn't be.

She pushed past the lump in her throat as she swept into the room and took a seat at the little table tucked in the corner. A small journal lay open, the handwriting delicate and smooth across the page.

Advisor Gibbs flipped it shut as he took a seat but not before Amya caught sight of what she thought was her name. She didn't know how she felt about Advisor Gibbs writing about her in his journal—and she wasn't entirely sure what it meant—so she told herself she'd read it wrong.

She had only caught a glimpse.

His fingers drummed on the cover of the journal as he looked at her levelly. "I'll admit, it was a surprise to find you on my doorstep."

"Sorry." Amya ducked her head.

"I didn't say it was an unwelcome surprise."

Why did he do that? Amya wanted to scream with frustration that it wasn't fair. Everything he said made her heart race and all rational thought fly from her mind. She understood why Rinity had committed treason for Tov, if he made her feel the same way the Royal Advisor made Amya feel; she'd move the very stars in the sky if she thought would give her even a fraction of a chance with the man who sat across the table from her.

"You'll probably change your mind when you find out why I'm here." She sucked in a breath. "You have to understand before I explain anything else, that Rinity doesn't know who her father is and that's always bothered her."

"I don't know that I can..."

"No," Amya interrupted with a shake of her head. "That's not what I'm here for."

Did he truly think she'd come to ask for such help? She didn't know him well enough for that. But he'd looked concerned, like maybe he couldn't help, rather than confused or angry that she'd asked at all.

"So apparently, someone approached Rinity and convinced her he could tell her who her father was if she helped him with something."

Advisor Gibbs' eyes narrowed, and Amya wasn't sure if he thought she was there to ask for his help with whatever Rinity'd been asked to do, or if he was starting to guess that they were there because Rinity had done something incredibly stupid.

"He wanted her to steal a book from the Royal Library for him." She regretted the words as soon as they were out. She'd just admitted treason to a royal advisor; they were going to go to jail for the rest of their lives.

"So, your friend is a thief then?"

"Excuse me?" Amya demanded before the words processed and she realized they were fair. Why else would someone ask her to steal something for them if she wasn't a thief?

"You said—"

"I know what I said!" She sighed and her tone softened. "I'm sorry, I'm just touchy."

"So, she's not a thief then?" His shoulders were tensed up, his whole body tight, as his fingers increased their speed as they tapped on the leather journal. She was stressing him out.

But it was too late to leave, she'd already said too much for that.

She was tempted to lie and just tell him no. But she was there for his help, so the least she could offer him was honesty. "She always brought the books back."

He sucked in a sharp breath.

"It's not her fault," Amya defended her. "It's the only Library in the city and they won't let her in because she's not rich or ranked or connected. I think that's part of why she wanted to find out who her father was—she was hoping for a ticket into the Library. You can't blame a girl for wanting to read."

"I can when it means she commits treason to do so," Advisor Gibbs argued.

Amya rolled her eyes; had he not been listening? "It's a stupid rule."

"So, we just get to break rules now if we think they're stupid?"

She shouldn't argue with him, not when she wished him to be an ally. But he'd never be on her side if he didn't understand.

Also, he was wrong, so she needed him to understand that.

"So, you think it's a good rule?"

He narrowed his eyes at her. "I never said that."

"So, we just blindly follow rules even if they're wrong?" Amya asked with a shrug. "Because I'm pretty sure every change that's ever happened in the galaxy was because someone decided the rules were stupid and changed them. Our independence wouldn't've happened if Alaric the Pendragon had just decided that 'You know what? I'd like to do something but that'd be against the rules.' Space travel itself is a defiance of the rules—we were never meant to fly, and yet we didn't let that stop us. History is about adjusting the rules."

She glared at him, her gaze boring into him. She knew she ought to look away, to be embarrassed by having fought with him, but she couldn't bring herself to. She hadn't known him long. but she liked to think she knew him well enough to know he wouldn't wither away at her questioning or pushing back. In fact, he seemed to welcome it.

She hoped beyond hope that was still true, because otherwise she just completely ruined their chances of making any sort of deal.

"I assume this book she stole for the man wasn't one she planned on returning?" Advisor Gibbs said after a moment, as his fingers drummed on the journal cover.

"I never said she actually stole the book," Amya said.

He didn't dignify that with a response, just raised an eyebrow at her and frowned. It made her feel even more stupid than if he'd actually accompanied the expression with any words.

She shrank a little in her chair. "She stole it for real this time, yes."

"And did she find out who her father is?"

It surprised Amya that he wanted to know that. Though she supposed it had some bearing on the situation. Still, his words were soft with care as he asked. "He took the book and left her. She didn't find out anything."

"I'm sorry." There was a heaviness in his voice. Was it because he really was sorry for a girl he didn't even know? Or was it because he was stressed about the situation as a whole? Amya guessed the latter. "So, what was the book?"

Amya cringed because she didn't want to have to explain that part. "The Book of the Lamp?"

Advisor Gibbs' eyes went wide. "Please tell me this is a cruel joke."

Chapter 26

Amya buried her face in her hands before she worked up the courage to pry them away and look at Advisor Gibbs. "I know it sounds crazy—I'm not even sure I believe any of it—but if it's true—"

"His Highness could lose his throne." There was an edge to Advisor Gibbs' voice. She didn't know why it cut to hear him say it—she'd already known that. But it hit then how much she'd disappointed him and just how much his opinion meant to her.

"I'm sorry."

It wasn't nearly enough but it was all she could think to say.

He snorted. "Oh good, that'll fix everything."

"You don't have to get snippy." What was she doing? She wasn't in any position to dictate what tone he should or shouldn't use.

He looked at her with a hard expression. "I'm not even entirely sure why you're here telling me any of this."

"So you can fix it?" she suggested.

"Do you really think it's that simple?" He shook so hard that the table and Amya's chair shook too. His fingers tapped relentlessly on the table's wooden surface. But his words came out cool and even, his face blank.

She didn't want him to yell at her, but she almost wished he would; she probably deserved it.

"Rinity can tell you everything she knows." Amya made her tone match his. If she showed emotions it would elicit sympathy she didn't deserve. And she didn't want Advisor Gibbs to think she sought to manipulate him with the action.

"Then why are we having this conversation without her?"

She drew in a breath; she had no right to say what she was about to, but it was her only chance. "Because I want your word that if she helps you and this is all resolved, she won't get in trouble."

"You think I have the right to promise that?" Advisor Gibbs snorted. "You overestimate my reach."

"I don't think I do," Amya said levelly.

He shook his head. "Even if I did have such influence, what makes you think I'd be willing to offer you such a favor?"

"Because you're a practical man," she replied. "I don't mistake this for a favor—I wouldn't dream of asking you for one—but Rinity has information you need. And she'll happily give it, in exchange for amnesty."

Advisor Gibbs snorted again. "I don't know your friend well, but I believe if I went in there and told her she legally had to give me the answers I needed, she'd give them without even questioning it."

Curse him for being so perceptive. "She made a stupid mistake. Don't make her spend the rest of her life paying for it. I'm only asking for pardon if things are resolved."

"Because if they aren't none of us will have the right to grant anything," Advisor Gibbs reminded her. "His Highness won't be king anymore and I doubt whoever else becomes king will want me for a royal advisor. You have nothing to bargain with, Miss Cole."

She let out a frustrated squeal. "Fine, blame it on me, I'll go to prison, let me take the fall for it. Just don't ruin

Rinity's life over this. It's not fair. I'll probably survive better in prison than Rinity would anyway. You can't do that to her. You just can't."

Gibbs didn't say anything, and Amya knew she'd made a mistake in coming. He was right—Amya had nothing and that powerless feeling ate away at her. "What do you want from me? Name your price and I'll make it happen."

How foolish she must sound. What did she even have to offer him?

"I shouldn't have toyed with you, Miss Cole." Advisor Gibbs's voice was soft. "And I certainly didn't mean to distress you. I just wished for you to understand the gravity of the situation. I've no intention of sending either you or your friend to prison. Now's the time to be allies—and I'd never wish to be enemies with you."

He held out a hand to her, to shake—a truce. Ought she say something in response to his words? But what was there to say? Anything she could think of rang empty.

So instead, she shook his hand and offered a simple, "Thank you."

He slapped his hands down on the table. "Well, now that that's settled, I suppose we ought to move this conversation to the parlor so we can see just what exactly we're dealing with."

It felt like hours that Gibbs and Amya left Rinity sitting in the parlor.

The seconds ticked by on the clock over the mantle, slow and steady and maddening. She wondered when they would come back and why Amya had insisted on talking without her. She assumed it was because Amya knew she'd do something stupid if she were in the room.

But no. Amya loved her.

She drew in a shaky breath. She'd been a fool for all she'd done but Amya was still by her side—well, metaphorically—in it all. She could have walked away when Rinity told her she'd stolen the book. They didn't know what it was. It could have been anything and there was no reason for Amya to get herself involved.

But there they were. Rinity knew how hard it was for Amya to be there, to be asking Gibbs for help.

The door opened and Rinity jumped to her feet. Amya and Gibbs stepped inside before Gibbs shut the door behind them once more.

"Advisor Gibbs has agreed to help us." Amya crossed to stand beside Rinity.

"I'm really sorry," Rinity hastened to say. "I know I was wrong—I do. And you being willing to help us, it's very generous of you. And if that means I have to go to prison—"

"You're not going to prison," Amya interrupted, glaring at Gibbs.

"If we can get this all sorted, there's no reason for such repercussions." He offered Rinity a soft smile that set her at ease. She could see why Amya liked him so much; underneath all his sternness he seemed kind, which made Rinity sad, because Amya deserved to have someone who would be kind and gentle with her heart.

"So, he needs you to tell him everything," Amya said, drawing Rinity back to the conversation and out of her thoughts. "About the man and what he told you and everything you can remember. He can't help us if he doesn't know who we're dealing with."

Rinity nodded as she sat on the couch once more. She kept her gaze on her hands as she twisted the ring on her finger. "His name was Isaias—at least, that's what he told me it was. He said to tell me anymore would be telling, and I had to earn his answers. He showed up at our apartment, and we spoke in the mail room—he claimed to be my uncle, and he gave me this ring. He said it belonged to my father."

"Can I see it?" Gibbs requested from his seat just across from them.

Rinity pulled it off slowly, reluctant to give it up even though she was sure it didn't actually belong to her father and was no doubt worthless.

Gibbs took it from her, and his expression was blank as he turned the small piece of silver over in his hands.

"There's a crest on it," Rinity said, though he could already see that. He didn't seem to be paying it much attention though. She'd expected him to study and exam-ine it, but instead he barely glanced at it before he looked up her.

"Can you describe this man?"

Isaias appeared vividly in Rinity's mind, too vividly, and she shuddered at the remembrance. "He was kind of lean and taller than me." That meant nothing, she was of average height for a girl, so most men were taller than her. "That is, he was tall—maybe a little taller than you? He had sort of wispy hair and was really well-dressed and put together—like, everything was pressed and perfect."

Amya's eyes narrowed as she studied Gibbs. Gibbs looked to Amya, and they made eye contact. He asked her a question with his eyes, though what the inquiry had been, Rinity wasn't sure.

"What's going on?" she asked.

Amya frowned. "Do you have any idea who the man might have been?"

Rinity opened her mouth to respond to her but shut it again because Amya was looking at Gibbs, so she wasn't asking Rinity. Because they had already established Rinity didn't know. She looked to Gibbs as well, waiting for an answer.

"I have my suspicions," Gibbs said slowly.

"Do you think there's a chance he might actually be Rinity's uncle?" Amya gave Gibbs a pointed look, and Rinity was all the more confused.

Gibbs' frown deepened, his brow wrinkling into hard, comfortable lines, as if he made the expression often. "I'd prefer to look into it further before giving a voice to anything that might be mere speculation."

Amya rolled her eyes but nodded. "Okay. So, what do we do next?"

"We don't do anything, Miss Cole." He seemed surprised by the question. "You gave me what help you can, I don't see of what further assistance you can be."

He was right. Rinity didn't know anything else and while she wished there was more they could do, the truth of the matter was she'd already done far, far too much.

Amya nodded. "Of course, it was foolish of me to think you'd need our help when you'll have a security team—"

"I can't tell anyone about this," Gibbs interrupted and Amya and Rinity both looked at him in surprise. "Don't get me wrong, I'd much prefer to have a team of security officers at my back, but what exactly am I supposed to tell them? That your friend here stole a priceless book that puts the fate of Liosa at stake, and then I made a deal with her to completely erase her treason because she gave me one brief description? No, I take care of this quietly, and we pretend it never happened."

Amya laughed. "You plan to go save the planet all on your own?"

"If you have a better plan, I'd love to hear it." There was a pointedness to his tone that made Rinity shrink back as her breath came in shallow breaths. Not because she was scared of Gibbs, but because she knew Amya well enough to know she wouldn't take kindly to his tone.

Chapter 27

Amya had no right to lecture Advisor Gibbs on his words or tone, not after all the help he'd offered them. But still, he was being foolish. Like one of the heroes in Rinity's stories, always trying to save the day on their own.

"I don't know, maybe we could offer some help instead of you just going off alone," Amya suggested. She fought to keep the annoyance out of her tone, but it had never been a battle she was going to win.

Gibbs snorted. "You think you have any help to offer when you can't even ask for it yourself?"

"Excuse me?"

Rinity stiffened beside her. Amya reached over to reassure her, and Rinity took her hand and squeezed it, like a child did when they were trying to be brave through a painful ordeal.

"You showed up at my doorstep, unannounced, to tell me your friend committed treason, and you can't just ask me for help." Gibbs' voice was heavy with pain. She'd hurt him, deeply. She didn't know she had the power to do that, and her chest squeezed at the realization that she did and the implications of what that meant. "You keep pretending you have something to bargain with when you don't. Why can't you just ask me for help?"

"Because I don't have the right." Amya shook as she spoke, her words strained and choked.

Rinity let go of Amya's hand to rub her arm instead, and Amya flinched at the touch. Rinity shrank back as she pulled away. Amya reached for her hand again and squeezed it, her turn to draw comfort and courage from it.

"I'm not here to ask for a favor, because if I am, it means there's something between us, and there can't be. It's as simple as that."

Advisor Gibbs frowned at her as he worked his jaw. Time ticked by on the clock over the mantle. Amya wondered if she ought to say something but didn't know what there was to say. Finally, Advisor Gibbs spoke and his voice was low and husky, heavy with emotion.

"If you think asking me to disregard the law isn't asking something of me, you clearly don't know me at all."

His words cut deep but Amya couldn't argue. She didn't know him, not well enough to be asking anything of him. Yet there she was doing just that.

She could see how she hurt him, the way his shoulders sagged and his expression was softer, sadder, than his usual schooled expression. She'd done that. But worse, there was a twinge of hope that rose in her to know she meant enough to him that she could have that kind of effect on him.

She pushed that hope away, though she knew that wasn't how hope worked. It was a pesky thing that had a habit of sticking around far longer than she wished and refused to be killed no matter how hard you tried. It was tenacious as ivy and twice as stubborn.

"I'm sorry." Not just for the situation they were addressing, but so much more.

Rinity squeezed her hand, reminding Amya she needed to talk to Advisor Gibbs about the man and the ring, and that she didn't want to do so in Rinity's presence.

Advisor Gibbs had been right not to give it a voice in front of her. It could get Rinity's hopes up and that wasn't fair. Not if it was going to turn out to be nothing.

"Could we maybe speak privately again?"

Advisor Gibbs frowned at her but nodded. When he spoke, it was directed at Rinity. "Feel free to occupy yourself with any books that strike your fancy."

Rinity was to her feet in an instant and circled the couch to start exploring the bookshelves along the far wall. It struck Amya that Advisor Gibbs had been considerate enough to find a way to occupy her—and one he knew would mean so much to her.

They stepped into the hall and, as soon as the door was closed behind them, he said, "I'm not entirely sure what there is to discuss."

"Maybe your sister?" Amya suggested. She knew her suspicions were correct too by the way Advisor Gibbs stiffened. His expression remained perfectly schooled though, as he strode down the hall in the direction of the kitchen once more. Amya hurried to catch up. "So, there's a chance."

Rinity had always wanted a brother but Amya wasn't sure her friend should ever know. It would make things worse, to discover she had a brother only for him to have to throw her in prison.

"The crest on the side of the ring?" he said as they stepped into the kitchen once more. "It's my family's crest.

And my uncle's name is Isaias, and the description does match, though there's little to go on. And my father wasn't exactly the picture of fidelity. What made you guess?"

"You have the same thinking face."

His brow furrowed in question.

Victory, there were two of them. Her best friend and the man she felt more than friendship for were the same person.

"Yeah, that one," she said with a laugh as she pointed to the little wrinkle in his brow. "You both scrunch your faces up the same way. And, well, when something as familiar as your best friend's thinking face starts to remind you of someone else, you get suspicious."

He nodded.

"Is that all you wished to discuss?" he asked with a frown.

There was so much more she wished to discuss. And not discuss—because why did his mouth look so kissable? She wanted to entwine her fingers into his wild mess of wispy hair and kiss the starlight out of him.

Victory, she wanted to kiss him.

She took a step back, as if she didn't trust herself to not do just exactly that; maybe he wasn't as exactly like her best friend as she'd originally thought. "I—um—just—we should discuss the plan. I recognize I pulled you into this and I am asking a lot, so if I can offer any help at all, it's the least I can do. To say thank you."

He snorted.

"Okay, that's stupid and I know it, but surely I'm better to work with than not having anyone at all." In truth, she didn't know how she wanted him to answer that. Because part of her wanted him to turn her down; she'd planned to never see him again, but she couldn't very well just walk away from the situation.

It was Rinity's fault and by extension hers. If she'd only stayed with Rinity that night instead of going for a walk. If only she'd gone to talk to her the night before instead of going to a party. She never should have gone to that stupid party and danced with Steward Newton with his stupid perfect face, and job, and family that she couldn't bring herself to love anymore because of the stupid Royal Advisor standing before her.

"What about Miss Rinity?" Advisor Gibbs asked, and Amya realized he didn't even know her last name. He'd agreed to wipe her record completely clean, and he didn't even know her name. He was right, Amya was an idiot—not that he'd said that, but it was implied—for thinking she wasn't asking so much of him.

"What about her?" They couldn't bring her. It was a bad idea. Rinity was amazing but she didn't do well under pressure, and Amya would be useless trying to make sure she was fine if they were anywhere, so Advisor Gibbs might as well leave them both behind.

And she didn't want to suggest that because then he'd leave her behind.

Not that she wanted to go.

Or did she?

She had no idea what she wanted.

"Is it wise to leave her alone?" Advisor Gibbs asked.

Amya glared at him. "She's not going to steal something else. She's not a thief."

"We're in this position because she is a thief," he reminded her. "But I was asking because it seems unwise to simply send her back home. First because my uncle—or whoever this Isaias person is—could come back. And there's the matter of her emotional state. She might, perhaps, want a friend by her side through this."

Rinity had committed treason. And Advisor Gibbs' concern was her emotional state.

He really was too good for her.

She nodded. "I guess I can take her home."

"I just said that's not a good idea." There was an edge to Advisor Gibbs' voice.

"Sorry, right," she said with a shake of her head. "Um..."

"I suppose it makes the most sense for you to stay here." He didn't sound too thrilled about it, and she didn't blame him.

She nodded. "We won't be any trouble, *rook di goo*."

She wanted him to know his greenstone would still be there when he got back and they wouldn't mess up what was clearly a fastidiously kept house.

Her words brought a smile from him and Amya hated that it warmed her to her toes as a smile of her own spread across her face. There was a tease in his voice as he spoke.

"It's a little late for that, Miss Cole."

Chapter 28

Rinity didn't look up from the book she was reading when Amya returned alone—she continued to read, grateful she'd chosen a short chapter to read. She heard the clock tick by and felt Amya's gaze boring into her as she read, and it was hard to concentrate on words rather than either of those things.

She tried to draw her attention away from the story, to simply close the book and be done with it, but the words itched and pleaded, and she couldn't bring herself to do it, no matter how hard she tried.

Her heart pounded as she read, the room growing unbearably hot in her discomfort.

But still she read.

It felt like it took ages to read those last two pages, the words drawing themselves out, meandering all the slower the harder she tried to hasten their pace. They plodded in a steady fashion, until Rinity herself grew annoyed with them.

"Hurry up," she muttered crossly.

But the words didn't listen. Instead, they moved all the slower, as if time had somehow frozen itself and the words had all but frozen with them.

Finally, she reached the end and she snapped the book shut. She tossed it onto the couch beside her and jumped up. "I'm so sorry. Where's Gibbs?"

Amya crossed to take a seat on the couch, flopping back. "He had a suspicion about who Isaias might be so he went to look into it. He asked that we wait here, for our safety."

He should have thrown them in prison.

Rinity knew that. She knew that the fact that they were still sitting there was a huge deal, and she was beyond grateful for the Royal Advisor's kindness.

But she wasn't stupid—she knew his kindness wasn't extended because of her. She could see it in the way he talked to Amya. The way he leaned toward her when they conversed, the way his eyes lit up when he looked at her, and the way his brow softened when she spoke.

Rinity had also seen the way his expression had fallen when Amya had said there was nothing between them. His shoulders sank just a little and she knew what it meant—disappointment. And if he was disappointed that there could be nothing between him and Amya after everything that had happened, Rinity doubted anything else Amya told him about herself would be a deal breaker.

"He's a good man." Rinity noted as she sat back down again beside Amya. "I can see why you like him."

Amya glared at her. "Please don't."

"What?" She knew full well "what." "I was just noting, that's all."

"You weren't, and you know it." There was an edge to Amya's tone that made Rinity's chest squeeze; she and Amya rarely fought because usually when they disagreed, they simply never spoke on the subject.

But Rinity didn't want to let it go. Gibbs was what Amya deserved and far more than she'd ever dared to allow herself to dream of. It wasn't fair to let him slip away without even trying.

"He likes you," Rinity said. "I don't think I've ever seen a guy look at you the way Gibbs looks at you."

It was as if Amya held the secrets to the universe, and he wanted to slowly unpack each and every one—there was an eagerness and a hesitancy; as if he wanted to jump right in but was holding himself back in order to savor it all.

Amya shook her head. "I keep telling you, that doesn't matter."

"It should," Rinity pressed. "If he doesn't care that you showed up on his doorstep, told him your best friend committed treason and you were hoping he'd help but that he doesn't mean anything to you, and his response is not to throw us in prison, I don't think any of the other things are going to matter."

"And what if you're wrong?" Amya drew in a shaky breath. "I love him, Rinity. As stupid and as foolish as that is, I let myself love him. And I don't think I can bear it if he doesn't love me back."

"He deserves a chance," Rinity said.

Amya let out a ragged sob that she tried to cover with a bitter laugh. "What exactly am I supposed to say? 'Hi, I come from a large family that's super poor. Also, I have a lot of emotional baggage and am too stubborn and judgmental for my own good. Plus, I know heritage is important to you, which is great because mine is both Liosi and Alisethian. But I really like you so would you be willing to overlook all that?' I think today proved how poorly that would work out. I couldn't even bring myself to ask him for help."

"But that doesn't mean—"

"No!" Amya sat up and looked Rinity in the eyes. "How many times do I have to say I don't want to discuss this?" She stood up and started for the door. "Just read a book or something. I'm going to go find the cat."

She stormed out before Rinity could ask about the cat or apologize for what she'd said or change the subject to something that wouldn't make Amya cry.

Amya didn't cry. Not over much. And never boys.

She'd said she loved him.

Amya didn't say that, not about guys. She loved dresses, and styles, and fabrics, and her family, and Rinity. But she didn't say she loved guys.

They were good kissers, or decent enough of a person, or from a good family, but Rinity had never heard Amya say she loved a man before.

Her heart was breaking over the Royal Advisor, and all Rinity had done was make it worse. That's all she ever did. She pushed, and pushed, and pushed until people were hurt.

She'd committed treason, and she hadn't even said she was sorry.

Not that sorry was enough.

But there was nothing she could do. She was so useless that she broke things she didn't know how to fix.

The tears came, and she let the sobs shake her as she thought about everything she'd done. The lies she'd told, the wreckage she'd left. She'd never meant for any of that to happen.

She'd just wanted to kiss her Librarian. He wasn't supposed to be a prince. And after she'd found out, she'd only meant to hold on for just a little longer. Just a few dances, and conversations, and kisses.

But she'd given her heart to that man with the sweet smile and earnest eyes. She should have known; she always got in too deep. It was how one time sneaking into the Library had turned into her saving grace. It was how a conversation with the girl across the hall had turned into a friendship that apparently not even treason could shake. It was why she'd committed treason to find out the name of a man who clearly didn't give her a thought or concern.

Because she cared. Once something got into her head it went straight to her heart, and she cared about it too hard and too deeply.

She stood, in need of comfort, and looked at the wall of books she longed to explore. Gibbs had no idea what he'd done, so casually and willingly offering for her to read his books. He'd given her a gift, and he hadn't even realized it.

But they weren't her books. They weren't the ones who'd been with her through her awkward teen years when she didn't feel like she fit in, through the few nasty fights she'd had with her best friend, through the days she missed her mother most, through the questions about her father.

Her books had been there, and she'd betrayed them.

She couldn't apologize to Amya—she didn't know what to say. There was no apology she could give to Tov—she'd cost him his throne. If she spoke to Gibbs, she'd probably blurt out Amya's secret. And she didn't even want to think about how disappointed Will would be if she told him about all she had done.

She needed her books.

As soon as the idea entered into her head it became not a desire but a need until it ate away at her.

She needed to apologize and to see if they would offer her some comfort and advice. Maybe things would be clearer if she could just be with them for a little while. And maybe she could find something useful to share. It wasn't right for Gibbs to do all the work when Rinity had been the one to get them into the mess in the first place.

She'd ask Amya.

Except, Amya would tell her there were plenty of books to read. Or else she'd want to come with Rinity, and hadn't Amya said they ought to stay there for their safety?

Rinity would stay there. She'd be fine. She'd read the beautiful books the Advisor had given her permission to read.

Except, she didn't want them. They didn't whisper their secrets to her; she was a stranger to them. She needed her friends.

She couldn't ask Amya to put herself in danger. Amya would do anything for Rinity, everything that had happened had proved that. And it wasn't fair of Rinity to ask any more.

So, she slipped from the parlor and out into the hall. She could hear Amya in the kitchen—it sounded like she was rummaging through the cupboards—and so Rinity moved softly to the door.

She eased it open and slipped out into the street. Then she closed it behind her and set off in the direction of the Liosi Royal Library.

Chapter 29

It felt wrong to be at the Library.

It felt wrong to run her fingers along the spines, to seek comfort in the cool leather and fabric beneath her fingers. It was like asking a friend for a favor after you'd broken their heart.

She didn't know how to apologize though.

"I am sorry." She brushed her fingers over the spine of one of her favorites—a volume of legends of Liosa. It had all her favorites and there were little line drawings that never ceased to warm and delight her. But she hesitated pulling it off the shelf. Was a simple "sorry" enough?

"I was hoping to see you today."

Rinity froze at the voice as a thousand thoughts raced through her, and yet her mind went blank all at the same time.

She focused on her breathing, reminding herself breath was essential for survival. *In. Out. In. Out.*

She turned, and her heart crumbled again.

Tov stood before her with an easy smile as he regarded her with earnest eyes. There was a soft smile on his lips, but the softness wasn't an indication of how deeply he felt it, she knew that. Her gentle Prince, whom she had no right to love.

He reached for her hand, and she took a step away from him. He pulled back, his expression confused and hurt.

"Is something the matter?"

He didn't know. Last she'd spoken to him he'd asked if he'd see her after his speech, and she'd left—true, it'd been because Siphone needed them, but the point was he didn't know about the fight with Amya, or Isaias, or the ring, or the book.

He didn't know what she'd done.

"I'm so sorry." How did she explain? Where did she even begin? And once she'd begun, how did she find the words to tell him the vileness of what she'd done?

Standing before him, the gravity of it hit her. She'd destroyed everything for him. And he didn't know. If she didn't tell him, he'd probably just keep kissing her until the end of time.

She'd done that. She'd betrayed him like that.

"Rin?"

The sadness in his voice broke her, and she began to cry. She buried her face in her hands and let out a ragged sob. He placed a hand on her arm, gentle and soft and questioning, as if he were unsure whether it belonged there or not. Because he didn't know what she'd done, how she'd repaid his kindness and love.

She pulled away and he stepped back. She could see the hurt in his expression. He deserved to know. He deserved to understand why she wouldn't let him touch her—because when he knew, he wouldn't want to ever touch her again.

"I never wanted to hurt you," she murmured.

"Come on," he said. "Let's sit down, and you can explain, and we'll work it out." He sat down on the floor, his back against a bookshelf, and patted the ground beside him.

Work it out. He thought it was something he—they—could fix. Ever the storybook hero.

They couldn't, but she sat down beside him anyway. Because it was hard to cry while standing up, and she did need to talk to him. But she made sure to keep some space between them, and he made no move to close the gap.

"I lied to you." That was where they needed to start. "I'm not rich or connected."

He snorted, and she looked at him in surprise. He looked offended. "We met because you were hiding in a vent. If you'd truly left your membership card at home, they wouldn't have let you in in the first place. I already suspected, but after your vehement speech about the limited access to the Library, it all but confirmed it."

She stared at him silently, trying to process what he said.

"I'm naïve," he continued. "But I'm not stupid."

He'd known. All along, he'd known.

"Why didn't you say anything?" Rinity asked, breathless.

He gave a little shrug. "You didn't want to talk about it, and I didn't want to push. I figured you'd tell me when you were ready. And it didn't—doesn't—really matter to me."

It didn't matter to him.

It always mattered to the Prince. Heroes in stories didn't marry civilians. They married princesses and warriors.

Rinity began to cry again. "It will though."

"It won't though." Tov's tone was gentle as he shook his head, and his soft curls bounced with the action.

She choked back a sob as she forced the words out. "I don't know who my father is."

"That's okay," he assured her.

"No," she snapped. "It isn't. It's hung over me ever since I was a child. I've wanted to know."

Heroes always knew where they came from. Because they were Liosi and that was the most important thing to a Liosi.

"Oh. I'm—I'm sorry."

It wasn't fair that he sounded hurt, because he had no reason to be hurt for her. But it would pass, and he'd be angry and hurt soon enough, she was getting to that.

"I had the chance to find out."

He sat up, a light in his eyes, excitement written plainly in his expression. "That's good!"

Why was he always so nice? Even the heroes in her stories were gruff or harsh sometimes. But not Tov. Never Tov.

"He promised to tell me who I was if I—that is—he wanted me to—I agreed to—"

She couldn't tell him.

She had to.

"I stole something for him."

"Oh."

There was so much in his tone for such a small word—confusion, defeat, sorrow, question. And she hadn't even told him the worst of it. How she wasn't just someone who'd made a mistake, but rather had made herself the villain of his story.

She shifted a little farther away from him and leaned back against a shelf of books she had no right to find comfort in. "It was supposed to just be a book—I thought it was harmless—"

She needed to stop justifying it. Needed to stop trying to keep him from thinking the worst of her. Of course, he would think the worst of her. And she deserved every nasty, vile, hurt-filled thing he would think of her.

"I stole the Book of the Lamp."

Tov's brows went in, but she saw the recognition in his eyes.

"I don't know what he intends to do with it," she said. "But when we spoke to Gibbs—"

"Gibbs knows about this?" Tov interrupted.

Rinity nodded. She drew her knees up and hugged them to her chest. "I told my friend, Amya, and she said we should talk to Gibbs. We think—that is—it's possible—we don't know for certain—but, the man could be hoping to reclaim the throne for the heirs from before the conquest.

He could be trying to take the throne from you."

"Oh."

It was the same word he'd said just a minute ago, but it meant something entirely different. Rinity wasn't sure exactly what all was contained in that one little word.

He sank back against the bookcase, and neither spoke. An apology seemed worthless and inadequate.

In fact, anything she could think to say would ring hollow. It was wrong to try to explain or justify—did it matter in the face of what she'd done? To tell him it had been unintentional, that she hadn't known how serious it was, would make no difference. She didn't want to seem as if she were trying to excuse what she'd done or make herself seem blameless.

She took full responsibility.

Finally, Tov said, "Would that be such a bad thing?"

There was silence between them as her mind raced. Had she heard him wrong or misunderstood him? Had she not explained herself properly and the misunderstanding was on his part? She'd thought she'd explained it clearly.

"You could lose your throne."

"Right," Tov agreed. "And would that really be such a bad thing?"

"How can you say that?" She'd expected his hurt, his anger, but the words he spoke? She was woefully unprepared to respond to them. The princes in her stories never said things like that. What kind of a hero gave up?

He sighed. It was tired and heavy, and Rinity felt it in her innermost self. "I've known for a long time I'm not a king of legend, like Alaric the Pendragon, or like my grandfather, or father. Surely Liosa deserves a better king than me. I'm not a warrior."

"Does Liosa need a warrior?" She knew Liosa's history and their legends. She knew how they'd carved out their existence on a planet that didn't want to be inhabited. They'd fought back when they'd been oppressed, and they had great pride in their warrior nature.

But what if the monsters had been slain?

He snorted; she shouldn't think about how much she loved the sound. "I don't think Liosa is ready for anything else. We're bold and brave. We act before we think, and we don't back down. But that's not me. I overthink, and I like to have all the options before I decide."

"You say that like it's a bad thing." She gave a little laugh. Maybe if she'd thought things through, had all the options, she'd have made a wiser choice.

He shrugged. "Isn't it? It's not Liosa. It's not what they want. I'm going to disappoint so many people. They're looking for a strong leader, and maybe the true heir is one of those. Maybe he's better than me."

"Gibbs seems pretty bent on keeping you on the throne," Rinity pointed out. She knew Tov respected Gibbs' opinion. And Rinity respected it too; from the little she'd seen, he seemed a man of good judgment.

"I made Gibbs a royal advisor against his will, and he's given me nothing but his loyalty and undying devotion. I don't deserve him."

He sounded like Amya; just what was so special about Gibbs that everyone thought him too good for any of them? Rinity had been impressed with what she'd seen of him, but surely Tov and Amya were being excessive.

"Did Gibbs say what he intended to do about any of this?" Tov asked.

Rinity shook her head. "He said he had a suspicion about who the man might be, so he went to speak to him. He gave me a ring, and I think Gibbs recognized the crest."

"What'd it look like?" Tov asked, and Rinity knew what he was doing—he'd avoided the questions about whether Liosa needed a warrior king. She fully intended to circle back to them.

"There was a crescent moon with a string of ivy around it that almost looked like stars." She could picture it clearly—so much so, she ran the pad of her thumb along her finger, expecting the ring to be there.

"You mean Gibbs' crest?"

Rinity wasn't sure she'd heard Tov correctly. "What?"

Or maybe he'd misunderstood her, because she'd spoken of both Gibbs and the crest. Perhaps he didn't realize she didn't mean to connect the two.

"The crest, with the moon and the ivy, it sounds like Gibbs' crest."

But that would mean—

If the man had said it belonged to her father then—

—it must have been a lie after all.

Which meant they could circle back to the other matter. "You can't give up your throne, Tov."

It was strange, to sit on the Library floor and speak so familiarly with the monarch of her planet. It was strange and familiar at the same time, and she wondered when it had happened. She was still a civilian—one who had committed treason at that—and there she sat and spoke to the Prince as if he were a friend.

As if he were more than that.

She wasn't a girl in a storybook. People often assumed she didn't, but she did know the difference between reality and stories. And she knew what passed between her and Tov, it belonged in a story, it wasn't meant to be real.

"I never wanted it," Tov said. He sat back against the bookshelf, his gaze upward, his tone heavy. "I've always known it was expected of me, but my father was never proud of me. If he could have given it to someone else, I think he would have. But there was no one else, and he died so unexpectedly. There was no time for him to tell everyone just how disappointed he was."

"Were you close to him?" Rinity asked. She knew what it was to not have your father's love, but not like that. Not as someone who knew him and was denied his love. Hers had just been absent her entire life.

He snorted. "No one was close to him."

"And do you think his pride is something that would have been worth having?"

He looked at her, and there was pain in his light brown eyes. "It's all I ever wanted, I don't know how to let that go."

Rinity understood that. It was why they were in that mess at all. Because Rinity hadn't been able to let go.

And deep down, a part of her thought when she found her father, he'd want her. He'd accept her. The way she'd wanted to be accepted her whole life.

Except it wasn't fair, because Rinity had Will who had done nothing but accept the strange girl who was a package deal with the woman he married. He could have run in the other direction. He could have gotten a cat instead. But, no, he'd gone out of his way to always make sure she was taken care of and that she was safe and loved. No matter that blood said otherwise, she was his girl.

Tov didn't have that.

He had his cruel and demanding father who wasn't even a very good king. And he'd been expected somehow to reconcile his good heart with whatever was expected of him from a man so at odds with that.

"Who's to say there even is an heir?" Rinity said. "And even if there is, there's no guarantee they'll be a better ruler than you. I think you're what Liosa's got. It's not a matter of whether there's someone better, but rather being the best you can be because you're what we have."

He sighed that heavy sigh of his, so hard she felt it shake the bookcase behind them both. He pushed himself to his feet. "I need to think."

"I offended you." She always said too much when she spoke. It was why she didn't talk or only told stories. Stories were safe.

"Never." He smiled down at her.

"I'm sorry."

He ran a hand through his curls. "I just said you didn't—"

"For the treason," she explained. "I never meant for—I didn't want to—that is, I never intended—"

"Did you get your answers?" His eyes were earnest and kind, and she hated him for that. For asking about her when she'd acted without a thought to him.

She shook her head. "He double-crossed me."

"I'm sorry."

She shrugged. "There's bigger things to worry about. And, if he hasn't wanted to find me in all this time, I can't imagine me showing up at his doorstep would make a difference."

"I'm sorry," he said again.

She pushed herself to her feet, uncomfortable with all his pity and concern. "I should get back to Amya. It was stupid of me to leave in the first place."

So stupid. Amya was going to be so upset.

Tov nodded, his gaze on the ground, shy all of a sudden. "Rin?"

"Hm?"

He looked up and met her eyes. "May I kiss you? One last time?"

One last time.

The tears threatened to come again, and she blinked them back. Their story was coming to an end right before her eyes, just as she'd always known it would. It had never been built to last.

She nodded.

One last time.

Chapter 30

Amya knew without a doubt that Advisor Gibbs would kill her.

She should have known better than to leave Rinity alone, but she hadn't expected her to do anything so foolish as to leave.

Where had she even gone?

And when Gibbs got back and asked why she'd left Rinity alone, what was she supposed to say? That she hadn't liked that Rinity had told her she and Gibbs stood a chance together? That would simply open up the exact conversation she wished to avoid.

She sucked in a deep breath and let it out in a huff.

The front door opened, and her heart skipped.

She was going to die.

"My?"

Rinity.

Amya stepped into the hall to find her best friend standing there, an apologetic smile on her face.

"Where have you been?" Amya shook as the words came out, not sure if it was from anger or relief.

Rinity sighed. "I went to the Library."

"You did what?" Amya demanded. Hadn't Rinity learned? Didn't she know it was time to stop?

Rinity shook her head. "I'm sorry. I just needed to clear my head and I thought it was a good idea—except I knew it wasn't—but I went anyway, and I didn't tell you because I knew you'd want to come, and I didn't want to put you in danger."

"Rin, if something happens to you and we don't get this all sorted, I'm going to prison."

She didn't mean to snap at her friend, but Amya had been so worried. And deep down, she didn't like that if it came down to a choice between Amya or her books, Rinity would choose her books every time.

Rinity shook her head. "But you didn't do anything."

"It's called being an accessory," Amya told her. She hadn't wanted to worry Rinity with that, but if she was going to be reckless, thinking only her own life was on the line, she needed to know the truth.

Rinity covered her mouth with her hand. "I'm so sorry. I—I didn't realize..."

"I know," Amya said. "But I need you to realize now. This is serious, Rin."

"I know..." Rinity mumbled, her head hung low as she moved the toe of her boot across the carpet in the hall. "I just...I needed to talk to my books."

Rage boiled inside Amya, welling up and threatening to spill forth if she didn't use every ounce of strength to hold it back. It was always the same with her books. No matter how many times Amya told her it was dangerous, that she was worried about the consequences, Rinity always assured her it was fine. She always swore she wouldn't get in trouble.

And she'd look at Amya with those huge hazel eyes of hers and besides, she had to do it, she needed her books. And Amya melted every time, a weak mess when it came to denying her friend the thing that made her feel alive.

"I saw Tov."

That drew Amya from her swirling thoughts. "What happened?"

She and Amya moved to the front room once more, and Rinity told Amya everything. It took everything in Amya to just listen and not interject every two seconds—Rinity hated that.

Plus, she knew if she spoke, she'd start yelling. Because Rinity wasn't supposed to just blurt out to people that she'd committed treason. That was part of the whole sweeping it under the rug that Advisor Gibbs was hoping for.

But Amya also understood that while she thought Rinity could be a little too free at times, she did appreciate her friend's ability to be open.

The front door opened again, and Amya jumped up from her seat on the couch. "We don't need to tell Advisor Gibbs about..."

Rinity frowned at her, but Amya shot her a pointed look that she hoped got the message across. If Rinity wanted to tell the man she loved everything, that was one thing, but they'd keep their secret from Advisor Gibbs.

It was wrong, she knew. He deserved to know. But she also wanted to live, and she'd already disappointed him so much.

He came into the parlor with a grim expression on his face. His hair was even more rumpled than ever, flat in some places and sticking up in others. His posture sagged, and he just looked tired. So very tired.

"I half expected you two to be gone by now."

Amya frowned at him. "Why?"

The tiredness melted away as he fixed her with a dark glare, and she stood taller under it. He was ticked off about something, that much was clear. She was sure whatever the reason it was her fault, but she wasn't going to wither.

"When I went to speak to my uncle, he was gone. I've a feeling he won't be returning anytime soon," he said. She was surprised he brought up his uncle—he'd been so hesitant to put a name to him before in Rinity's presence. "And then, when I went to the palace to check on His Highness, I was informed that His Highness went to the Library, spoke with a woman"—he glared at Rinity—"and then intimidated one of his guards into giving him some space."

Amya laughed, and Advisor Gibbs shot her a glare that said he might bite her head off if she said one more thing he disapproved of. "I'm sorry. I'm just having a hard time picturing it. His Highness intimidated a guard?"

"His Highness can be quite commanding when he sets his mind to it," Advisor Gibbs said. "And the guard was an inexperienced one, who will be demoted for more training if things are sorted out and tried for treason if they aren't."

"If what things are sorted out?" Rinity asked with a frown.

Advisor Gibbs looked to her, his frown still in place, a shade darker than her own, but matching it all the same. "His Highness has disappeared."

Chapter 31

Amya let out a little gasp as Rinity stepped back, as if stricken. "What's happened to Tov?"

Advisor Gibbs shook his head. "Your guess is as good as mine, Miss Rinity."

"And what does that mean for us?" Amya asked, though she already knew. It wasn't right to ask, not really, it came off as demanding and uncaring. But Rinity and Advisor Gibbs were worried enough about Tov; someone had to worry for Rinity and Amya.

Advisor Gibbs didn't look at her as he spoke. "You're to be escorted to a safe house, where your fate will be decided when—if His Highness—is recovered."

A safe house was just one step away from prison. It was for high profile offenders awaiting trial. Even if Tov was found it was no guarantee that they'd be spared. "Please..."

Advisor Gibbs still refused to look at her as his fingers tapped incessantly at his side. "I know it's easy for you to assume the worst in people, Miss Cole, but I assure you, I fought tooth and nail for you both. Security Head Elis wanted to throw you both in prison immediately. This was the best I could do, *rook di goo.*"

She hated the way he was looking at the ground and not at her. She hated the hitch and conviction in his voice. She hated the way his shoulders sagged. She hated that he'd sworn on his life that he had fought for her when he owed her nothing.

"Thank you," she said and he looked up and met her eyes. There was pain in the rich, dark depths, and she wished more than anything that she could simply say something awkward to make him smile. But they were well past that.

"I'm sorry," he said, and she knew he meant it. Amya wasn't the trusting type, but she trusted Advisor Gibbs. And if her life were to be in someone's hands, she supposed there was no one else's she'd wish it to be in.

Amya wished there were some other reason for her and Rinity to be at the safe house because it was the nicest suite Amya had ever been in in her entire life. Located in the palace, it had two bedrooms with a washroom in the middle, a parlor, and a little dining nook.

It was exactly the sort of apartment she only dreamed of being able to marry into affording—or recently, had hoped to sew her way into. But as she stood there, it felt so empty. She would either go to prison or the planet as they knew it would be destroyed.

She and Rinity opted to share a room—or rather, Amya made the decision because Rinity had started crying as soon as they'd left Advisor Gibbs' home and had continued to do so on and off since. She'd shut down completely and was in no position to make any kind of decisions.

Rinity threw herself down on the bed Amya had chosen and buried her face into a pillow that Amya guessed cost more than her sewing earned her in a month. Amya left her to cry; she knew Rinity well enough to know it was time to let her have her space to process through her emotions in her own way. And it wasn't as if she could leave, so Amya didn't have to worry about her slipping away to the Library again.

And besides, as much as Amya would have liked to comfort her friend, to offer her some peace or reassurance, Amya had none to give. She was tired. Tired and terrified.

For all her bravado as she'd begged Advisor Gibbs to send her to prison, for all her assurance that she'd survive better, she was scared. She'd finally figured out what she'd wanted out of life, but it was gone. Her life was over. True, they weren't yet in prison, but it was only a matter of time, Amya knew that.

Amya wandered the little apartment and inspected their situation—there was no food, so she assumed that would be delivered. They weren't going to starve them, were they?

The sitting room was filled with books; Rinity would be happy about them when she'd stopped crying. It wasn't fair, that her friend would have her comfort to get lost in but Amya's involved scissors and pins and would probably be considered too dangerous to let her do.

She kept picturing Advisor Gibbs' face. His tired expression fighting his dark glare. She'd hurt him. Deeply. She didn't have the right to do that.

He'd fought for her.

Those words rang in her ears over and over again. She replayed them in her mind, as she pictured the way his hair had fallen across his forehead as he kept his dark eyes on his fingers that tapped against his leg, as if the fate of the planet depended on it. The way his voice, usually so smooth and schooled, almost squeaked.

He'd fought for her. Like she was someone worth fighting for.

Not that it meant anything. It couldn't mean anything. Because she was going to prison.

She paced the length of the sitting room as her heart raced.

She'd always thought Bender would be the Cole who went to prison, not her.

Her poor parents would be devastated. That wasn't even strong enough a word. It would ruin them—

—when they found out!

Her hands went to her head, weaving into her hair at her temple, as the thought struck her. Her parents didn't know where she was. They'd be so worried. They had a lot of kids but they kept track of them all. Mrs. Cole even had a little calendar where they were supposed to write their appointments and work schedules in so she could keep it all straight.

She'd just written that she was going to see Rinity. She hadn't run back home to write "gone to the Library to stop treason," nor had she told anyone she was going to the home of one of the most powerful men on the planet.

They didn't know where she was.

She dropped down onto the couch, sinking into the plush cushions, as the tears started to fall and the hopelessness sank in.

She might never see her family again.

She never should have encouraged Rinity to pursue Tov, especially when he'd turned out to be the Prince. She should have walked away from Advisor Gibbs and dragged Rinity out of there. She never should have stayed to dance.

She never should have let her heart get involved.

But instead, she'd stayed, and she'd fallen in love.

Victory, she was a fool.

She pulled her legs up and curled herself onto the couch, tucked into a little ball as she let the tears fall freely. The sobs came—for everything that had transpired that day, for her family, for her dreams, for Rinity and how Amya had failed her. And she cried hardest of all for the man her heart had no right to love.

"Rin, you need to wake up."

Rinity's head pounded as she came awake, slowly, groggily. She swallowed hard, her mouth dry. She opened one eye to see Amya standing over her, her friend's usually carefully pulled back hair, rumpled and messy.

She rolled over in the bed—the plushest bed she'd ever slept on—and sat up. "Did they find Tov?"

She didn't care about going to prison—not for herself. She'd committed treason, and if that was the price she had to pay she would. She just wanted Tov to be okay. Whatever had happened to him, she needed him to be okay.

Amya frowned and Rinity's heart sank.

"There's a Security Officer here," her friend said. "He needs to ask us some questions."

Rinity rolled from the bed. "I told Gibbs everything."

"That's what I told him," Amya said, her tone displeased. Had she fought with the Security Officer? Rinity wouldn't be surprised; Amya was always so collected under pressure and never afraid to stand up for herself or those she loved.

They stepped from the bedroom and into the little sitting area. Rinity immediately noticed the rows and rows of books, but she didn't let them distract her. She couldn't.

Instead, she focused her attention on the silver-haired man who stood on the far side of the room, arms crossed over his chest, scowl on his lined face. He seemed taller than his average height because of how straight he stood, back like a steel rod, chin out. His green uniform was pressed and formal.

"I told Gibbs everything I know," Rinity told him when he didn't immediately say anything.

"Advisor Gibbs," the man corrected, his voice a low growl, and it took Rinity a minute to understand the need.

Had she truly been calling a royal advisor by nothing but his last name? But...it was what Tov called him and she'd adopted it from him.

But he was the Prince, soon to be King. And she was a civilian. She couldn't address people in the same manner as he did.

"Advisor Gibbs," she amended in a mumble as Amya took a seat on the couch and pulled Rinity down beside her. Rinity sank into the plush cushions and wished more than anything that she could simply be absorbed into them. "I told him everything, sir."

"Yes, well, Advisor Gibbs is no longer a Security Officer," the man replied. The information was new to Rinity; she hadn't known Gibbs had ever been a Security Officer. "I'm Security Head Urian Elis and I've a few more questions."

"You don't have to be so rude," Amya said crossly. Rinity gaped at her.

The man's scowl darkened. "Make no mistake, Miss Cole, you and your friend are in serious trouble. You ought to be in prison, and would be if not for Advisor Gibbs' foolish recommendation to the contrary. But don't mistake your being here for being absolved of responsibility. You committed treason—we consider that a grave offense."

"We know that!" Rinity hurried to tell him. They did know that. And if he didn't stop reprimanding Amya, her friend would bite his head off. "I'll answer whatever you want me to."

The man—Security Head Elis—nodded once, curtly. "Please describe your first encounter with the man for me, as clearly as you can recall."

So Rinity did, for the fourth time that day—had she really only told Amya about it that day? It felt like an eternity ago. Security Head Elis asked her questions, pressed her for more detail, and she gave it. Amya, to her credit, didn't speak more.

Rinity tried her best not to let her voice shake as she told him everything. But every time she told it, her reasons felt shakier. She could no longer justify why she'd done it. She didn't care about her stupid father. All she cared about was Tov and his throne. And Liosa. She wouldn't lie and say there weren't things she didn't question, but she did love her planet. It was her home, her heritage, and it would be destroyed because of her.

If that didn't make her a villain, she didn't know what did.

Finally, Security Head Elis stood with a curt nod. "That's all I'll be needing for now, Miss Garrick."

He moved to the door and Amya jumped up. "Wait!"

He turned and regarded her with a frown. "Do you wish to argue more, Miss Cole? Because I assure you, it's not a battle you would win."

"No." She shook her head and some of her hair came loose of her bun as she did. She pushed it behind her ear as she said, "I just wanted to know how long you intended to keep us here."

He cocked his head to one side and regarded her thoughtfully. "Why? Do you have an appointment you hope to keep, Miss Cole? Because I would put that from your mind. There are two ends to this—in three days, His Highness is supposed to be crowned. If he returns in time for his coronation, it will be put to His Majesty to determine what is to be done with you. If he doesn't, in place of his coronation we'll hold your trial. Advisor Gibbs might plead for you, but I doubt anyone else will."

Rinity shrank under the harshness and gravity of his words, her breath short, her heart racing. She expected Amya to argue, to make a bitter remark about his tone or his threats, but instead, all her friend said was, "Our parents will be worried about us."

Rinity hadn't even considered what Will would think. She'd been so worried about what he would think of her when he found out, she hadn't even thought of how worried he'd be before he found out—he'd have no idea where she was or if she was okay. He'd be so worried.

"You should have considered that before you committed treason, Miss Cole."

She frowned and Rinity recognized her friend's determined face. "Surely you can tell them where we are—it won't take the worry away, but it will ease it. They'll think we've been kidnapped or that we're dead."

"My job isn't to nurse the feelings of a traitor's family, Miss Cole." How could a man be so disconnected? Surely, he just didn't understand.

"Do you have a daughter, sir?"

The man scowled at Rinity, but it was different than the scowl he'd given Amya; the one he fixed on Rinity held pain so deep it hurt for Rinity to see it. "That is none of your concern."

"If she disappeared without a trace, I would be willing to bet you'd tear the galaxy apart looking for her," she said softly. "Because that's what a father does."

"If she were a traitor, I would only do so to see her brought to justice," he said curtly and Rinity wondered what his daughter had done to cause him such pain. "I'll no doubt be back with more questions."

He nodded once again and then left them alone. As soon as the door closed behind him, Amya gathered Rinity into her arms for a hug. Somehow Rinity knew the hug was as much for Amya's benefit as it was for Rinity's. And Rinity knew that if even Amya was without hope, she might as well give up too.

Amya and Rinity remained there for three days, though time would have ceased to exist were it not for the regularity with which meals were delivered.

Aside from that, they were left on their own, with guards outside their door, but none inside. Twice Security Head Elis came to question them, but he stopped coming when he realized they had little to tell him outside of what he already knew.

Amya didn't ask again about getting word to their parents because she knew it would be to no avail. Her words had fallen on deaf ears, and she wouldn't bother pleading a case she would never win.

The days passed slowly, time ticking by. It gave Amya and Rinity the time they needed to talk through all the things they'd avoided saying for fourteen years. There were a lot of tears—from both girls—quite a bit of tea consumed, and a few times when the conversation got heated with long suppressed resentment.

But in the end what they'd always known was true remained—they were still friends. Only not quite as they'd always been because they were both determined that no matter what else happened, they would be a better friend to the other.

Finally, their three days were up. It was either to be the day of Tov's coronation or their trial, and when Security Head Elis returned for them, his schooled expression didn't give any clues as to which it was.

"You're to come with me," he said, as if that were enough.

"Where are we going?" Amya demanded. Why must he toy with them? He could just tell them which it was to be, there was no profit in him playing his games with them, save his own pleasure.

"Have they found Tov yet?" Rinity asked. She had asked it both times he'd come before, as if that were her only concern. And Amya supposed it was.

Rinity had broken down sobbing that first night about how it was all her fault he was gone and while Amya didn't agree with the sentiment—it had been his decision to send his guard away and whatever had happened after was his own fault—she couldn't ignore her friend's concern. And Rinity wasn't just concerned because Tov's fate was tied to theirs; whether she could be with him or not, she was concerned about the man she loved.

"I won't wait," the man said, as if that were a reply.

Amya stood. She didn't doubt the man would drag her and Rinity kicking and screaming from the room if they didn't go. And the fastest way to answers was to go with him. "Come on, it'll be all right."

Amya had never lied to Rinity before, and as soon as the words were out of her mouth, she regretted them. But they were said, and she didn't know how to take them back.

They were led down several long hallways, a handful of staircases, and through far too many rooms to count until they came to a large set of doors, intricately carved to rival even the detail of the carving in Siphone's home. The guards on either side opened the doors, and Security Head Elis led the way inside.

It was a large open room with rows of desks and benches, the rows in the back raised so that those seated there could see over those in the front. They were filled with well-dressed men and women who'd been speaking and busying themselves but fell silent as the Security Head, Rinity, and Amya entered.

Straight ahead was a long table with chairs around it. Seated in one of the chairs was Advisor Gibbs.

Amya's heart pounded as her breath caught in her chest.

Tov was nowhere to be seen and Amya's heart sunk as the reality sank in. She and Rinity would be tried for treason. They'd go to prison. And Liosa as they knew it was still at risk.

She shuffled forward, as directed, to the table and chairs at the head of the room.

"Lord Advisor," she said softly so only Advisor Gibbs, Rinity, Security Head Elis would hear, dipping her head more to avoid his gaze than out of respect.

"My Lady," he replied.

She looked up and met his rich brown eyes. He gave her a sad smile as he motioned for her and Rinity to sit.

She sat as instructed, though the motion was almost automatic, as she fell into a daze, no longer in control of her own actions. There was only one outcome to the trial. And somehow it was worse that Advisor Gibbs would be the one to try her. Could the galaxy be any crueler?

Advisor Gibbs turned his attention to the room before them. His hand tapped at his leg at a rapid speed, hidden from the group by the table, but his voice rang out loud and clear. "Attention! I'd like to call this meeting to order."

All eyes turned to the front of the room. Rinity slouched down in her chair, so that she was shorter than Amya, even though, in truth, she had a good several inches on her. Amya sat up straighter. If she was going to prison, she wanted to at least be present while she was tried.

"No, I'd like to call it to order."

As quickly as the attention had turned to Rinity and Amya, it turned away from them, to the back by the doors where the man who'd spoken stood. He was tall and angular, with wispy hair and dressed rather well.

Rinity let out a sharp gasp and based on her petrified expression—and the description she'd given earlier—if Amya were to venture a guess, she would say that the man was the one Rinity had stolen the Book of the Lamp for.

Chapter 32

The man who claimed to be her uncle—no, the man who had lied to Rinity—stood in the back of the room, a smug grin on his face.

It was the same one he'd worn when he'd taken the book from her and told her that the only payment she would receive was that people lied.

"Not again," Gibbs muttered.

Rinity pushed herself to her feet. "Where's Tov?"

All eyes turned to her and she realized her mistake. Well, there were several, actually—first, she'd referred to the Prince by his first name in a room full of people who thought she was a traitor. Second, she'd spoken directly to the man who was there to destroy the planet as if she had any right to. If she were sane, she'd have shrunk in fear.

But she wanted to know if Tov was okay.

Isaias' eyes narrowed as he looked about the room. "Is...His Highness not here?"

Gibbs frowned at the man. "You know perfectly well where he is."

"I assure you, I don't," Isaias said as he strode toward them. "But my business can be conducted without him." He frowned at Rinity and his expression matched Gibbs'—the man must be his uncle after all. "I am surprised to see you here."

Rinity glared at him. "I might be stupid but I'm not a coward."

"That's still no way to talk to your uncle." He said it so casually, but she saw the way Gibbs winced, and it hit Rinity.

He wasn't lying.

The breath was sucked out of her as her mind raced in a million directions, trying to process what it meant, but there just wasn't time.

"What are you doing here?" Gibbs hissed, his eyes narrowed at Isaias—her...uncle? Gibbs' uncle?

Were...she and Gibbs related?

Isaias smirked back at Gibbs. "I intend to make you King. It turns out my brother wasn't as much of a fool as I thought, marrying your mother."

Before Gibbs could reply—before Rinity could even fully process the words—Isaias turned to face the room before him. "It seems our future monarch has fled, which is a pity but not a surprise. Did any of us really expect him to have what it took to rule Liosa? He's a sweet boy, but not fit to lead."

Rinity wanted to protest but she didn't know what to say. That he was trying? That he wanted to do his best? The words meant something to her, but would they sound sincere to the people who filled the room? Would they be enough?

"I have here in my hands the Book of the Lamp," Isaias continued. He held it up and waved it as if everyone could get a better glimpse at it that way. "I don't need to remind you of the legend—that it's said to know the identity of all who write their name inside. And of how it will reveal the true heir—the one lost when Philosanthron stole our heritage from us."

He had a commanding voice, Rinity had to give him that. Everyone in the room was held under his spell, hanging on his every word.

"We've not needed him until now—we've had good rulers, strong rulers. Men who had honor and strength in their veins. But I ask you—is His Highness such a man?"

"I'd like to be."

The spell was broken as all eyes turned to the door once more, where Prince Tov stood. He wore the same clothes he'd worn that day at the Library, the last time Rinity had seen him, though they were torn and dirty as he stood in the doorway. His hair was a mess—sticking up in all directions, the usually glowing curls rather dingy—and his face was smudged with dirt.

He strode into the room, carrying himself proud and tall, a stark contrast to the state of his appearance. He carried himself like a king from a legend. Rinity could have cried—both from relief and from how utterly perfect he looked.

He came to stand beside Isaias, who wrinkled up his nose, no doubt from the smell that exuded from him.

"This is your King," Isaias said with a smirk as he gave a dramatic sweeping wave to indicate Tov's filthy frame. "This is the boy you would make your ruler—his planet was thrown into danger, and he disappeared. He abandoned his people."

"Never!" Rinity sprang to her feet. Her chair clattered as she pushed away from the table and the sound rang through the hall. It wasn't her place to speak but she wouldn't hear anyone talk about Tov that way.

Not when he'd come back. Not when his heart was for his people, always.

And the way he smiled at her, that dazzling smile of his, it gave her courage. She had no right to be the hero. But she wouldn't be the villain.

"He'd never abandon his people, he loves them," she stated. "It's all he talks about. He wants to be a better king—he wants to make Liosa proud of him."

Isaias scoffed. "And yet he lets a woman plead his case."

"What's wrong with being a woman?" Amya demanded.

Gibbs squeaked beside her, and Rinity wasn't sure if it was from shock or laughter.

Tov smiled at Rinity, and it felt as if everything was right with the galaxy. He grinned, first at her, and then as he turned to address the room before him. "I know I'm not my father—I've spent my whole life trying to be, but you all know as well as I do that I'll never be him. I'm not King Isambard, and I'm certainly no Alaric the Pendragon."

Rinity wanted to tell him to stop talking because he was putting himself down, and he didn't want to do that. He shouldn't. He had so much to offer. And how could he say those words with that grin? As if he were happy with the realization.

"So, you admit it?" Isaias asked with a taunting jeer. "You admit Liosa deserves a far better man than you for king?"

The man was right—Liosa didn't deserve Tov. But Rinity knew it was because Tov was far too good for it. If they didn't see that the man standing before them would do whatever it took to lead his people well, they didn't deserve him.

"I spent the last three days trying to run away from all this," Tov said. "I was willing to hand my planet over to whoever this heir might be. Because they're no doubt stronger and bolder and braver than me. You could have a king who was like my father.

"But those three days were spent on the streets of the city my father ruled and honestly, I wasn't impressed."

Rinity wanted to hug him—and probably kiss him too—but she didn't move because she couldn't. He had the room in such a spell that she doubted she could if she tried.

But the thought scared her, so she wiggled her toes, just to check, and was happy to find she could in fact still move.

"I won't be a perfect king, but neither was my father," he stated with more conviction than she'd seen him possess before.

His speech was fit for a story, and she hoped someone was writing it down. It would be a shame to lose it forever. It ought to be recorded, preserved. Even if she could never read it.

"And I intend to be my own king—one who puts Liosa first, who strives to serve them in everything, and who won't be pushed around any longer. I'll hear no more talk of replacing me on the throne. I'm to be coronated today and nothing short of celestial intervention will stop that. Guards, you may escort this man out of here."

The guards looked from Tov to Isaias and then back again, as if they weren't sure what to do with such an order. Tov looked to Gibbs with a question in his eyes before he shook his head and turned back to them, standing a little taller.

"Now. That's an order."

Chapter 33

Isaias narrowed his eyes at Gibbs. "I was going to make you king."

Tov's eyes grew wide, and he let out a little gasp as he looked from Gibbs to Isaias. But Gibbs' expression remained graced with his usual schooled features as he reached and took the book from his uncle's hands. "If you think I'd want that, you don't know me at all."

Rinity didn't think Gibbs would make a bad king, but she was glad he didn't want the job; it would put a damper on his relationship with Tov, and she knew how much he meant to the Prince.

Isaias was dragged away, screaming about how they would regret it.

"This meeting is adjourned," Tov announced to the room. "Unless anyone else has any treasonous claims they would like to make."

A murmur moved through the room in a wave, though it must have been to deny any such claims because soon everyone was shuffling from the room.

Tov turned to Amya, Gibbs, and Rinity. "What are you doing here?"

"They were going to be tried for treason," Gibbs explained. "Since, you know, Miss Garrick was the one who stole the book in the first place and the last person you spoke to before you disappeared. Since we couldn't find my uncle, the council was content to let them take the fall for his crimes."

"Rinity's innocent."

"No, I'm not," Rinity said as Gibbs said, "That's not exactly true."

Tov shook his head. "I mean, no one is holding either Rinity or her friend for any sort of trial."

Gibbs dipped his head in acknowledgement. "Thank you, Your Highness."

It was a strange thing to say, Rinity thought, until she realized. He wasn't so much grateful he'd let Rinity off, but

Amya wouldn't get in trouble, and Rinity had a feeling that was important to him.

"It would probably sit better with some if there were some sort of repercussions though," Gibbs continued as he took a step to the side in an attempt to make the conversation a little more private, between himself and Tov.

Tov glared at him. "I'm not sending them to jail."

"I appreciate that," Gibbs said, his voice low as he cast a sideways glance at Rinity and Amya. "But treason was still committed, and there will be some who are concerned about that. Surely there is something halfway between a prison sentence and getting off with a warning."

Tov looked at Rinity and Amya and then back at Gibbs. He frowned. "I do see your point. But I just spent three days on the streets, I ate food out of a can—like, straight out of a can—and then I came in and saved the day and…I don't have it in me to arrest them too. Can't you just say you're happy to see me and we leave it at that?"

He looked like the boy Rinity had fallen in love with—not the legend or the King, but the boy who wanted to be the best he could but was terribly afraid of failing every time.

Gibbs' expression softened, and the faintest hint of a smile tugged at the corner of his lips. "I'm glad you're back—and not just because the fate of the planet was at stake. And you're right, this is a discussion for another time."

"Thank you," Tov said as he turned back to Rinity and Amya. "Don't worry, I won't let him do anything terrible to you."

Gibbs let out an exasperated sigh but offered no other rebuttal.

"Does that mean I can go home?" Amya asked. "My parents will be worried sick, not knowing where I even am and—"

"They're obviously worried, but I have tried to reassure them as best I can," Gibbs interjected.

She furrowed her brow. "You spoke to my parents?"

He dropped his gaze as he ran a hand through his hair, which only caused it to stick up all the more. "I—uh—I knew it wasn't exactly comfort I offered, given the circumstances, but I thought knowing where you were would perhaps be better than the worry of the unknown."

"Oh. I—I see. Thank you."

He was a keeper; Rinity started to understand what it was Tov and Amya saw in him.

"So, I'm free to go?" Amya clarified.

"You both are," Gibbs said, though he looked to Tov for conformation.

Tov nodded as he looked to Rinity. "You're both free to go, but I'd like to speak to you if I might first, Rinity?"

Rinity looked to Amya.

"I'll see her home once she's ready," Gibbs promised Amya, and her friend offered him a grateful smile before she hurried off.

Rinity ought to go too. She needed to speak to Will, needed to assure him she was okay. But that would be the last time she'd speak to Tov, and as much as it would break her heart, she knew she needed to stay; she'd regret it if she didn't.

Gibbs stepped away so that Rinity and Tov could speak privately.

"I'm sorry about everything." Had she already apologized? She couldn't remember. She'd been so selfish, and she'd almost destroyed everything.

Tov shook his head. "Don't be. I've been having this pity party my whole life. You reminded me of who I'm capable of being when I stop holding myself back."

"You'll make a good king," Rinity told him.

Tov shrugged. "I'd make a better one if you were by my side."

Rinity drew back as he tried to take her hand, and she hated that he let her go. Because he always respected her. Always. She shook her head. "Tov, I committed treason. And I'm a civilian."

"I don't see why that matters," he told her. "You're smart and clever, and you always remind me of who I am. And you know people really well. Better than I do. I want Liosa to thrive, and I can better accomplish that with you by my side. Besides, just think how many books you'll have access to if you say yes."

Rinity laughed, and suddenly she felt like they were the Librarian and the girl in the vent again—it was comfortable and right between them.

She loved the man sitting before her. Loved him with her whole heart. And if she walked away, she'd lose herself. It was foolish to say yes, but she didn't think she could survive if she said no.

"You truly mean it?" Rinity clarified. "You're not going to change your mind tomorrow? You could marry someone better."

Their story either needed to end then or not at all. She couldn't bear it if he promised her forever and changed his mind after he'd had time to think.

"I will never love anyone as much as I love you," Tov told her. "I know it's not perfect, and we'll probably tell it wrong sometimes, but this? What we have? It's my favorite love story. And I never want it to end."

She gave a little gasp, because he'd said the words her heart had spoken again and again.

He reached a hand toward her, cautiously, questioningly, and she leaned into it. He caressed her face with his fingers as he gazed into her eyes. Then he leaned closer and their lips met.

As much as Rinity didn't want to say goodbye, she did have to go home. While she'd said yes to Tov's proposal, it wasn't that simple; there was still a lot left to work out. And Tov really needed to take a shower.

As promised, Gibbs escorted her home.

They sat across from each other in the vehicle in awkward silence until Rinity said, "Should I have told him no?"

Gibbs hadn't commented on the match, but Rinity was sure he had an opinion. And she didn't know how else to ask. She cared about his thoughts—Amya and Tov both respected him greatly. And he'd given up the chance to be king. He could have taken the throne from Tov; she didn't want to do anything that would make Gibbs regret his choice.

Especially when she and he were probably related.

Gibbs' brow wrinkled in question. "Do you regret it?"

"I know you don't approve of me," she mumbled as she ducked her head.

"I don't recall saying that," he replied. "And I certainly never meant to imply it. I barely know you. And while we have only met under...less than ideal circumstances...two people I respect and care for hold you in high regard, and that does recommend you to me more highly than my first impression might."

It was a sweet compliment. She ought to say something in response. But what was there to say? And then she realized—

"Did you say you cared for Amya?"

He dipped his head as he drummed his fingers on the seat beside him. "I do. Though I confess I am unclear on how she feels about me."

"She told me she loved you." Rinity clasped her hand over her mouth. "I knew I would let that slip if I was left alone with you. I wasn't supposed to tell you that."

The hope in his eyes warmed Rinity. Despite what Amya said, there was a chance they could work it out. If Rinity could marry a prince, surely Amya could marry a royal advisor who had made it clear he was willing to do anything for her.

"She doesn't want you to break her heart."

Gibbs shook his head. "I would never—"

"She's afraid you'll reject her when you find out the truth about her—her heritage and her faults," Rinity explained. "But I've already said too much. You should talk to her, if—that is, if you truly care for her."

"I do," he said again. "*Rook di goo,* I do."

Neither said anything for a moment.

"Did you catch what all was said?" Gibbs finally broke the silence. "About my uncle and—yours?"

So, they were related after all.

"I assumed he was just toying with me—telling more lies," Rinity said, not looking up at him. She picked at a scab on her finger. She almost wished that were so. She didn't need a name to get into the Library, not when she was going to marry Tov. She'd made up her mind, whoever her father was, he wouldn't want her. Why should the Royal Advisor be any different?

"As much as I wish that were true, there's a good chance you are in fact my sister."

Her heart squeezed. It shouldn't hurt. Why should he want her for a sister? "I'm sorry if it pains you to—"

"No!" Gibbs interrupted, his expression horrified. "I didn't mean I regretted the connection. As I said, you're thought highly of by people I trust, and I look forward to getting to know you better. But Amya said you wished to know your father. And that can never happen. Our father is currently in prison, being investigated for war crimes. And even if he weren't, he was never a man worth knowing. I'm only sorry for your sake—you deserve more than him."

He ran a hand through his hair again, and Rinity put a hand to her own hair; the texture was different since hers had been bleached and dyed. But she knew the texture well. How else did she and he resemble each other? How was one supposed to react to a stranger who shared your blood?

He was right, it hurt to know. But she was also relieved. She had her name. She knew who she was. *Victory*, she had a brother.

And Amya had been right all along—she already knew who she was. At that moment she was going home to her stepfather who had loved her more than most men loved their own blood. She was proud to carry his name and to call herself his daughter.

"He wouldn't have accepted you; he barely accepted me." Gibbs sighed, and it was heavy and tired. "I spent my whole life trying to live up to my name, wanting to be worthy of it. And in the end, I guess I'm the only one who actually even cared if it was worth anything."

"I'm sorry," she said. His father was in prison for war crimes, and his uncle had just been arrested. And the sister sitting across from him was a stranger who had committed treason.

He offered her a smile though his eyes were still sad. "I've no experience at it, but I'll try to be a good brother. You won't be entirely without family."

"I have a stepfather," she told him and realized it probably sounded like she was rejecting his goodwill. She hastened to add, "He kept me even after my mom died—they'd only been married a year—and it probably would have been easier to send me away, to pass me off to someone else. He's been my constant. I'd bet if you ever needed a dad, he could be your constant too."

She shrugged. "And I don't know how to be a sister either, so I'd be willing for us to figure that out together."

That time the smile reached his eyes. "I'd like that a lot."

Rinity accepted Gibbs' offer to walk her to the door of her apartment. Not because she needed the company—it was a walk she'd made thousands of times in her life—but so she could point him in the direction of the apartment across the hall. Just in case he wanted to talk to Amya.

Then she stepped inside her apartment and shut the door behind her.

"Rin?" Will came out of the kitchen and dropped the towel in his hands, letting it fall to the floor. He grinned at her as tears welled in his eyes. It brought tears to her eyes as well. "You're home."

She nodded, not sure what else to say or where to start. "Yeah."

He closed the gap between them and drew her into a hug. "I thought I'd never see you again."

"I'm sorry." For all the mess she'd caused, for the choices she'd made, and forever hurting him.

He broke the embrace and gripped her shoulders, holding her at arm's length. "Let me look at you."

"I need a shower," she said with a laugh.

"I was worried sick."

"I wanted to tell you where I was, but they wouldn't let us."

He nodded. "Gibbs told me as much."

Of course, Gibbs had come to talk to Will when he'd talked to Mr. and Mrs. Cole. He really was a good man.

"He's my brother," she blurted out because she didn't know how else to work it naturally into the conversation.

Will's widened. "He's what?"

"My brother," Rinity said again. She shook her head. "I have so much to tell you."

Will nodded. "I'll make tea."

Chapter 34

Amya was swarmed by her family and siblings as soon as she walked through the door.

They smothered her with hugs and questions, all talking over each other, and she had to hold back the tears as she thought about how she had missed them and how close she'd come to losing them.

She tried her best to explain everything, but they kept talking over her, asking more questions than she could ever answer and trying to fill her up with food and tea.

Finally, she got it all out, and everyone started to grasp what had happened. Her mother hugged her a little tighter, and her father regarded her with steady eyes. Her siblings had more questions, and she laughed as she tried to tell them everything and repeated once more how tired she was.

A knock sounded on the door, and she jumped, grateful for a chance to extract herself from the entanglement of hugs and familial affection for just a minute.

Alana made a joke as Amya walked to the door, and she laughed as she pulled it open. The expression disappeared, however, as soon as she saw who was on the other side of the door.

"My Lady."

"Lord Advisor."

There was a quirk of a smile as Advisor Gibbs regarded her with a steady gaze, and she pushed him away so she could step into the hall and close the door behind her.

"What are you doing here?" she demanded.

He drew in a breath as he tapped the fingers of his right hand on his thigh. "I wanted to talk to you."

"Well, I hardly thought you were here to kiss me," she said crossly before she winced. Why wasn't she capable of having a normal conversation with him? "Sorry, I just—I didn't expect to see you again."

"I can leave if it's unwelcome." There was an earnestness to his voice that told her he meant it; if she told him to go, she didn't doubt that he would do exactly that without a question.

As much as she knew it would be simpler to tell him to leave and be done with it, he was there, and so they would talk everything through. And then she'd go back inside and let her family see her cry. And she'd discover just how much tea it took to mend a broken heart.

"No, we should talk."

He nodded, and the tapping slowed to just one finger tapping a gentle, steady beat.

There was silence, and she wondered if maybe she should just start listing her faults. But what if he'd come for another reason? That would be awkward if she just assumed he felt anything for her. He'd implied as much, but hadn't said it. Maybe she'd misunderstood.

"Did you want to start?"

He looked up to meet her eyes and offered her a sheepish smile. "Right. Sorry. I—that is—I hope it's not presumptuous of me to—"

The door opened, and Amya's father poked his head out. "Are you all right, Amya? Ah! Advisor Gibbs."

"Just Gibbs," he said as he offered the man an amiable smile. "And it's good to see you again, sir. I'm sorry to have pulled your daughter away so soon after her being returned to you, but I hope you'll allow me just a little more of her time."

Her father smiled back at him. "Amya is her own woman, and she can do with her time what she wishes."

Amya liked the way her father smiled at Advisor Gibbs and the easy way with which Advisor Gibbs spoke to him. There was respect there; he didn't see her father as someone beneath him. It was why she admired him as much as she did.

"I'll be in soon," she told her father.

He nodded. "You're welcome to bring him inside when you're through with your talk."

She doubted Advisor Gibbs would want to come inside after she told him everything, but she didn't bother arguing, especially since her father had closed the door already. The two were alone once more.

"You're good to him," Amya noted.

He leaned easily against the wall, and his fingers tapped out a steady beat on the surface. "He's a good man."

"He's Alisethian." That was a good way to get that out into the conversation.

"Ah," he said, understanding lighting his face. "That's what his accent is, I couldn't quite place it."

"So, I'm Alisethian as well," she clarified, in case he hadn't picked up on that.

"That would make sense," he agreed.

"So, I'm only partially Liosi," she added.

He nodded slowly, as if he weren't following. "That's how genetics work. Though, I wouldn't say you were 'only' anything."

She frowned at him. "You don't care?"

"I mean...yes?" he said. The tapping grew faster. "But also, no? It seems a privilege to have two heritages, though I'm hardly qualified to tell you what you're about."

He was an infuriating man.

"I'm not rich or connected."

He looked at the dimly lit hall around them in feigned surprise. "I hadn't noticed."

She smacked his arm, and he winced; she might have hit him a little harder than she'd intended.

"In case it's unclear," he said, still holding his arm. She felt certain he was exaggerating; she hadn't hit him that hard. "I think the galaxy of you. I think your parents and Liosi-Alisethian heritage are beautiful because you're beautiful, and they're part of you. You're the most interesting woman I have ever had the pleasure of knowing. And, for the record, my mother was a merchant's daughter. In case that changes anything for you."

"What?" she demanded.

"My father married a merchant's daughter," he explained. His hand was still on his arm, and his fingers tapped his bicep. "For her money. They were very unhappy, and I wouldn't recommend the arrangement. That—that doesn't actually change anything for you, does it?"

There was a panic in his eyes, and she laughed. "No. It doesn't change anything. Though, maybe don't sell yourself short—you were almost made king today."

"Please don't remind me," he said as his one finger tapped all the faster.

"Do you think there's truth to it?" It didn't make a difference to her, but she was curious. And as long as they talked about that and not whatever was—or couldn't be—between them, things were okay.

He shrugged. "Possibly? Probably? If it had been false, he would have tried to make himself king, not me. Never me. I wish my mother were alive to know. Father always liked to put her in her place, to remind her she was only worth her money, as she had no other connections. Maybe she would have believed she was worth more."

Amya recognized the pain in his eyes. It was the same pain Rinity got when she spoke of her mother, and Amya knew it was pain she could never fully understand—not when she had two parents who adored each other waiting for her on the other side of the door.

"But I believe we were discussing something else," he said, and his voice was soft. He met her eyes, and she wished more than anything to get lost in the rich, brown pools.

But he was right, they had been discussing something else. And she needed to get the conversation over with. Though she was no longer sure what direction the conversation was headed, and she hated the swell of hope that rose in her.

No, she needed to be clear, direct. So, there were no regrets later on. "I have a lot of flaws. And I don't know if I want to get married."

"But you're thinking about it," Advisor Gibbs pointed out. His mouth pulled into a faint smile, and she couldn't help thinking how kissable it looked. *Victory.* She wanted to kiss him. "Because I never mentioned it."

He was right. She had been thinking about marrying him.

"I've always thought the only way to get ahead was to marry well," she explained. "But I started finding clients, women who want me to make dresses for them, and I think I could make a go of being a designer. I'd like to see if I can."

"Do the two have to be mutually exclusive?" he asked. "I've no objections to you starting a business—I'd be happy to offer you financial advice, if you'd welcome that. And we don't have to work all this out now. I'd like to court you, if that was agreeable. We have time."

She liked the sound of that.

"I'd like that," she said. "If you were to court me, that is. If you're sure."

"I'm sure," he said. "*Rook di goo.*"

Well, if he was going to swear it on his life, she supposed she would have to believe him.

"Okay," she said.

"I'd very much like to kiss you now," he said. "If that was agreeable to you."

It was. So, she told him by closing the gap between them and kissing him herself.

The door opened and she jumped backward. Her father stood in the doorway, a little smile on his face.

Advisor Gibbs cleared his throat. "Sir. I hope you know my intentions toward your daughter are nothing but honorable."

"I'm glad to hear it," her father said. "Though I assumed as much. Amya would have sent you packing if you were any less than she deserved." He looked to his daughter. "Your mother wants to know if your young man is staying for supper."

"Oh!" Amya looked to Advisor Gibbs—perhaps she ought to call him Gibbs, as they were dating. Or, no. She ought to learn his first name.

Victory, she didn't even know his first name!

She couldn't introduce him to her whole family, not when she didn't even know his name. Not when they'd only just started to figure things out. She'd also forgotten to mention her large family in her list of reasons why he'd never want her. But he surely already knew about them. He'd met her parents at least and probably some of her siblings.

Maybe it'd be okay.

"I have to get back to the palace," he said with an apologetic expression.

Her father nodded. "Another time then."

"I look forward to it, sir, thank you."

The door closed again, and they were alone once more.

"I really should go," he told her with a frown.

She nodded. "But you'll come back?"

"That is how courting works."

He leaned in to kiss her again, and it lasted longer that time, uninterrupted. It was different—better—than any kiss she'd ever shared before. She didn't want it to end, and she whimpered when he pulled away.

"My Lady," he said with that teasing smile of his.

"Lord Advisor," she returned and that was that.

He walked away, and she watched him go. He cast a glance at her over his shoulder and gave a little wave before he rounded the corner and she waved back until he was gone from view.

On the other side of the door, she could hear the sounds of her family yelling, and laughing, and living. Across the hall she knew Rinity was there and they'd have so much to talk about.

And in that moment, she was standing in the hall watching the man she loved walk away. But it wasn't in the way she'd expected.

She'd expected to be going back inside with a broken heart, but instead her heart was so full.

He'd promised to come back.

And while she'd forgotten to ask, so she didn't know his first name, there was one thing she knew about him for certain—her Royal Advisor always kept his promises.

The End

Playlist

- *Once Upon a Dream* by Evynne Hollens, Peter Hollens—Tov and Rinity's song
- *Honey and the Bee* by Owl City—Tov and Rinity's song
- *The Real World* by Owl City—Rinity's song
- *Lost Boy* by Ruth B.—Rinity's song
- *Appalachian Wine* by eleventyseven—a song for Rinity's stories
- *We'll Be A Dream* by We the Kings, Demi Lovato—Tov and Rinity's song
- *I Don't Care* by Ed Sheeran, Justin Bieber—Amya and Gibbs at both balls
- *Gold* by Owl City—a song for both Rinity and Amya
- *Long Live* by Taylor Swift—on here for the vibes
- *Call Me Maybe* by Carly Rae Jepson

- *Easy* by Camila Cabello—both Rinity and Amya feel hard to love
- *Grand Adventure* by JJ Heller—for Rinity and Amya's friendship
- *Atlas: Nine* by Sleeping at Last—Rinity is an Enneagram type 9
- *Too Much* by Carly Rae Jepson—Amya's song
- *She Is* by ben Rector—Amya's song
- *Atlas: Three* by Sleeping at Last—Amya is an Enneagram type 3
- *Atlas: Two* by Sleeping at Last—with a strong wing 2
- *The Book of You & I* by Alec Benjamin—Tov and Rinity's song
- *Better Place* by Rachel Platten
- *King* by Lauren Aquilina—Tov's song
- *Happy Not Knowing* by Carly Rae Jepson—Gibbs and Amya's song
- *Tonight I'm Getting Over You* by Carly Rae Jepson—for the scene with Steward Newton
- *So Will I* by Ben Platt—pick a dynamic in this book, this song will fit most of them
- *Holding the Key* by Jason Gray
- *Overthink* by Addison Grace

- *Let's Sort the Whole Thing Out* by Carly Rae Jepson—for the final scene
- *Happily Ever After* by He is We—the first end credits song
- *Perfect Color* by SafetySuit—the second end credits song

Character Love Letters

Somewhere in the midst of working on my books I like to write the main characters each a love letter that details how they came into being, why I love them, and my hopes for them. It is one of my favorite writing exercises I do and I love getting to share them—and a piece of my heart—with you.

Dear Rinity,

I was sitting at church—Trinity Fellowship—and I looked down at the bulletin and went "if you take off the 't' Rinity is actually a really cool..." and that's how you were named.

You're one of the characters I've had the longest and one I thought I'd set aside, a fond memory from my childhood day, but not someone I'd ever actually write about. But you'd wormed your way into my heart all those years ago and refused to go away. You insisted your story be told because for all your quiet gentleness, you're fierce when it comes to going after what you want.

You were originally the Miller's Daughter and your story was a Rumpelstiltskin retelling. You could "turn straw into gold" only with your words—you were a storyteller and while couldn't physically change things, you had a way with words, of persuading people. You made the extraordinary out of the ordinary.

You were always a poor girl who dreamed of having more. You came from a crappy family and your stories were your solace—you got lost in them because they were the only riches you were able to steal for yourself. And it was the prince's mother who was the villain, not the king, because I wanted to be okay with you and the prince ending up together.

Because, our sweet, innocent prince wasn't about to imprison anyone.

I don't remember why your story changed from Rumpelstiltskin to Aladdin. The shift happened when your story became part of the Evraft Galaxy, but I don't remember where the inspiration came from.

A lot of things changed—your desire to find your father, your reason for meeting the prince, your story goal in general. But a lot of things stayed the same—your name, your love of stories, your dreams for more than you had, that restless discontentment.

Your stepfather was originally a jerk, but then I went "why are stepfathers always jerks???" and decided there was no reason for yours to be. So Will was born—sweet, earnest Will who only wants the best for you. It added depth to your story, your desire you find your father while already having a father figure, but having the questions anyway.

Identity is complicated. I don't understand it fully and I don't know why I decided to tackle it in this story. I guess because it's your story—it's the story I'm supposed to tell.

You're such an interesting character to write—book smart but not always smart in other ways, a good-natured girl who just wants to read stories and know who she is.

I write broken girls but you're broken in a different way than I usually write. Your life is good, there's just a restlessness under it all, a discontent, a desire for more. You have a wanderlust without the desire to leave Liosa. You want to pour over dusty volumes for the rest of your life and to be denied that, it's stifling. You hide too in your stories because they give you a sense of being connected to something that you're missing in reality. And inside your stories you're safe because no one makes you feel like you're not enough or that you're too much.

I hope you know you're so much more than the stories you tell. You're more than your father's name. You're more than the civilian you think you are.

You're too good for the galaxy, Rinity Garrick—Amya's right, you're far better than her. You're innocence and goodness and purity. You're heart and soul and fire. But not the "burn it all" kind of fire. More like "sit beside me for warmth and comfort" kind of fire.

The rest of the books in this series are heavy. They deal with brokenness and loss and deeply hurting people. And not that your story doesn't deal with those subjects but it's by far the lightest in the story. It's warm and comforting. My hope is that people will find rest within its pages, that they'll come to it weary and find comfort.

I hope this story does for them what all of yours do for you—that people can get lost within it and find their own heart within yours.

Thank you for sticking around for so long. Thank you for being willing to grow and change as I shifted you from world to world and story to story.

I hope this version does your story justice. I hope it shows people the Rinity I know.

You're going to go far, firefly, don't ever let anyone tell you otherwise. You've got stories to tell and hearts to touch. And you've got a sweet prince to love and kiss you for the rest of your life. It's going to be okay.

With Love,
Jenni

Dear Amya,

I don't even know what to say about your creation. In true Amya fashion, it's less that you were created and more that you simply swept into my story and said "I live here now."

You changed the story completely. There was originally an actual genie character with actual magic (but we don't talk about her, because then people will be disappointed that they got this book instead of that one). But you and her were both filling the same role and it became clear that the story wasn't big enough for the two of you.

And somehow, you won out over a character with real, actual backstory and a plot connected to their story. I threw out a whole plot for you. I don't have plots to spare. But you were Rinity's best friend and you held my heart. And you wanted to be the genie character. I couldn't have told you no if I wanted to. Like Gibbs, I'm weak when it comes to anything related to you.

I also changed two characters' names because of you. I don't like having names that are too similar in my series and even though the other two were established characters I've had for longer than you, I couldn't change yours. You're Amya. And I couldn't change you if I tried.

You're the girl who wears gold eye shadow and bold lipstick and crop tops. You're the girl who says what's on her mind. The girl who knows what she wants and what she is willing to sacrifice to get those things.

You became a gold-digger from the start—pragmatic, confident, sure. I love your depth—that you manage to be exacting and ambitious while still being sympathetic and endearing. There's so much more to you than meets the eye. You carry a heaviness—a desire for things to be different, for more. There's a restlessness to you, a simple desire for more than you have and a drive to get it.

You're all the things I wish I was—clever, confident, open about your weaknesses and insecurities, extroverted, sure of what you want out of life, and capable of connecting with people. But you're no "wish fulfilment character" where I live vicariously through you in all your perfection.

Because you're not perfect. You're weak in so many ways and you hate showing that—that's one of your weaknesses. But you let me see them. You let those weaknesses add depth to your character, and you let me see parts of you you're scared to show to others.

I hope other people can understand that. I hope they see the Amya I love—who loves the life she was given but knows it isn't enough for her. Who is willing to work hard to achieve the life she wants. I hope they can see the way you wear your confidence as a mask, a security net.

I love you. I know we're not supposed to have favorites, but you're one of mine—don't tell the others. I think it's because three of my closest friends all found parts of themselves in you. Maybe I did it on purpose without meaning to. Maybe it just happened. But you hold pieces of my favorite people, so of course that's going to make you extra special.

I hope you know you're safe, that you can let people in and let them stay. That there's more to you than the usefulness you serve. I hope you know it's okay to show the people closest to you your weaknesses and your emotions. It's okay to have needs. You don't always have to be the one who is needed, sometimes you can be the one who needs people. You're not bothering anyone by having emotions, by having needs.

Thanks for letting me be your author. Thanks for letting me love you. Thanks for letting me see the messy, vulnerable sides of you that not even Rinity gets to see sometimes. Thanks for trusting me with your story.

You're someone worth knowing and loving. You're worth the space you take up, not because of the usefulness you serve but simply because you exist and that's enough. I'm glad you're here.

Chin up, lover, and never forget that you're made of starlight.

With all my heart,
Jenni

Dear Tov,

You are one of my oldest characters.

I created you as the losing side of the love triangle probably fifteen years ago. That story was revamped again and again but you were always the sweet, earnest prince, desperately in love with the girl, but in every version she went for the other guy—who, admittedly was perfect for her, sorry.

But then along came Rinity, and you got to have a happy ending. It was a different retelling in a different world, but you were still you.

In fact, it was when I wrote the scene at the end of Rook Di Goo, when El choses Captain Behnam over you—who, admittedly is perfect for her, sorry— I recognized you instantly. And I felt less bad for the rejection because I knew Rinity would move to this world and her story would be told. I knew that after this heartbreak would come the happy ending you deserved.

You've always been a challenge to write. You're a mix of the insecure boy who only ever wanted his father's approval, who had too much responsibility placed on his shoulders, and the confident prince who was born to a role, who accepted that because he never had a choice.

You wear a mask but it falls off far too often. People see your weaknesses, your insecurities, and I don't think they know what to make of you. You're naïve and trusting and you fall in love far too easily. You give your whole heart when you should be cautious and guarded.

They aren't the qualities of a good prince, which is why you struggle so much. You trust and then remember to ask questions. You give your heart and then remember you were supposed to guard it. You don't know how to not be earnest and true.

You're what we call a pure bean. A cinnamon roll.

You're so special to me, the prince looking for his place in the world that I created when I was ten, who hasn't changed much now that I'm twenty-five.

You remind me of who I was before I was broken. You remind me of my innocence. You're pure nostalgia. I miss the parts of your story I had to scrap because they didn't fit with the Rook Di Goo storyline but I'm grateful that the heart of you is still there.

You remind me that underneath it all, goodness doesn't die. I didn't lose the parts of me that I had before everything changed. When my world fell apart it didn't end. There in the rubble are still pieces of goodness, the purity I once had, the innocence. And you've shown me the strength in those things. That they aren't synonyms with weakness or less than.

So many of my stories have shifted, darkened, as I've rediscovered them. They've changed along with me. But not you. And while I don't regret the changes that have been made—they're better stories for it—I love knowing that those pieces of me are still there, still good.

They remind me in turn that God is still good. There are constants in this ever shifting world. There is innocence, there is purity, there is hope.

The stories I write, I'm reminded, haven't really changed. The girl I was has grown up, but she's still there, and she'd be so proud of how far we've come. She'd be proud of the stories I'm telling.

I never thought a wide-eyed prince looking for his place in the world would mean so much to me. But here we are.

You, Prince Tov, remind me of my heart.

I hope people can see that heart of ours that we share, that they can share in a piece of it too. I hope they see what I see when I look at you—someone who's trying. Always trying. Someone who cares too deeply and too painfully, but who can never seem to stop, no matter how ill-advised and impractical that may be.

I suppose shouldn't call you Prince Tov, not anymore. So let me end by saying this:

King Tov Kinsley Daedric Kallovenris, you are worthy of that title. You will rule Liosa not as your father or your grandfather did but as only you can. Learn to trust a little less openly, but once your trust is earned, never withdraw it. Continue to be openhearted and innocent and pure.

Liosa was built by warriors, ruled by warriors, their independence won by warriors. Show them that softhearted warriors exist too.

Gratefully Yours,
Jenni

Dear Gibbs,

YOU GET YOUR OWN BOOK.

When I wrote your love letter for Rook Di Goo sometime around draft 3 or so, I remember writing that I didn't want to get too attached because I was afraid I'd want to give you your own book. And at the time, I didn't think I could afford to add another book to this series.

But then I was working on Rinity's book and up popped this wispy haired security officer. And then plot twists were added and I knew you weren't going anywhere. As her story shifted to Aladdin, you played a number of roles—the genie at one point as well as a myriad of random non-Aladdin characters—and then it all fell into place: you got to play my favorite character from the original tale.

A lot of people don't know the Grand Vizier's Son because he's not in Disney's version and I almost didn't include him. I was always sad with the way his story ended anyway. And while you might have to look hard to find where your role overlaps with his—you don't marry the prince, after all, as he marries the princess—you and the genie do spend quite a bit of time together while the Aladdin in your respective stories seeks to win the heart of their true love.

But personality-wise? You share the same earnestness, the same desire for nothing but the best for the people you care about, and a decided grumpiness over the situation you're forced into and the inconvenience of it all. It was already all there, even more so as I did final edits for Rook Di Goo. And in finding your role from the original, it solidified the part you'd play in this story and just how large of a role that would be.

In my first draft of this book you were still just a security officer. And you were married; not sure why I thought that was a fun throw away detail to include, but you were. Now you're one of the most powerful men on the planet and you aren't married.

Yet.

Amya's pretty awesome. I didn't mean to create a gold-digging social climbing girl as your love interest. I didn't even really create her though. She just sort of swept into the story and said "I live here now" and then took one look at you and said "also, I'mma spend the rest of my life driving that man crazy, because I love him."

And honestly, I can't picture anyone more perfect for you. She's going to drive you crazy, tear down all of your walls, and break every single one of your rules. But you're going to spend the rest of your life loving that woman.

It's so strange to be writing about you, especially since it's more intimate now. I get to be in your head a lot more, even though the book is never told from your perspective. I get to see the weaknesses, the coping mechanisms, the doubt.

I get to see who Carrigan Gibbs is without the mask. And I just have to say, I love you even more than I already did. You're no longer the angry boy from Rook Di Goo, but instead you've grown into a man, and one I'm proud to say I know. You're also very smooth when talking to Amya. Who gave you permission to be that smooth? Because I know it wasn't me.

I know what happened in Rook Di Goo broke you—you and your father have always had a rocky relationship, but his betrayal hurt. A lot. But you've come so far.

I'm proud of you for all the ways you've grown. For not letting your anxiety define you. For being someone not worthy of the Gibbs name, but someone even better. Because we all know apart from you, the Gibbs name doesn't mean much.

And I'll see you again—not that you're happy about that, I'm sure you suspect that means more treason—because I'm not ready to say goodbye yet. And I will be writing you into every future book I can. You're my favorite, Gibbs. I never expected you to worm your way into my heart the way you have, but here we are. (If Amya tells you I said she was my favorite, I didn't; I said she was "one of my favorites," which is different.)

I can't wait to see how you continue to grow. How you continue to press on despite—despite the anxiety, despite the betrayal, despite all the voices telling you that you're not good enough. I look forward to writing you more, for putting you through more stress because…well, treason is going to happen and there's no one else who's as good at taking care of it.

Yours in Earl Grey,
Jenni

Dear Siphone,

I almost didn't write this letter.

You're not a main character, after all. You only play a small role in this book and it's not even part of the main plot. But it felt wrong not to include you.

You were supposed to be a random character Amya meets at the ball. You were going to compliment her dress and that would be that. I hadn't even given thought to naming you. But then I wrote two sentences with you and I knew beyond a shadow of a doubt that your name was "that one Greek name, but not the first part." I searched lists of names until I came across Tisiphone and knew that's what you meant.

As Amya's story fleshed out and you became part of her arc, I started to dive more into who you are. It doesn't come across on the page, but knowing it all helped me write the parts of you that did make it into the book. And you told me something very important: that this isn't the last we'll see of you.

You have so much more story to be told, and I can't wait until I get to write more of it. I never wanted to leave you alone after the ball that night, but this story wasn't yours. I couldn't follow you inside, couldn't give you the closure you needed. I couldn't even make sure you had tea and a hug and someone to cry to.

But I'll be back to tell your story properly. Because you have so much heart and light and joy to share. And I can't wait to share that beautiful, bubbly heart of yours with the rest of the world.

I know how much you struggle to feel like you're too much for people. Too much and not enough at the same time. It's why you clung to Amya so fiercely when you met her, because she made you feel like someone worth knowing.

Someone worth loving.

I can't tell you how your story will end, how your heartbreak will be dealt with or what it will do to you. Because I don't know yet. I don't know how the story ends. But I've seen inklings of it and I can tell you I love what I've seen. Because you're still all the things I fell in love with. Insecurities, and quirks, and affection, and all. You're still you.

I know it hurts. I know it feels like nothing will ever be okay again. And I know you're going to make a very wild, daring choice to deal with it. But I promise it will be okay. You're one of my characters, it has to be okay in the end. I can't make any promises about what that will look like, but I promise it's coming.

Thanks for letting me tell a glimpse of your story and being willing to wait for the rest to be told. Thanks for trusting me with your story and with your heart. I promise to take good care of it.

Don't let this dim your light. Don't let this make you feel like you're not someone worth knowing or loving. Because you are worth every ounce of love the galaxy has to offer. Grow and heal, and keep being you.

I need more people like you in this world. And if I need you, there's got to be others out there who need you too.

Hold tight, until we meet again. I promise, your story is coming.

Affectionately yours,

Jenni

Acknowledgements

This is always my least favorite part because I'm certain I'll forget someone. If you're looking at these because you think your name deserves to be here, it probably does. And I'm sorry if it's not.

Mom and Dad, you're the best, plain and simple. Thanks for putting up with me all these years and pushing me to become the person God wanted me to be. And for encouraging me to believe that maybe, just maybe, "writer" was part of that person.

Yentl for always believing in me. Always. You hype me up and love me more than I ever dreamed possible. It's funny when I say you're the Amya to my Rinity because I haven't known you forever, but it feels like I have. It feels like I've known you my whole life and I can't imagine living without you. You make me feel like I'm someone worth loving, someone worth believing in. Also, your love for Gibbs gives me life—even if I am slightly scandalized by it sometimes. xD

Selina for dealing with every early morning crisis, all the drama and excitement, and all the "I'm moving to a small town and never writing again" messages. For the pep talks, and virtually whacking me with me a broom when needed, and keeping me on track. For accepting "you're the one who pointed out the problem, so you gotta help me fix it." For being a better friend than I ever dreamed I'd have. You really are the Gibbs to my Tov, dealing with every metaphorical 1 am insomniac episode and reminding me I can do this, I just need to slow down and breathe first, sometimes.

Gabby for letting me always talk about all the story stuff and being interested. And for letting me lie on your dining room floor while you sewed and talk about all my favorite bits and where I was discouraged. And for the screenshots, and emojis, and comments. I love all your emojis and comments.

Hannah, for being a person who stayed. Through the craziness that has been both of lives, you've always held into me, made a point of being my friend. And when others have shown me that "see, you're not worth sticking around for," you still make me feel as if I'm never too much or not enough. I'm glad we started talking more, because I seriously can't imagine what my life would be without you.

Savanna Roberts for all your amazing help. You're the best editor, and this book is infinitely better because of all your suggestions and feedback. I was feeling so lost and discouraged and you helped me pinpoint the problem areas, and how to make them stronger, and added so much depth to this story.

Jessie because you love Tov as much as I do and he needs all the love he can get. Also, for always being as excited about all the random things, for making the treason jokes, and always asking me to sort my characters by the most random criteria. And because you helped me decide what Amya wears, which inspired her being a seamstress. Which inspired her entire character arc. She seriously wouldn't be the person in this book if not for that one conversation. You have no idea what an impact you have, just by being passionate about the things you love, and for always showing up for people.

Meredith because you always show up for my stories. Thanks for taking a chance on me, even though I don't write your usual genre. Your feedback is invaluable and your encouragement means the world to me.

Austin for all your encouragement, for loving my baby draft, and for all phone conversations that keep us both but are so healing. And for all the tea blend inspiration. Also, thank you for catching all my typos, I promise I know words.

Rosie and Joyce for being the founders of the Gibbs fanclub. And for all your beta feedback and encouragement.

Betsy, thank you so much for your feedback and all your love.

The Evraft Galaxy Crew group chat for always putting up with my nonsense. Whether you're there because you love me, or my stories, or both, you really do help so much by giving me an outlet of endless encouragement. It fuels my stories almost as much as tea does, and I hope you know you all mean the world to me.

Rita whose shop, Scents and Sensibility candles is no longer running—so you know this isn't sponsored xD—because your candles fueled my drafting and editing. I adore them so much, the seriously set the mood as I wrote.

For the Bookstagram community that never fails to show up for me. Helping with my cover reveals, playing story games, every comment of "I can't wait to read this." Everything you do, no matter how small you think it might be, means the world to me.

And Isabel, because I promised.

About the Author

Jenni Sauer is a 20-something city girl from New York (but no, not The City). A pragmatic optimist, she writes fairy tale retellings woven with realism and laced with hope, striving to offer light that shines in, rather than denies the darkness.

When not writing she spends her time nannying, overanalyzing stories, and drinking too much tea. If you're looking for her, she's probably bent over her laptop somewhere plotting her next step in world domination— er, the next book in her series— or procrastinating on that by investing in the #bookstagram and writing communities.

Mount Laurel Library
100 Walt Whitman Avenue
Mount Laurel, NJ 08054-9539
856-234-7319
www.mountlaurellibrary.org

CPSIA information can be obtained
at www.ICGtesting.com
Printed in the USA
LVHW020445090721
692210LV00001B/73